The Jetsetters

Amanda Eyre Ward is the critically acclaimed author of seven novels, including *How to Be Lost*, *The Same Sky*, *The Nearness of You* and the *New York Times* bestselling *The Jetsetters*. Her bestselling novels have been featured in *People* magazine, *The New York Times* and more. Amanda's work has been optioned for film and television and translated into fifteen languages. She lives in Austin, Texas, with her family.

amandaward.com
Twitter: @amandaeyreward
Instagram: @amandaeyreward
Find Amanda Eyre Ward on Facebook

The Jetsetters

Amanda Eyre Ward

PENGUIN BOOKS

PENGUIN BOOKS

UK | USA | Canada | Ireland | Australia
India | New Zealand | South Africa

Penguin Books is part of the Penguin Random House group of companies
whose addresses can be found at global.penguinrandomhouse.com.

Penguin
Random House
UK

First published in the United States of America by Ballantine Books,
an imprint of Random House, a division of Penguin Random House LLC,
New York 2020
First published by Viking 2020
Published in Penguin Books 2021
001

Printed and bound in Great Britain by Clays Ltd, Elcograf S.p.A.

The authorized representative in the EEA is Penguin Random House Ireland,
Morrison Chambers, 32 Nassau Street, Dublin D02 YH68

A CIP catalogue record for this book is available from the British Library

ISBN: 978–0–241–49132–4

www.greenpenguin.co.uk

MIX
Paper from
responsible sources
FSC   FSC® C018179
www.fsc.org

Penguin Random House is committed to a
sustainable future for our business, our readers
and our planet. This book is made from Forest
Stewardship Council® certified paper.

For my first reader, my best friend,
Claiborne Smith

Contents

The Jetsetters

Prologue / Hilton Head Island, 1983

THE LARGE OIL PORTRAIT of Charlotte and her children began with a photo snapped on a Hilton Head Island beach at sunset. Charlotte wanted the night to be perfect. She packed a cooler of beer and Cokes in glass bottles. They were sunburned, light-headed. Winston considered himself an amateur photographer.

In the portrait, Charlotte looks happy but not too happy. She is thirty-nine, thin and sunburned, perched on a blanket in the sand. Her three children surround her: Lee, blond hair wispy in the salt-smelling wind; Cord, dressed in seersucker shorts and a white polo shirt; and baby Regan, barefoot in a sundress.

Lee, just six, was eager to please. She read her parents like a ghost story, alert for danger. Winston had spent the day in their vacation villa smoking cigarettes and watching television. Although he had showered, he still smelled sharp. Lee had thought weekends, when Winston was home, were the worst. She was wrong.

It was the sun, making Lee's skin hurt, even after Charlotte applied sticky aloe. It was the hours not knowing when he would emerge from the bedroom, and if he'd be angry or just blank and sad. Charlotte was more nervous than usual: it seemed desperately important that their weeklong holiday be perfect, and Lee tried to understand what this meant. Staying quiet was definitely good. Seeming excited by lighthouses, sand dollars, and collecting shells was imperative. If you were stung by a jellyfish, you should tell Charlotte quietly and not "be dramatic," no matter how much it hurt. No sand in the condo. No talking back. No "gimme gimme gimme." If you got an ice cream, you ate it, all of it, even if it wasn't the flavor you wanted, and you did not allow a melted drop to spill. If you ordered chicken fingers at the Salty Dog, you did not leave half-cooked fries in the paper tray like a spoiled brat.

Lee did her best but sometimes, as soon as she figured out a rule, one of her siblings would break it. She understood that Regan was an infant, but just that afternoon her little sister had started crying with Winston in the room. Lee's stomach hurt as their father looked at them, his eyes narrowing. Lee was learning to be a ghost herself, even while her body remained in Winston's line of fire. Nobody could tell. She'd just take her brain somewhere else, somewhere safe. But when she left, it meant nobody was protecting four-year-old Cord and baby Regan. So Lee tried to stay, sometimes biting the side of her mouth to keep from making a sound.

Cord, Lee could tell, was starting to get it. He didn't run up the stairs anymore. He pretended to enjoy crabbing with his father, though Lee saw the flash of despair when Winston handed his son a chicken neck to put on the hook. It was so hot. Cord was fragile. Lee saw him blink back tears and grip the crabbing pole. Winston would slap his son on the back, but Cord steeled himself, did not recoil. When Winston looked at the water, it seemed as if he was seeing something else, something heartbreaking in the distance.

Lee and her father were the early birds in the family, and would hold hands and walk along the boardwalk to the beach to watch the sun rise. The sand was still cool. Her father said kind things to her: he loved her golden hair, she was his superstar. But he also said strange things. "I really am trying," Winston said, speaking maybe to himself. "It's like a fog. I wish I could make it go away but I don't know how."

Lee hugged him hard. Many years later, she would understand what he was talking about, but that morning, his words were a mystery.

TIME FOR THE PHOTO. Charlotte was laughing in her high, frightened way, fluffing her hair back. "How do I look, honey?" she said.

"Fine, you all look fine," said Winston. "My family. There you are."

It was as if he couldn't believe it himself, as if they were a movie he wanted to like but just didn't. Cord rested his head on Charlotte's knee, gazing placidly at the camera. Maybe he knew how to take his brain elsewhere, too.

"Cord, you look miserable," said Winston.

Cord blinked, as if woken from a deep sleep. Baby Regan was silent in her mother's arms. Charlotte lifted her chin.

"That's right, that's right," said Winston as his expensive Nikon clicked.

Regan gripped Lee's finger in her tiny hand and Lee reached around Charlotte to touch her brother. At least she had Regan and Cord, thought Lee. Because of them, she would never be alone. She yearned to make things okay in her family: to fix her father's "fog," to keep her siblings from making Winston yell, to tell her mother she was beautiful and could stop fishing for compliments.

"Lee!" said Winston. "Come on now, give me that smile."

Lee smiled with brilliance, hoping to make her father proud. This day, and the two more excruciating days that followed—days of sand and beer-scented misery—would be the last time Lee went on vacation with her mother and siblings.

Until thirty-two years later, when they became jetsetters.

ONE

Baggage

1 / Charlotte

SOME EVENINGS, CHARLOTTE FOUND herself standing in front of the family portrait. It hung in her Savannah, Georgia, condominium, above the gas fireplace she rarely turned on. In the painting, her hair was a marvel of burnt umber and gold, falling in loose waves around her jawline. Her face was inscrutable with a "Mona Lisa smile," as they called it, alluring in its standoffishness. No actual person smiled in this way. It was an expression meant to be gazed upon, not the sort of smile that came spontaneously, from joy. And yet, Charlotte concluded, she looked lovely, much better than she'd ever looked in real life. And certainly much better than she looked now that she was seventy-one years old, her gray hair frosted to Marilyn Monroe platinum every third Tuesday by Hannah at Shear Envy.

CHARLOTTE DECIDED TO WEAR a little black dress to her best friend's funeral. Minnie had made gentle fun of Charlotte when she bought a neon-pink cardigan at the Ralph Lauren outlet store, so Charlotte tossed it over her shoulders and added a white Coach purse. Charlotte could have called her daughter Regan for a ride, but then she would have to hear about the Weight Watchers gift certificate again, so Charlotte drove herself.

Charlotte and Minnie had discussed caskets more than once. Charlotte felt an open casket was both scary and kind of tacky. Minnie disagreed. She believed that saying goodbye to an actual face gave you more closure afterward. "I deal in reality," Minnie had said, "and you live in denial. Or you try. But it's going to catch up with you one day, Char."

Perhaps today was the day.

CHARLOTTE WALKED SLOWLY TO the altar, weak and dizzy. She could see Father Thomas watching her, and appreciated his concern. She peered inside the open casket, as Minnie would have wanted her to do. Minnie was wearing too much bronzer, but then she had always worn too much bronzer. Charlotte had tried to tell her, "Minnie, go easy with the bronzer!" But Minnie hadn't listened, had gone on doing whatever she wanted. It was part of why Charlotte had loved her, ever since they'd first met at a St. James pancake breakfast, soon after Minnie had moved to Savannah. The pancakes had been awful—mealy, drenched with cheap syrup—and Minnie had turned to Charlotte and said, "Eyuck!"

Charlotte had looked down. She considered herself refined, not the type to insult pancakes at a church.

"Did you hear me?" said Minnie. "I said, 'Eyuck!' "

"I heard you," murmured Charlotte.

"Your pants are fabulous," said Minnie.

Charlotte touched her leopard-print culottes (which matched her cheetah-print shoes). They *were* fabulous.

They'd both been lonely. They went to art openings, Wine Down Wednesdays, and the Driftaway Café. They went to Marshwood Pool and Franklin Creek Pool, zipping along the golf-cart paths, past magnolia trees and winter-flowering camellias. They played golf and watched people play tennis. Minnie had a Blue Demon golf cart with a forty-eight-volt motor and leather seats. Somehow—how?—twenty years passed, and now Charlotte was officially old and Minnie was dead.

"Too much bronzer, honey," whispered Charlotte. Her throat grew hot. She touched Minnie's cheek. "A nice blush. Why not a nice blush, Min?" she said softly. Once, after they had split a bottle of Barefoot Chardonnay, Minnie had allowed Charlotte to give her a makeover. In Charlotte's bathroom, Minnie offered up her face. Charlotte applied foundation, mascara, lip liner, and lipstick. She curled Minnie's sparse lashes, dusted her with loose powder. At last, Minnie opened her eyes. Charlotte ran a brush through her best friend's hair as Minnie took in her new and improved visage.

"Well?" said Charlotte, crossing one arm over her chest, resting her chin in her opposite hand. "Aren't you beautiful?"

"I look like a prostitute on Saturday night," said Minnie, turning her head side to side to survey Charlotte's expert contouring.

"It's Wednesday," said Charlotte primly.

And then they both collapsed into laughter. How good it felt, thought Charlotte, to allow yourself to laugh, to let your guard down for an instant. The next day, when they met for their sunrise walk around the lagoon, Minnie's face was as naked as a baby's. A few years later, after her daughter sent her bronzer for her birthday, Minnie began showing up each morning in her usual visor and track pants, her cheeks carrot-colored. For evening events, Minnie went orange from her hairline to her décolleté. The more Charlotte advised her, even buying Minnie subtle, tinted sunscreens and liquid blush at T.J.Maxx, the more defiantly Minnie bronzed.

Charlotte remembered Minnie's warm cheekbones under her fingers, Minnie's small sigh as she enjoyed the pleasure of being touched. Now, Minnie's skin was ice.

"Ma'am?" said the woman behind Charlotte in line. She turned, but the woman was a stranger.

IT WAS POURING RAIN outside St. James the Less Catholic Church. A young man offered his umbrella. Charlotte shook her head, hating to depend on anyone.

She had trouble getting her key in the lock of her VW Rabbit. The rain was relentless. When she was sitting inside her cozy condominium, she loved Savannah thunderstorms. But now, in a parking lot, she felt afraid. Everything seemed too loud. All Charlotte wanted was to drive home, pour a cold glass of Barefoot Chardonnay, and drink the cold glass of Barefoot Chardonnay. How could it be true that she couldn't call Minnie to gossip about the funeral? Who had dressed Minnie in her least favorite floral blouse— the one with the tulips—and an unflattering, high-waisted skirt?

Minnie had two children: a ne'er-do-well son and a divorced daughter. Both lived in New Jersey, the state Minnie had fled after her husband's death. Charlotte had received an Evite to a brunch being held at Minnie's townhouse "directly after the burial of our beloved Mama," but had deleted it. Charlotte couldn't bear to see Minnie lowered into the ground and was upset on Minnie's behalf that her children couldn't be bothered to send actual paper invitations. Though Minnie wouldn't have cared. But Charlotte cared! It was simply gauche to send an Evite for an après-funeral brunch. Minnie deserved better—an eggshell-white or pale pink invitation; handwritten calligraphy on heavy card stock.

Did Charlotte's own children know to send paper invitations? Did they know she'd like a lunch held at Marshwood after her funeral? She made a mental note to tell Regan, who would remember. For a moment in the rain, Charlotte felt a wave of gratitude for her overweight, thoughtful daughter. She resolved to make more of an effort to be kind.

The battery on Charlotte's key fob had run out months before. She *knew* she was jamming her key in the right place! But the door remained locked. "Mrs. Perkins!" cried the young man Charlotte had walked away from moments before. "I can help!"

What Charlotte wouldn't give to slide into her car and zoom away.

"I can help," he called, walk-jogging across the lot, his enormous golf umbrella keeping him dry. "Mrs. Perkins," he said, his voice overly solicitous. Charlotte knew he saw her as elderly, an elderly lady in the rain. She wanted him to know she'd been a stunning beauty once—that inside, she was still that graceful young *bohème*. But strangers seeing you as someone you couldn't bear to be was simply one of the indignities of age. You could accept it, rail against it, or just pretend it wasn't happening. Charlotte moved between acceptance and willful ignorance, too elegant (and perhaps too worn out) to bother with nips, tucks, and the Beach Booty videos her friend Greer swore by.

"Let me help you, Mrs. Perkins," said the man. He took her keys right out of her hand and she let him. "I offered you my umbrella," he reminded her.

When she was inside her car, the young man lingered, saying, "I know you and Mrs. Robbins were thick as thieves. Always saw you cackling together after mass! I'm sorry for your loss. I'm really sorry."

Charlotte felt antipathy rise inside her toward this man—his cologne-y smell, his close shave, his use of the word "cackling," as if she and Minnie were nothing more than withered crones. His useless condolences. And worst of all, the fact that he was living and Minnie—kind, sarcastic, thrumming with mischief—was not.

"I said I sure am sorry," repeated the man.

"Thank you," said Charlotte. Finally, he shut the door and walk-jogged back to the church steps. Charlotte closed her eyes. Rain hammered down.

On the drive back to her condominium, Charlotte tried to focus on the road. She drove around Tidewater Square (where once Minnie had made Charlotte stop the golf cart so she could watch a scissor-tailed flycatcher *forever*), took a right on Brandenberry (the grass still ruddy from where Minnie had missed the curb years before), then another right on Boar's Nest Lane. The Spanish moss hanging from her live oak trees danced bewitchingly in the wind. But it was hard to keep a very painful question at bay.

What now?

Minnie's evening heart attack—out of the blue, no heart trouble that Charlotte had known about, and Charlotte *would have* known, as Minnie shared her ailments perhaps a teensy bit too much—made it clear that Charlotte could be next. Who knew how much time she had left? And did she even want to be here, now that Minnie was gone? And if she didn't want to spend her remaining time here, inside a gated community on the outskirts of Savannah, Georgia, where should she go? None of her children were sending Evites to come visit.

Oh. Charlotte's children.

To her great sadness and bewilderment, Charlotte's three adult children were lost to her, and perhaps to themselves. Learning how to navigate the world without a husband had been painful—finding a job, trying to spruce up their badly lit rental home with Laura Ashley wallpaper, fielding questions about what had happened to Winston— but sometimes Charlotte actually missed those days. They had all been together, crammed into a tiny colonial, sharing one bathroom with a leaky shower. Although she hadn't realized it at the time, Charlotte now understood that proximity mattered.

It seemed impossible that they had traveled from that place, where they were together every night, aware of one another's favorite morning repasts, to the present day. Charlotte had no idea what her children ate for breakfast now, or if they even ate breakfast at all. Cord had always appreciated a bowl of apples-and-cinnamon instant oatmeal sprinkled with sugar. Regan adored donuts so much that Charlotte would set her alarm clock for 5:45 A.M. so she could have time to run to Publix and deliver a fresh glazed donut to Regan, her sweet baby girl, before she headed to work at Lowcountry Realtors. (Regan in her L.L.Bean flannel nightgown, saying sleepily, "Oh, Mom! It's still warm!" made every early rise worthwhile.) And Lee drank SlimFast milkshakes, which she made herself before school, leaving a trail of brownish powder and revolting cups half-full of sludge in her wake. Charlotte herself enjoyed a heavily buttered English muffin and three to four cups of black coffee.

Back at home, Charlotte changed out of her funereal dress and into snug white pants and a neon-pink-and-white-striped top and pink sandals. Father Thomas had once, five or so years ago, stopped by in the evening, and Charlotte wanted to be ready in case he did it again. She made dinner (Triscuits, wedge of cheddar, Chardonnay) and nibbled through a *20/20* about young people taking hallucinogenic drugs to find serenity, which seemed a bit much when Chardonnay was easily available, or Pinot Grigio if one preferred. She had dessert (one mint Milano, Chardonnay), then rinsed the dishes and settled in the living room to see what old movies caught her fancy. Her Siamese cat climbed into her lap.

Godiva purred and the wine lent the evening a buttery luxuriance. After her children left, every quiet evening had been painful, and Charlotte was proud that she had come to peace with being alone. But without Minnie—Minnie popping by for a drink; plans to meet Minnie for their sunrise walk around the lagoon; her phone ringing in the middle of *20/20*, Minnie on the other end with opinions she just "had to share"—Charlotte was back in a sad place, the hours moving slowly toward bedtime. No one cared when she went to bed. No one—besides Father Thomas—was waiting to see her in the morning. Her Triscuit dinner was pathetic.

Charlotte was flipping toward the Turner Classic Movies network when the face of a handsome man appeared on the screen. "I am here tonight," he said, "to tell you about the most amazing contest in the history of contests.

But first, I've got a question. And here it is. Do *you* want to become a jetsetter?"

Charlotte paused, wineglass halfway to her lips.

"Is your story a love story?" asked the man. "An adventure story? Now is your chance to *tell your story* . . . and become a jetsetter!"

Charlotte had a story all right—the kind of story that deserved a prize. She sipped, cozy on her lemon-colored sofa, watching images of European hotspots scroll past: the Colosseum, the Acropolis, a sun-drenched beach lined with navy umbrellas.

The winner of the Become a Jetsetter contest would receive first-class tickets to Athens, Greece, followed by a nine-day cruise to Barcelona, Spain. Hmm. A first-class flight was hardly a jet, but then again, Charlotte had only flown economy. She hadn't been abroad since she was sixteen, and not one of her children had ever left the country. Charlotte was somewhat embarrassed to admit—even to herself—that museum visits and sightseeing didn't really appeal. But suddenly she wanted nothing more than to walk through a European city again—to feel that thrill of a foreign and more glamorous place—a place where *she herself* was foreign and glamorous.

Charlotte allowed herself to remember her sixteenth summer. The heat, the thrill of being chosen, being passionately kissed. Why not enter the contest? She could almost hear Minnie whispering from the Great Beyond, saying, "Go for it! Go type up the story of your first love!"

Telling herself she didn't have to show the pages to anyone, Charlotte changed into her nightgown and robe, refilled her glass, and sat before her Dell desktop computer. Next to the monitor was her faded wedding photo. Winston, he'd been tall. But he had never made her feel cherished. Their lovemaking had been perfunctory at best and, at times, desperately sad. (Once in a while, Charlotte would walk by a man who smelled of the previous night's whiskey and she would wince, remembering her nighttime encounters with Winston.)

Marrying out of desperation had probably been Charlotte's biggest error. The aftermath of her erotic summer had left her lonely and bereft; according to her mother, she was "spoiled goods." So when Winston happened back into her life, still saw her as a shining girl, she jumped at the chance to begin again. Maybe she was making amends. Maybe a part of her had really loved him, once. She hadn't been able to imagine any other path forward, and that was the truth. If Winston rose from the grave right now and just told her what to do, she'd probably do it.

Charlotte logged on to the contest website. My, it was bright. The pictures kept moving and flipping around, but Charlotte placed her cursor in the window under the command "Win first-class flights to Europe and an all-expenses-paid Mediterranean cruise! Tell your story HERE."

Charlotte clicked and wrote:

It may be hard to believe, but once upon a time, I was unpeeled like a banana, my rich fruit eaten raw.

She stared at the words in shock. A banana! Where had that image come from? She erased the revolting sentence and started again:

My first lover was as strong as a bull. He impaled me with his

Her face was hot, her mouth open. She deleted the statement, shaking. Whatever in the world! What if some late-night dog walker happened by? Charlotte gathered her bathrobe at her neck. She tried to look as if she were paying bills online, or checking weather.com for approaching thunderstorms.

She took a deep breath, then typed without stopping, letting the memories come, chronicling her sixteenth summer without censure or shame. She wrote it all down, every blistering detail.

Periodically, she refreshed her drink with a teensy splash.

When Charlotte finished, the bottle was empty and her mouth was dry. What would her children think if they knew? What would her *church* friends think? She'd be kicked out of Bible Study, and that was for sure. This story did not belong to the narrative Charlotte had created about herself, the one that led her from Paris to Savannah, from the ashes of widowhood to a sturdy, purposeful life. This story exposed her as the wanton woman she secretly feared she was. Weak! It made her seem weak, and this was horrible. Only Minnie knew this story, and she had kept Charlotte's secret (as far as Charlotte knew) to her dying day.

Charlotte was paralyzed above her keyboard, still in control, still considered . . . if not perfect, then at least free of sin. Respectable. Someone her mother would admire. Oh, Charlotte was so tired of caring what Louisa would think! And yet she still yearned to impress her mother, still heard her disdainful, brittle voice, even though Louisa had been buried at Bonaventure for twenty years.

Charlotte ached to have her children around her, to believe she was still connected to them, still necessary. If she won the contest, they could fly to Europe! They could be together on a cruise ship for nine whole days! It would be like old times, but luxurious.

And then there was sex. Something had been happening to Charlotte. Where once she'd found it possible to ignore sexy thoughts, now she spent hours conjuring imaginary encounters. She gathered parts of the men she saw around the Club and at church: a pair of strong shoulders, a cleft chin, the way a fellow shopper at Publix let his hand graze hers in the string bean bin. Alone, she fit these pieces together and imagined being trapped in country houses, closets, furtive embraces in the rain. She reread the dirty parts of her romance novels, even tearing out juicy scenes to savor later.

Mightn't a ship full of men have one man for Charlotte?

From the moment she had rushed, too late, to Minnie's bedside, the question had remained in her mind: What now?

She bit her lip and clicked on the button that proclaimed: *Submit.*

2 / Cord

CORD STARED AT THE champagne in his refrigerator. Who would know if he had a glass, just one glass, to fortify himself for his marriage proposal? His company had paid for the rehab that had finally stuck, but he'd taken the day off. He had at least an hour to himself—more than enough time to have a glass or two, shower, and brush his teeth. He could almost feel the buoyant calm the booze would bring.

Cord took the bottle—someone had brought it over months ago—out of the refrigerator. It was cold, so cold. Ah, if only he could return to the halcyon days before he knew he was an alcoholic . . . before he understood that the *pop* of the cork and tickle of champagne bubbles were harbingers of painful dread he could scarcely survive.

Cord's heart beat in his chest.

It's too hard, said the lonely voice. *Just drink it. Just drink it.*

He twisted the wire *collerette*, ripped off the foil, and pulled the cork free. He jammed his thumb over the bottle's opening to save every drop.

He had time. He could drink it all and still shower and

be ready. He could drink it all *in* the shower, which briefly struck his lizard brain as a clean and streamlined plan.

Cord felt feverish, but maybe it was his close kitchen, more useful for arranging a selection of appetizers than for baking. He had never actually prepared an entire meal from scratch before, excepting the time he woke in the middle of the night, binge-watched *Top Chef,* and found himself naked in the kitchen at dawn, various egg creations congealing before him. That was the first time he tried to stop with the Ambien.

Cord wanted the night to be flawless. He'd selected ten kinds of cheese, his last remaining vice. Not only had he ordered a pasta maker and rolling pin from Amazon Prime Now but he'd *used them*, reveling in his flour-coated hands, turning the wooden handle to create lovely strands of fettuccine, which he'd strung from wire hangers around the living room to dry. There was a bag of salad. Warm baguettes from Levain. And the pièce de résistance, a flourless chocolate torte it had taken Cord three times to get right. Three times! He had actually made two failed tortes (one a sinkhole, one burned) before triumphing with *numéro trois.*

By the time the torte, now cooling elegantly on a platter, was served, Cord imagined he'd be betrothed, cozied up on the faux Herman Miller divan. After years of mean and unattractive lovers, a wedding in his mom's Savannah backyard. He could see himself in his mind's eye: his still-full head of sandy brown hair, his toned six-foot-two physique, just a hint of sexy "I was at the beach and forgot to shave" stubble. His eyes pale blue, like Charlotte's. He looked a lot like her, in fact, but younger, taller, and macho. With a man's haircut. And stubble.

Cord looked out the kitchen window of his apartment on West Eighty-sixth and Riverside. He'd probably never stood here in the afternoon; the light on the trees was sort of sad and pale.

His father had told him to be strong, to be a man. Cord wished he could ask his father about the lonely voice. Had Winston heard it, too? If nothing else, Cord's father had shown by example what could happen if you let your demons take you down.

Cord put his shoulders back. He walked to the sink and poured the champagne down the drain, all of it. He inhaled the smell, which made him feel both ill and desperate for oblivion.

Day 534.

En route to the shower, Cord paused in his dining room. He'd set the table with care: silver salt and pepper shakers, brand-new Williams-Sonoma place settings, a tablecloth and pressed napkins. And one elegant rose.

The shower was too hot and too hard, but if you wanted prewar, you had to roll with the punches. As Cord lathered up, he allowed himself to picture the backyard of his mother's townhome, lined with azalea bushes. They could erect a pergola for the ceremony, hire some Savannah caterer. Cord pictured himself in a linen Cucinelli suit, holding a mini crab cake. But try as he might, he couldn't insert Charlotte into the scene. She'd be crying in her golf cart, more likely, or pulling a Blanche DuBois at her makeup table, topping off her glass of crap Chardonnay. Cord put his mother out of his mind. This was his life, maybe his last chance. He'd handle his mother in due time. She'd still love him if she knew him, wouldn't she?

"What matters," his AA sponsor had told him, "is that

you love yourself. Do you hear me?" Cord had nodded, scoffing inwardly at yet another AA platitude. Love yourself? What did that even mean?

CORD SHAVED, USING THE horsehair soap brush his older sister, Lee, had sent from Los Angeles for his thirty-sixth birthday. (Poor Lee. She tried to act successful, but they all knew she was struggling, even doing that tampon commercial and the Walmart Summer Shoes flyer. She'd always had excellent toes.)

As he surveyed his closet with a towel around his waist, Cord's chocolate Labrador, Franklin, plodded into the bedroom. "Hi, you," said Cord, scratching behind the dog's ears. And then, as he was about to reach for an ice-blue shirt (to match his eyes), Cord heard an awful heaving sound. Alarmed, he turned to see dear Franklin vomiting on Cord's Louis Vuitton sneakers. "What are you doing?" he asked, panicking. "What are you doing, Franklin? What are you doing?"

Cord ran to find a dish towel, realizing in moments that his dog had eaten every last handmade noodle. And in the kitchen, all that remained of the "Marry Me?" torte were a few wet crumbs. Cord's buzzer rang, and Giovanni's rich voice came over the intercom. "You gave me a key!" Giovanni sang. "I'm letting myself in!"

As he surveyed the wreckage of his careful plans, Cord jammed his fists into his eyes, breathing in deeply. From the bedroom, his beloved dog continued to retch.

Giovanni burst into the apartment, a bottle of Italian lemonade in one hand, a lit cigarette in the other. "Thank God it's Friday!" he cried, but then he halted. Bewilderment transformed his young and lovely face. "Honey?" he said.

Cord swiped the tears from his eyes. Giovanni came close, wrapped Cord in his arms, and rested his head against Cord's chest. Franklin slunk into the kitchen and collapsed at their feet. "What is it?" said Giovanni. "Honey, what is it?"

"It's . . ." said Cord. How could he possibly express all the feelings crashing around inside him? His knowledge that he would be abandoned, coupled with the fierce desire to hang on to love . . . his sense that something was wrong and that he had to fix it, but had no idea what it even was? His yearning to be drunk and how much he missed his mother and the way Giovanni's smile changed the color of everything, brightening his days as if a heavy curtain had finally been lifted . . .

"What?" said Giovanni.

"It's that I love you," whispered Cord.

3 / Regan

REGAN SLOWED HER WALMART shopping cart and allowed herself to touch a bag of rat poison. What drink would mask the taste of a RatX pellet? A strong cinnamon latte from Starbucks? She imagined the first sip, the strychnine convulsions beginning . . . But no: She'd already run that scenario. As appealing as it was, rat poison wasn't going to play out. And Regan was in for the long game.

After her Walmart errands, Regan headed to her favorite spot, Monet's Playhouse at the Oglethorpe Mall. When she had begun painting pottery, Regan had pretended she was waiting for a friend, or creating a gift for a child's birthday. She'd even dragged her daughters along a few times, enduring their fidgety annoyance to get her fix. But she was beyond the subterfuge now. Kendall, the Monet's Playhouse manager, knew and accepted Regan, who perhaps kept them afloat.

"Oh, hey, Mrs. Willingham," said Kendall, as Regan perused the ceramic figurines.

"Good morning, Kendall," said Regan.

"You doing good?" said Kendall.

Regan nodded, smiling, not correcting Kendall's grammar. She picked up a large white dinosaur bank. She could paint it turquoise, or green.

"There's a monkey bank, too," said Kendall. "And one there with two cats snuggled up."

Regan nodded. She knew about the monkey bank: she had three of them in her secret pottery cupboard at home. She had four dinosaurs, too, and countess salt and pepper shakers, plates, platters, and ceramic wine goblets. Clearly, her Monet's Playhouse purchases were not items she'd actually use. But sitting inside the cheerful studio made her calm. In Monet's Playhouse, Regan could ignore the desperate sense that her life was a car that had hit a wall, crumpled, and remained still and broken, no air bags deploying, no metaphorical ambulance en route. No: Her life had sailed over the guardrail into the air, then landed in an ocean of dread and ennui, sinking slowly, its inhabitant (Regan) running out of time, gasping, her metaphorical seatbelt (a symbol for marriage if ever there was one) jammed and holding her tight against her seat, ensuring her flailing, watery demise.

Regan listened to Kendall's boy-band playlist as she squeezed paint onto a clean palette. She selected brushes of various sizes.

Regan had thought she'd be an artist once. Sometimes, when she opened her secret pottery cupboard, sitting cross-legged on the floor and admiring her glossy creations, she felt as if perhaps she *was* an artist. Sure, she'd jettisoned her schooling to hold on to Matt, to make a generous, lush life that was the opposite of her penny-pinching childhood. But Regan went to the mall every few days and painted, feeling as if she were under a happy spell, making something from generic molds, something that hadn't existed before and wouldn't exist without her careful, constant work. And wasn't that the point of art? (And, come to think of it, motherhood? Life itself?)

When Regan had finished painting the dinosaur bank, she gave it to Kendall for firing and set down her credit card.

After Monet's Playhouse, Regan walked around the mall, searching for things she could acquire that would make her feel less like a goldfish trapped in a Ziploc bag. She caught a glimpse of herself in a shop window. She was no longer adorable. She hid her formerly size-six body under size-fourteen dresses. Her thighs rubbed together when she walked. She'd had babies, she'd nursed babies, and she tried to be proud of the havoc this had wreaked on her body. Regan loved preparing—and enjoying—good food. Her mother had spent her life on one diet or another and Regan was trying to set a healthier example for her girls. Still, being invisible instead of cute kind of sucked.

In front of a travel agency, Regan stared at a poster of a chaise longue and sun umbrella. The tagline read *Get away . . . to anywhere but here!*

Regan put her hand to her throat. She felt choked with yearning. "I want to get away," she said, gazing at the pink chair, the fruity drink beside it. Rat poison, pillow suffocation, cutting the brakes on the Tundra truck . . . but none of these plans would result in what she most desired, which was to be free.

Regan made herself walk past the travel agency without going inside. She was due to volunteer in the gymnasium at Savannah Country Day in a half hour. It was an expensive school, but every time Regan drove up to the campus and saw her children in their smart uniforms, she felt a surge of accomplishment. Her father had been a lawyer, but after he died, money was tight. Charlotte had kept them afloat by getting her real estate license.

Charlotte had been a mediocre realtor. Once in a while, she'd sell a big house to a retiree from somewhere expensive or for a friend from church, and these sales supported them during Regan's high school years. Regan could remember lean times, too: Charlotte hunched over a stack of bills wearing her CVS reading glasses and pecking at a calculator. There were weekends when Charlotte brought Regan and her homework to her open houses, pasting on a smile when lookie-loos meandered in. At those times, Regan was touched by her mother's effort, but it was hard to see Charlotte later in these evenings: exhausted, worried, eating a sad McDonald's cheeseburger for dinner.

Somehow, Charlotte had found enough money for Cord and Lee to finish up at Savannah Country Day, then hightail it out of town to college. But Regan was sent to public school in her sister's hand-me-down sweater sets. Her art teacher called her gifted, but there was no money for "extras," such as art classes at the Telfair or SCAD.

Regan allowed herself a deep sigh. She'd worked so hard for her big, new home, her big husband, her two delightful daughters. She'd surrendered herself to give her girls the mother she'd always wanted: present, attentive, enthusiastic. But she knew that as soon as she struck the match, her life was going to explode. She was both terrified and so very ready.

Regan parked her minivan in the visitors' lot at Savannah Country Day. She grabbed her Tory Burch gym bag, used her volunteer badge to enter the school, and changed into track pants and a pink T-shirt in the teachers' restroom. It was Volleyball Appreciation Week.

In the Pledge-scented gym, Regan stood to the left of Coach Randy (*What a name!* was a joke Regan had told to no one). She mimed his "ready position," feigning excitement. Regan's daughters, nine-year-old Isabella and seven-year-old Flora, smiled at her, lit up by her presence. Regan knew there'd be a day when the girls didn't want their mom roaming the privileged halls of their school. She read blogs titled "I Forgot to Cherish Every Moment" and "The Last Time My Son Wanted a Hug—If Only I'd Known." So Regan did her best to cherish the damn moment.

After school, Regan took the girls for ice cream. At home, on She Crab Circle, she made them take a bath and combed out their long blond hair with No More Tangles. She fastened them into sundresses, gave each some bubbles from the dollar bin at Target, and sent them out to play in the backyard. Isabella pretended to think bubbles were babyish, but Regan knew her elder daughter was still darling beneath her eye-rolling and hip-jutting poses. As soon as Flora blew through her bubble wand, Isabella dropped her airs and ran barefoot with her sister.

By six, Matt was not home. Regan's calls to his cell went unanswered. She fed the girls pasta with butter and let them watch *Finding Nemo*. When the movie was over and Matt still wasn't back, Regan put the girls to bed and took the phone and a mug of tea into the backyard.

For a few minutes, Regan hesitated. She tried Matt again but the call went to voicemail.

Get away . . . to anywhere but here!

Regan knew she should hold off, just console herself with After Eight mints and her mother's cast-off romance novels. (They lacked the dirty bits, which Charlotte piously ripped out, causing jarring lapses of continuity.) But she was tired of being patient.

Regan gazed at her garden, where she'd considered planting deadly oleander or belladonna. She'd even googled "plants that kill no trace" and then erased her search history. Now, she dialed her oldest friend, Zoë, in Atlanta.

"Hi, stranger!" said Zoë. "To what honor do I owe an evening phone call?"

Regan was careful with her words.

Zoë was silent for a moment, then said, "Hmm. Do you think you should hire a tail?"

"What?" said Regan, biting her thumbnail.

"Believe it or not I know a guy in Savannah," said Zoë, a police officer.

"I believe it," said Regan.

"He's good. Kind of an investigator slash bounty hunter slash sculptor."

"Okay," said Regan.

"I'm calling him for you," said Zoë. "I know you won't call him yourself."

"Oh," said Regan. "Okay, thank you."

"It might be nothing," said Zoë.

"Right," said Regan, pushing against the ground to lift herself into the air. She closed her eyes and imagined everything catching fire: her manicured lawn, her house, every item of clothing in her closets. She would save her girls, and that was all.

4 / Lee

FOR THREE DAYS, LEE drove from Los Angeles to Savannah, where she would take refuge with her mother. Her credit cards maxed out and her bank account empty, she drove all day and curled up in the backseat of her leased Prius at night. Like a child. Or a dog. She paid with Charlotte's ATM card (given to Lee when she went to college to use "in an emergency") for gas and snacks. She called Charlotte as she filled the tank in Atlanta, four hours from Skidaway Island. When Charlotte answered her landline, Lee said, "Hi, Mom, it's me."

"Lee Lee!" cried Charlotte. It warmed Lee that every single time she reached her mother, Charlotte said, "Lee Lee!" as if the call were the greatest thing in the world.

"Mom, I have a surprise," said Lee, her voice rusty from disuse. How long had it been since she had talked to anyone? A week, maybe ten days?

"Oh, honey, what is it?" said Charlotte. "Is it a big new movie role?"

"Not exactly," said Lee, looking upward at the wires above the Sunoco station, where hundreds of grackles roosted in a horrifying spectacle of urban proliferation.

"Is it a small new movie role?" ventured Charlotte.

"No," said Lee. She decided that after this conversation, she'd treat herself to a Twix or a Snickers bar. Maybe both.

"Are you and Jason getting married?"

"Mom . . ." said Lee. She braced herself. The Perkins family didn't talk about things, not really. They forged ahead, pretending everything was perfect. Anyone who made note of a problem or insecurity was a troublemaker and/or "dramatic." Lee had learned long ago to coat her words, no matter how dire, in bulletproof cheer. It was only recently that she was beginning to admit to herself how much it hurt to have to be fine.

Lee was not fine. She hadn't really slept in a long time, and her mind felt as it had when she'd snorted Adderall in college—buzzy, sped-up, full of brilliant ideas and insightful connections. She didn't feel depressed—quite the opposite, in fact: she felt euphoric, driven by a weird, fabulous energy. When her La Quinta key card stopped working on the door to her West Hollywood motel room, she'd realized with a sunlit clarity that she needed a road trip. She wanted to see her mom. And so she gathered her mail (old credit card bills, new credit card offers, a bat mitzvah invitation), gassed up her Prius, and headed east.

"I'm coming home," said Lee.

There was a momentary silence.

"That's the surprise," said Lee.

Charlotte regained herself. "Well, that's the *best news ever*!" she cried.

"It is," said Lee. "It sure is."

"We're going to have *so much fun*!" said Charlotte. "Is Jason with you?"

"No," said Lee. She swallowed, and lied. "He's busy with work. But sends all his love."

"By the way," said Charlotte, "I don't want to get your hopes up, but I entered a contest and I think I might win. It's an all-expenses-paid trip to Europe! A nine-day cruise from Athens, Greece, to Barcelona, Spain!"

"Wow, Mom," said Lee. She worried about Charlotte's fragility. Ever since Lee had found her father's body, she'd felt as if she had to protect Charlotte. It was, quite simply, her job. She called Savannah so often that Jason had complained Lee's "brain space" was so filled with Charlotte that there wasn't enough "brain space" left for an adult romance with him. When Jason began to make money, Lee had used it to send Charlotte fresh flowers every week. Lee still had a credit card in Jason's name, but was too proud to use it, now that he was living with Alexandria Fumillini.

"I can't wait to all be together on the Mediterranean Sea," said Charlotte dreamily.

Lee's stomach clenched. She knew her mother wouldn't win the contest—nobody won these things. But she couldn't bear to see Charlotte disappointed. "Me neither," said Lee weakly.

"Will you be here in time for dinner? I'll make that shrimp stir-fry. The one from *Martha Stewart's Quick Cook*," said Charlotte.

"That would be so great," said Lee. She was overwhelmed with gratitude. No one had made her dinner in a long time.

Lee had subsisted on egg whites and cocaine for years, believing it was just a matter of time before she got the job that would change everything. She'd been so close—called in, called back, singled out, chosen for enough small roles that she could stay afloat—but as Lee grew older and the calls dwindled, she'd begun to recognize that it was entirely possible that everything was never going to change.

What had Lee even wanted in Los Angeles? She'd been told she was beautiful, more beautiful than other people, since she was four years old. (And maybe even before that, but her first memory is her father looking her dead in the eye and saying, "You think you're more beautiful than everyone else, don't you? Well, you're right.")

Throughout high school and college, Lee was cast as the lead in every amateur production from *Guys and Dolls* to *The Seagull*. But was she even a good actress? Classes had always bored her: Lee wanted to be famous, not to delve into sad childhood memories. And sometimes being *too practiced* an actress could work against you. You needed to be relatable, vulnerable. Appealing. You had to be what the casting agent "had in mind." But Lee suspected that often the casting agent didn't even know what this meant. It was a gut thing, like love. And you couldn't train to be beloved. It just happened.

Or it did not.

When Lee's agent, Francine, booked her an audition, Lee prepared by reading the sides, highlighting her lines, stapling her head shot to her résumé. She and Francine would strategize about how she should style her hair, what she should wear, heels or high-tops. The other women in the audition waiting room afforded clues about what the casting director "had in mind": in Lee's early days, the other chairs would be filled with buxom stunners. (This observation had led Lee to her first appointment with a well-respected plastic surgeon and her second line of credit.)

More recently, Lee had found herself in a room of middle-aged character actors. She was up for "MILF" roles for a while, then just regular, nonsexy moms or hot women gone awry. Slowly, calls to Francine stopped coming. Then calls *from* Francine stopped coming. Then Jason (a psychology major turned actor) threatened that if she wouldn't go to a psychiatrist to delve into her "fear of long-term commitment, codependency issues, probable serotonin deficiency, and possible manic tendencies," he would leave her. But Lee had been taught to soldier on, not to delve. Revisiting her father's death was not going to happen—no fucking way.

And so, as promised, Jason left.

Lee had gone to Los Angeles because it was where you went to become rich and famous. For a while, she thought she wasn't smart enough, that she should try harder, really *read* the hardcover Stanislavski she kept on her coffee table. But becoming a serious actor, studying how to change herself into another person, how to inhabit roles—this was not, in the end, very interesting to Lee. She'd curl up with *An Actor Prepares* and a cup of coffee and her mind would just wander. She tried! But it didn't matter how long she stared at the page; she just wasn't into it. She hated it, in fact.

Jason had gotten the Big Job. It was the role of a robot on a sitcom called *Me & My Robot*, but still. In short order, Jason bought a house in the hills, emailed Lee that he was "officially breaking free of my own codependency and moving on," and began dating his costar, a woman in her twenties who was "stable" and "open to having a family." (The new gal pal was "Me" to Jason's sickeningly quirky "Robot.") Her head spinning, Lee vacated their rental apartment at the last hour and checked into a motel.

In a matter of weeks she had used up every scrap of favor and was persona non grata at the hairdresser, gym, yoga studio, Pilates-yoga studio, Whole Foods, and Whole Earth. And her friends! When you moved into a La Quinta, Lee learned, no one wanted to come over for happy hour.

Lee Perkins, voted Most Popular and Best Looking at Savannah Country Day, was an official has-been. She'd truly thought leaving Savannah, moving on from her boyfriend, Matt, was the best decision for all of them. She certainly hadn't thought he'd go and marry her sister!

Although Lee hadn't spoken to Regan since what had happened at the wedding, Lee followed her sister obsessively on social media. Seeing her nieces' bright smiles made Lee feel heartsick. She had never seen Flora and Isabella in person, and longed to meet them.

Regan had once hung on Lee's every word, dressed up in her older sister's clothes. Regan had always been chubby, never a guy magnet like Lee. But she'd been so earnest. A little mother from the start, running to hug Lee after school, offering back scratches and homemade snacks. It made Regan happiest to care for others. Unlike Lee, Regan seemed to have made all the right decisions, and now had grown into the woman she'd been all along inside, her two babies tucked one on either side of her in her Facebook profile photo.

Lee had actually wrapped her arms around two La Quinta pillows one night, imagining, drifting sweetly into sleep.

CHARLOTTE GREETED LEE WITH unreserved enthusiasm, her hair freshly styled and her outfit bright and fashionable. It had been six months since Charlotte's last visit to Los Angeles, and although Lee and her mother spoke often, it gave Lee a start to see her mother looking so, well . . . old.

"I've been a bit down since Minnie died," said Charlotte over their delectable dinner. She poured more awful wine.

"You guys had been friends a long time," said Lee. "Of course you feel down."

Charlotte nodded. "It's hard to know what to look forward to," she said, a rare sorrowful tone in her voice.

"Well," said Lee, scanning desperately for a way to make her mother feel better, "there's the big prize, right? A trip to Europe?"

"Oh, Lee," said Charlotte, her face alight. "We'll sail from Athens all the way to Barcelona! It's called the 'Become a Jetsetter' contest. Even though you don't actually get a private jet. You get first-class tickets. But still."

"It's going to be amazing," said Lee, reaching out to touch her mother's hand. "So we can look forward to that. Right, Mom?"

"Right," said Charlotte. "You're right, Lee!" Lee gulped another sip of wine. Charlotte gripped her hand so hard it felt as if she were hanging on for dear life. "You always make everything better," said Charlotte, and something in her voice—fear, hope—made the words sound less like a compliment and more like a desperate plea. Lee felt nervous, and wanted to wrest herself free. But she didn't move.

5 / Charlotte

IN THE MORNING, CHARLOTTE went to mass. When she knelt after communion, during the time she felt she had the most direct and clear line to God, she prayed, *Dear God, please let me win a Mediterranean cruise.*

Charlotte felt lighter as she navigated the road home, rolling down her car window and taking in the marsh-scented air. In town, brick row houses lined historic squares, while on the Landings, giant, new homes had been made to look historic and *Gone-with-the-Wind*y: imitation Taras with basketball hoops out front. Charlotte lived in a row of condominiums facing the ninth hole of the Deer Creek golf course. She parked her Volkswagen Rabbit and took a moment to revel in the fact that when she climbed the three brick steps to her front door, let herself inside, and called, "Helloooo!" someone would answer. Lee was home.

The first time Charlotte held newborn Lee, her first baby, Louisa was bustling around her hospital room, arranging flowers and neatening up, nattering about how thankful Charlotte should be that Louisa had insisted the doctors induce "twilight sleep," which was on its way out

of vogue. As later exposés predicted, Charlotte would en-
dure flashbacks of horrifying bits of memories over the
years, her brain having experienced Lee's birth no matter
how much morphine and mind-erasing drugs she'd been
given that night. The exposés wrote that women were tied
down as they labored, left screaming and terrified, doctors
blithely monitoring their progress under the assumption
that the women wouldn't remember a thing.

A nurse handed Charlotte her daughter. She looked
down blearily at the child. Lee's eyes bored into Charlotte's—so blue! So intense! Charlotte met Lee's gaze and
thought, *Oh. At last. Here is the person meant just for me.*
Charlotte smiled at Lee, and Lee's eyes fell shut. Pride
made Charlotte warm and weepy.

"Look at her," Winston said, appearing at Charlotte's
bedside, reeking of the cigars he'd been handing out in the
hospital hallways and puffing in the TV lounge. His face
was kind and flushed. He seemed happy—for the moment,
at least. Or maybe—the wish flickered in Charlotte's mind
like the flame from Winston's silver lighter—the baby
would cure him. They had named her Elizabeth Lear, combining Winston's grandmother's name with the name of
Charlotte and Winston's favorite Shakespeare play, which
they had seen performed outdoors in Paris at the very start
of their friendship. Her name would be shortened to Lee
within days.

"Look at our girl," said Winston.

Charlotte nodded, her arms tightening around the infant. She thought, *She's not our girl. She's mine.*

IN FACT, WHEN CHARLOTTE climbed the brick steps and
called, "Hellloooo!" no one answered. Lee was still asleep.

Charlotte changed into her one-piece bathing suit and terry-cloth cover-up, then packed her monogrammed beach bag with two towels and three romance novels. When Charlotte was halfway through *The New York Times*, Lee emerged in a negligee. She held her cellphone to her ear, grabbing the coffeepot, pouring herself a cup, and heading back toward the guest room, waving to Charlotte wordlessly and gesturing to her phone, as if she were transacting an important business deal in her underpants.

"Would you like an English muffin?" Charlotte called to her daughter's backside.

"Sure, Mom, thanks!" said Lee over her shoulder.

"Toasted? With lots of butter?" said Charlotte.

"Sure! Thanks!" cried Lee, moving up the stairs and down the hall, shutting the guest room door.

Well! Charlotte returned to the kitchen and pulled an English muffin apart, placed it in the toaster oven. Something was wrong with the toaster: it worked, but took fifteen or more minutes to make anything brown. Charlotte thought of replacing the appliance, but she wasn't in any hurry—who cared if her muffins took a while? When Lee's breakfast was finally ready, Charlotte carried it (on a china plate, with a folded napkin) toward the guest room. Charlotte heard Lee speaking, but couldn't make out the words. When Charlotte knocked and delivered Lee's breakfast, Lee was sitting on the bed with the phone still pressed to her ear, surrounded by junk mail. "What are those?" said Charlotte. "Credit card applications?"

"What?" said Lee. "No, no. I'll be out soon. Thanks for the muffin!"

When Lee finally emerged, she and Charlotte went to the pool, where they read romance novels in the sun, shared lunch with margaritas, and then headed back to

Charlotte's house in the golf cart. "I'm going to Publix. Do you want anything?" said Charlotte.

"We might need some wine?"

"Got it." Charlotte slowed the cart to stop at the mailbox, reached in, and placed a stack of envelopes on Lee's lap. Moments later, Charlotte pulled into the garage. She'd hung a tennis ball from the ceiling: when the ball hit the windshield, Charlotte halted and plugged in the golf cart to recharge.

"Well, I'd better call my agent again," said Lee, hopping off the cart. "See what's new."

"Ooooh, yes," said Charlotte, gathering their wet towels and magazines. Lee dumped the mail on the counter and grabbed her phone. Charlotte sorted through a stack of catalogs and coupons before discovering a large white envelope with her name and address typed on the front. "Oh," she said, hope like a hot balloon in her chest. It couldn't be. It couldn't be. But it was: a letter from Splendido Cruise Lines.

"What is it?" said Lee.

Charlotte realized she was shaking. Was this another manifestation of old age, or simply nerves? Most likely it was shock. She gripped the letter, opened it slowly. Its words swam in front of her eyes: *Congratulations! Pleased to inform; Please call as soon as possible; Charlotte Perkins; first-class; Athens, Greece.*

Charlotte was suffused with joy. If only he could see me now, she thought, the "he" referring to a few men: the one she had written the essay about (those strong hands on her), the husband who had never known her (those small hands, kind of stubby and soft), the golf pro whose hands (she really did think, though perhaps she was deluded) lingered a bit too long on her hips as he adjusted her swing.

A lover. A fighter. A winner: Charlotte Perkins.

Of *course* she was too classy for cruising. She was elegant and refined, more suited to posh hotel rooms in London or Paris. But Charlotte hadn't been able to go anywhere, posh or otherwise, in fifty years! She was above the sorts of vacations she could afford. And so she had stayed put. But now, her insides buzzed as if she were filled with champagne. *So what* if cruises were cheesy?

Charlotte took a shaky breath. She and her children would enjoy European wonders, then sit in a row on a cruise-ship deck as the sun set over the Mediterranean, toasting one another with overfilled glasses of Chardonnay!

Maybe she would even meet a man who wanted to kiss her, who would run his warm hands down her back to her bottom, cup her buttocks and pull her into him . . . Oh, here she was in broad daylight, imagining her dream lover's erection straining at his expensive gabardine slacks. She tried to make herself stay in reality, but her brain allowed her dream lover to press himself into her private place, his mouth on her neck. She flushed, hot with desire and embarrassment.

"Are you okay, Mom?" said Lee.

"Oh, honey," said Charlotte, meeting the eyes of her firstborn. Lee's gaze was as direct and penetrating as when she was a baby. Charlotte grabbed her girl, wrapped her tight. This cruise would fix whatever was broken in Lee, would repair and renew them all. "Oh, honey," said Charlotte. "I won!"

6 / Cord

IT WAS A RUNNING joke between Cord and Giovanni: Cord's mother always called when they were having sex. It was as if she had a sixth sense. Cord had begun leaving his phone and his dog in the kitchen with the door shut when things got going. "I'll be back soon," he told Franklin on Thursday evening.

The dog looked at him knowingly.

"Okay," said Cord. "You're right. It might be a little while. You understand, right?"

Franklin sank into his Hermès dog bed and sighed.

When he'd finally gotten sober (for the last time—really!), Cord had bought an aromatic diffuser and noise machine to protect his fragile nervous system. If he did say so himself, his bedroom was an oasis of calm. "Lavender or ylang-ylang?" he said, entering the room and brandishing two tiny blue bottles.

"Who cares?" said Giovanni. "Come here."

Cord shook his head, loving Giovanni, his innate happiness. Had Cord ever been whole, even when he was twenty-one, a newly minted Princeton graduate with a fancy job in venture capital and a secret midnight life in

Alphabet City, drinking and drugging and sleeping with every boy in sight? God, those had been good days. But fake days, impossible to sustain. He looked at Giovanni, impatient, erect. "I said," repeated Giovanni, "come here."

Cord hurriedly dumped lavender oil in the diffuser, pressed Mist, breathed deeply, and launched himself across the room toward his fiancé.

Fiancé!

Midway through the proceedings, Franklin escaped from the kitchen and entered the bedroom, trying to make his way stealthily onto the mattress. "Your . . . damn . . . dog," said Giovanni.

"Our dog," said Cord. "Yes, yes, he's OUR DOG, GIOVANNI!"

Franklin watched them both with disdain.

Afterward, Giovanni lit a cigarette. "What's the plan with the dog, anyway?" he said.

"The plan?" said Cord, watching Giovanni's face. The lonely voice in Cord's brain said, *He's going to tell you to get rid of Franklin. He's going to tell you it's him or the dog.*

"The wedding plan," said Giovanni. "I mean, does he walk with us down the aisle, with, like, rings around his neck? Or is he going to be a flower girl, with your sister's kids and my many, many adorable nieces?"

Cord's stomach—always seconds from chaos—eased. "Ring bearer," he said.

"Yeah, I like that," said Giovanni.

Cord watched Giovanni's smoke trail toward the ceiling. He closed his eyes, so happy it overwhelmed him. This was one of the pleasures of recovery: you opened the door to the pain and gnawing tedium, but joy came in as well. All of it, all of it, brilliant and clean and true.

Giovanni continued to speak, but Cord tuned it out,

took long inhales of the lavender-and-cigarette-scented air.

"I know you can hear me," said Giovanni.

"Sorry, what?" said Cord.

"I said," said Giovanni, "we've been together for over a year. We're *engaged*. When am I meeting your mom and sisters?"

"I'll keep you posted," said Cord. He sat up. "I've got to go in."

Giovanni looked pensive, clearly deciding whether he was going to drop the subject. He sighed, then said, "Are you having a meeting about the super-duper secret company that's going to make us rich?"

"I could tell you, but then I'd have to kill you."

"Yeesh. When can I retire?" said Giovanni, who was twenty-five, and had been teaching middle school art and Italian at Dalton for three years.

"Soon," said Cord. The IPO for 3rd Eyez was fast approaching, and with his firm's stake in the company, Cord was going to be very rich. *If* the 3rd Eyez virtual reality product was as amazing as Cord was pretty sure it was. He'd allegedly "experienced" the product 535 days ago, during his last booze blackout.

Giovanni put out his cigarette in an ashtray Cord had stolen from the Plaza in his youth. "Are you just with me for my money?" said Cord, his tone joking, but the lonely voice answering, *Yes*.

"I'm with you for your body," said Giovanni.

Cord smiled. He did try to make the most of his appointments with his personal trainer, Thatcher.

"You'll keep me posted?" said Giovanni. "About meeting Charlotte Perkins?"

"Please stop calling her that."

"What should I call her?"

"I don't know," said Cord, climbing from bed. "I just don't know."

"I'm not the type to wait around," said Giovanni. Though his tone was light, the words felt like a slap. (The lonely voice would repeat them all day.)

Giovanni had come out to his Italian American family when he was thirteen. He'd been president of his high school LGBTQ club. Savannah Country Day had not had an LGBTQ club. Officially, in 1980s Savannah, there was no such thing as being L, G, or B, and certainly not T or Q. Cord had kept his worlds separate for so long that he'd become two people: the Cord who existed in Manhattan, and the Cord he became when he visited Savannah.

Holiday Cord: a straight man, just picky, a person who glossed over real questions and flew back to New York when he couldn't take another minute of subterfuge. By ignoring the pain he was causing his mother, he hadn't been Holiday Cord in seven years. But he couldn't stay away from his family forever . . . or could he?

He could certainly try.

His relationships with his sisters were limited to emailing and texting. They'd send photos, chain-letter jokes, bons mots. (Never copying each other—Cord's sisters' Shakespearean feud was a brick wall between them.) Regan texted animated GIFs of women in various stages of disarray—pulling their hair out with acronyms such as "OMG" or "WTF" superimposed above them, hoisting giant glasses of wine ("TGIF!!!"). Lee and Cord exchanged photos of unfashionable strangers every few days, adding snide commentary—amateur Joan Riverses on the red carpet of life. Were these even relationships, or just data trails, vestiges of the love between people who had once been family?

Did all siblings revert to their childhood selves when they were together, or was there a way to transition to functional adulthood even while being in one another's lives? Was estrangement normal, healthy even? And if so, why did it feel as if he were missing a limb sometimes? Missing two limbs—two appendages that wouldn't speak to each other because of a surgeon named Matt.

Matt! Most of the time, Cord just felt sorry for the guy, caught up in the Perkins girls' web of drama. But Cord would be lying if he didn't admit that once in a while he wished Matt dead. What a joyful reunion they might have, at Matt's funeral!

Cord tried not to mind that no one in his family asked about his personal life, and didn't want to examine his own motives in keeping his orientation under wraps. It was probable that his sisters knew he was gay and just didn't care. The dysfunction almost certainly lay inside Cord, a snake of self-loathing and childish fear. It was something he should "unpack," in the words of his AA sponsor, a former child actor called Handy. But Cord was just fine with his emotional suitcase remaining zipped tight and locked.

"Did you hear me?" said Giovanni, following Cord into the kitchen, where (of course) his phone showed three missed calls from his mother. "I said, I'm not just going to wait around. This is sick, honey!"

"I hear you," said Cord. He hoped that Giovanni would drop the issue eventually, because Cord's feelings about a meeting between his mother and his lover were *hell no, never ever, not happening.*

That evening, Cord bought a bouquet of pink roses in

Grand Central as he waited for the 5:54 train to Rye. He was nervous, even though he'd met Giovanni's enormous family before and they'd always been kind to him. Giovanni's father, Cosimus, spent his free time on his La-Z-Boy couch, watching football and accepting the food and drink set before him by Giovanni's mother, Rose. Their small house was always filled with relatives, friends, and the smell of baked ziti. Still, Cord wasn't sure how the Lombardis would take the news of their gay son being engaged.

Oh, how he wanted a beer, or seven beers. It was still hard for Cord to "feel his feelings." He ate a Twix as the Stamford local rumbled out of Grand Central. If he waited, he knew, the edginess would fade on its own. And Giovanni, his salve, would be picking him up at the station.

"I told them," said Giovanni, as soon as they were strapped in his mother's Toyota, heading for the house on Mead Place.

"Please," said Cord. "Tell me you didn't."

"I did," said Giovanni. "Don't worry."

"I feel like I'm going to throw up," said Cord. He rolled down the car window, hoping the fresh air would help. Rye's Purchase Street rolled past: June & Ho, Crisfield's Prime Meats, Rye Eye Care, Royal Jewels of Rye. Giovanni had grown up walking to the Smoke Shop to buy his parents cigarettes, he'd told Cord. Rose had always given Giovanni an extra dime for Swedish Fish candy.

"I don't know what you're so ashamed of," said Giovanni now.

Cord looked at him. Giovanni's mouth was set in a grim line. "I . . ." said Cord.

"This is a happy occasion," said Giovanni. "I've been to eight thousand wedding showers for my sisters and cousins and tonight it's about *me*. Sorry, *us*. I find it pretty disturbing that the only person who thinks we're doing something wrong, Cord, is you."

"I'm sorry," said Cord.

"Get yourself sorted out," said Giovanni, pulling into his parents' driveway.

Cord felt a sense of dread; there was no other way to put it. The lonely voice was his father's, telling him to *focus and get your act together, for Christ's sake* when Cord couldn't catch the baseball in the backyard.

"We're here," said Giovanni.

"I'm sorry," said Cord. He had a hard time getting out of the car. He felt foggy, disoriented, as if he might pass out.

"What is it?" said Giovanni, his face pained. "Why can't you just be proud of who you are?"

Before Cord could answer, the door to Giovanni's childhood home opened, and Rose came running out. She was overweight, wearing polyester slacks, a T-shirt, and an apron. She had shoulder-length gray hair and wore Pan-Cake makeup and fabulous fake eyelashes. Right in the driveway, she enveloped Cord in a hug that smelled of floral perfume and tomatoes. Cord relaxed in her embrace. The lonely voice was silent. "I made ziti for you, Cord," said Rose. "I made ziti."

How wonderful it felt to be held by a mother who knew you.

7 / Regan

REGAN WOKE IN HER daughter's bedroom. It wasn't un-
common for her to sleep next to Flora—Regan was an in-
somniac and she just felt safer snuggled next to her
sweet-smelling daughter than next to her husband.

For a moment, Regan lay still, watching Flora breathe.
The curve of her nose, her lashes against her impossibly
milky skin! For a moment, Regan questioned her plan. She
promised herself that she would make sure Flora was okay,
even afterward.

Regan rose, stretched, and padded down the hallway in
her silk pajamas. Matt was fast asleep in the master bedroom, one arm tossed out, as if reaching for something. His
mouth was open and he snored loudly, without shame.
What must it be like, wondered Regan (not for the first
time), to access such abandon? Regan thought that her in-
somnia likely had roots in her fear of losing control. Her
high school art teacher, Alphonso Ragdale, had once told
her she was most beautiful while she slept. Besides the
obvious-in-retrospect creepiness of the comment, Regan
wondered if it had made her feel (on some unconscious

level) that she must *always* be lovely in sleep, a belief that
kept her from being actually, messily, at rest.

Regan's mind whirred. Her mother had called the day
before with the bizarre news that she had won a Mediterranean cruise. Charlotte wanted Regan to join her on the
cruise, along with Regan's siblings. "Please, honey," said Charlotte. "Please, let me fly you to Europe before I'm gone."

Regan's mother loved theatrical pronouncements.

"Please!" cried Charlotte.

"I don't know what to say." The last thing on earth
Regan wanted was a trip without her children and with
her mother and siblings.

Five sessions with an online therapist had taught Regan
how toxic her family was. She should, said the online therapist, accept that they were estranged. She should make
peace with it. And she was trying. But Regan missed them;
she just did. Sometimes she dreamed of playing with her
sister and brother on a giant trampoline while Charlotte
watched, pouring lemonade. They were so happy, jumping
and jumping! In the dream, Regan didn't even pee a little
the way she did in real life when she jumped on a trampoline.

"Come on, honey," said Charlotte. "Come on, cute little
Regan-doodle!"

Something in Regan relaxed when her mother called
her "Regan-doodle." After Winston died suddenly of a heart
attack, Lee and Cord were always too busy to spend time
with Charlotte. When they moved into a rental home, it
was Regan who hung out in the tiny kitchen when Charlotte got home from work; Regan resting her elbows on the
butcher-block table, settling on a tall stool and swinging
her legs.

"What would I do without you, my Regan-doodle?" Charlotte would say, easing off her high heels and pouring a glass of wine, poking through the refrigerator for a snack.

Regan would flush with a ten-year-old's happiness, telling Charlotte to sit down, arranging a vegetable platter with hummus, refilling Charlotte's drink. Sometimes, Regan would make up stories about imaginary mean-girl friends. Charlotte loved to hear that Regan was happy and very popular, though in truth she was lonely and embarrassed by her used clothes and wrong-side-of-the-YMCA address.

Every weekend, when her mother and siblings slept late, Regan gathered their discarded laundry and washed it in the basement, placing baskets of folded, clean clothes outside their rooms.

Regan sighed, missing being a barefoot ten-year-old with French braids and freckles. What would that girl do in Regan's situation? Regan winced, understanding how pathetic that girl would think the adult Regan was: so passive! And a *housewife*? That girl, Regan knew, would jet out of town.

Regan had tried to make Matt love her again. For years, she had tried. And then she gave up slowly, and told herself it was enough to live as roommates, as friends. But Regan would never let a friend treat her the way Matt treated her. Worse: the girls saw him treat Regan badly, and he had begun to make comments about the girls as well. Regan had broached divorce only once, after a few glasses of wine. "Maybe we'd both be happier . . ." she ventured, "if we tried a separation . . ."

He had turned toward her, his face cold. And then he'd

thrown his glass to the floor, where it landed with a very scary *thud*. "Shh," said Regan. "The girls."

"The girls?" said Matt. "Now you're worried about *the girls*?"

"Matt, I just—"

"If you leave me," said Matt. "You'll have nothing. I promise you."

"But, Matt . . ."

"No!" he said, grabbing Regan's upper arm so hard that she gasped. Matt stared at her and then released her arm roughly. "I am not a fucking failure," he said.

Neither am I, said Regan, to herself.

"ARE YOU READY TO be a jetsetter, Regan-doodle?" said Charlotte.

"What about Flora and Isabella?" said Regan.

"Send them to sleepaway camp," suggested Charlotte. "You *loved* sleepaway camp!"

"No," said Regan. "That was Lee. I went to day camp." A memory surfaced: standing in a giant gymnasium, realizing that she was the only girl at basketball camp. The smell of boys' armpits and socks. She'd taken her sketchbook from her backpack and hidden under the bleachers, drawing mermaids in underwater kingdoms until it was time to go home, wincing at the sound of dribbling basketballs and piercing sneaker squeaks.

"That's right. Well, anyhoo," said Charlotte.

"I don't have a passport," said Regan.

"Mine is expired," said Charlotte. "We'll expedite them. We can figure out the paperwork together!"

"Is this really happening?" said Regan.

"Yippee!" said Charlotte.

———

REGAN HAD FOUND A horseback riding camp in eastern Georgia. The girls were thrilled. All that remained was telling Matt. She watched him sleep. He was tall and stocky, with thinning black hair and a bit of a paunch. Regan could still remember him as a teenage football star, Lee's impossibly wonderful boyfriend, the one person Regan had thought of to call when she changed her mind about running away with Mr. Ragdale. And Matt had come, rescuing Regan from her art teacher, bringing her home on the back of his Harley-Davidson. Lee was gone by then, having ditched Matt to move to Los Angeles. Matt came by some evenings to sit on the porch swing with Regan.

Their romance had developed slowly. Matt had helped Regan talk about Mr. Ragdale, had insisted it wasn't her fault. Matt thought they should press charges. But Regan just wanted to forget the whole episode, and Charlotte agreed they should never speak of it again. Regan transferred to a different high school for her senior year. Matt, who had enrolled in the premed program at Savannah Technical College, worked in town at a bar called Pinkie Masters. When Regan stopped by with her friends, he gave her free drinks. (She was partial to Alabama slammers, as her fake ID said she was from Montgomery, Alabama. Never a big drinker, she'd have one and then switch to Sprite.)

One night, Regan came on her own. It was karaoke night, and Regan nursed a soda and studied for her English final exam. She was stunned when she heard Matt's voice through the speakers. "This one goes out to my angel from Montgomery," he said. Regan looked up and saw that he was smiling at her. His voice singing the Bonnie Raitt song was smooth and low. Regan couldn't breathe. It was the first moment she glimpsed the possibility of her greatest dream coming true.

"Just give-a me one thing," crooned Matt, "that I can hold on to."

Regan bit her lip. She nodded.

They made love soon afterward, on the night of her eighteenth birthday, just weeks before she was accepted to NYU. As Matt looked deep into her eyes and entered her, moved inside her gently, saying her name, she knew she would never leave Savannah. He was her love; he was home.

Regan stared at her sleeping husband. For a moment, she regretted what she had done at Bonna Bella Yacht Club. But it was too late.

Matt opened his eyes. "Hey," he said.

Just give me one thing that I can hold on to.

"My mom won a cruise," said Regan. "I told the girls they could go to sleepaway camp and I'm going. With my family. On the cruise."

"What?"

"I'm going away for a while," said Regan. Her voice wavered.

"Mmm," said Matt. He closed his eyes. Regan thought he had fallen back asleep, but then he opened his eyes. His gaze locked with hers.

"I'm coming with you," he said.

8 / Lee

LEE CERTAINLY HADN'T THOUGHT she'd take her first flight to Europe with her mother. But one of the joys of social media was its ability to obfuscate. For example, a shot she made her mother take in the airport waiting area would show Lee looking serene, one leg crossed in front of the other, showing off her beautiful shoes. (As soon as she made sure her photo was postable, she could switch them out for the flip-flops in her bag.)

Lee's mother was having a hard time hefting her old suitcase, which she'd refused to check. As soon as Charlotte had gotten the news that she had won the contest, she had begun digging around in her condo crawl space, unearthing a suite of old luggage, repeating that she had *so much to do* to prepare for the trip. When Lee asked what was making her feel so overwhelmed, Charlotte wrung her hands and just said, "Everything! Hand sanitizer! Peanut butter crackers!"

Lee had taken the golf cart to Publix and loaded up on mini hand sanitizers, travel-size cracker packs, women's magazines, and wine. She'd slowed next to a small refrigerator labeled FLORAL SECTION and grabbed a bouquet. "I love you, Mom," she said, when she got home, handing Charlotte the flowers.

"Oh, my," said Charlotte, visibly moved.

The timing *was* rushed, but Lee was glad for an adventure to take her mind off the incessant tabloid coverage of Jason and Alexandria. Their romantic days biking in the Los Angeles sunshine; entering and exiting gyms; walking a new puppy they'd adopted from the ASPCA. (A "schnoodle" puppy, a cross between a schnauzer and a poodle that could not be any cuter.) Their sultry nights: sushi for two; Lionel Richie's birthday party; ice cream cones after dark as they walked Noodles the schnoodle.

When asked about the adorable pup's name, Alexandria's laughter rang out. "I guess I just love noodles!" she confided.

Her smitten hunk added, "She really does love noodles."

"Who doesn't love noodles?" Lee had cried, throwing her phone across Charlotte's guest bed.

"What's that, dear?" Charlotte had called.

"NOTHING!" Lee had screamed.

"You want noodles for dinner?" Charlotte had said, appearing at the door in a golf visor and bathing suit.

Lee, tears at the corners of her eyes, had nodded sadly.

AT GATE C-22, LEE rushed to help her mother with her circular suitcase. What was this thing? A hatbox? "I've got it, Mom," said Lee. She grabbed the handle and it came off in her hand.

"My bag!" cried Charlotte.

"We'll just have to get you a brand-new one in Europe," said Lee.

"But these were the bags I had last time," said Charlotte. "They're French."

Last time? Lee's mood darkened. She had read that older people sometimes became hoarders. It was a way of maintaining control or something. Lee had, in fact, played a hoarder on an episode of *CSI*. She'd been a prostitute-hoarder and they'd made her wear a red wig and a maroon negligee. She and Jason had hosted a big party to watch the episode, and everyone had lifted their champagne glasses when she said her two lines: "I thought you were coming tomorrow. I haven't had time to tidy up."

Clink, clink! Life had been good.

Lee slumped next to her mother in the boarding area. Charlotte was examining the torn luggage handle, looking utterly lost. Where was Cord when they needed him? He had always been the one to placate Charlotte, taking care of her, soothing her. He'd become the man of the house at fourteen. But they wouldn't see Cord until they arrived in Athens.

Lee, at her brother's behest, had called and changed Cord's ticket so he could fly directly to Greece. Lee and Cord had a text stream going about jetsetting fashion. Every time one of them saw someone with a fanny pack or awful sunglasses, they texted each other an image with the hashtag #jetsetter. Lee loved texting with her brother. It was so much better than having to speak. In some ways, she was closer to her brother than to anyone else—they texted many times a day! She figured he was as lonely as she was, and was similarly looking forward to sharing stories about how their lives had dead-ended over cocktails in some weird cruise ship bar.

"I'm really sorry about your bag, Mom," said Lee. Charlotte seemed bewildered, and Lee felt a bolt of fear. Any sign of weakness in her mother made Lee feel completely unmoored. Charlotte's frankly appraising looks, her bad wine and wonderful dinners, the absolute *fact* of her, and knowing what she was doing every night (watching Brian Williams with Godiva, the cat) were things Lee depended on. It was honestly embarrassing how much Lee still needed Charlotte. As long as her mother was around, Lee could still be a child messing up, knowing that Charlotte would come along behind her, pick up after her, and make things right. Oh, how she'd loved as a teenager the way Charlotte had gathered her dirty clothes and returned them, perfectly folded, in a basket outside her bedroom door!

"Mom," Lee said gently. "You know we're going to Europe, right?"

Charlotte looked up, her face almost childlike. "Europe," she said.

"Yes."

"Lee," said Charlotte.

"Yes?"

"You're too old for a skirt that short."

And just like that, the bitch was back. Lee was filled with relief and familiar anger. "I am not," she said, sounding in her own ears like a petulant teenager. How she missed being a petulant teenager! Adulthood was the worst.

"I beg to differ," said Charlotte. "Here's your phone, dear."

Lee felt hurt, dejected, and frustrated that she felt hurt and dejected. When would her need to win Charlotte dissipate?

Lee scrutinized the photo of herself, applied a filter to brighten her face, and cropped. Then she instagrammed,

facebooked, tumblred, snapchatted, and tweeted, caption-
ing the shot, *#jetsetter #offtoeurope #jimmychoos #bonvoy-
age!*

For a moment, Lee savored the fact that she was living
the life she'd imagined when she cut out magazine pictures during a vision-board workshop. She had actually vi-
sualized world travel. She'd meditated upon these very
hashtags, when Jason had made her meditate every morning for three mornings in a row. And now they were hers.

Maybe everything was going to be okay. Lee did feel
calmer after two weeks of home-cooked meals, Tylenol
PM, and a captive audience (Charlotte) who hung on her
every word and trusted Lee when she said she was on a
hiatus before a big film project. The more Lee bragged
about her career, the more she almost believed herself. Her
stomach had stopped cramping, her racing thoughts had
slowed a bit, and she'd bought a neon bikini at T.J.Maxx
with Charlotte's money that had been an absolute sensa-
tion when she waltzed around Marshwood Pool. The attention of men: Lee knew it was a makeshift and ultimately
useless ice pack held to the burning fact that her life was a
mess, but comfort was comfort, no matter how fleeting.

Lee had been afraid she'd run into Regan around the
Landings—pass her on the golf cart path, spy her splashing down the waterslide with her girls at Franklin Creek
Pool—but it never happened. She thought of stopping by
the Willingham McMansion, but it just seemed easier to
put off their inevitable reunion. They hadn't spoken in ten
years. Ten years! Lee had called Regan dozens of times
in the months after the prewedding blowout, but Regan
hadn't answered, and eventually, Lee had been hurt enough
to give up. This mess wasn't her fault! Well, not entirely.

Still, Lee and Regan had been so close once. Lee could

remember roller-skating with Regan, staying out until dusk. They would hold hands, whizzing along the streets of their neighborhood, the evening air warm across their faces.

What could Lee have done differently? For one thing, she could have kept Matt's words to herself. Many times, she wished she had kept silent in the bathroom of Elizabeth on 37th, just given her sister a hug and whispered congratulations. But that would have felt as if she were hiding things from Regan.

Matt, in the rain, gripping Lee's shoulders. *I'd stop all this if you want me back. Please?*

LEE SWALLOWED, TRYING TO quell a decade-old confusion. She glanced down at her phone. Her post was racking up the hearts and likes already.

"Regan!" cried Charlotte. "Regan's here!"

Lee looked up and saw her sister. Regan looked resplendent—that was the word. She had put on some weight, but in a smart, black pantsuit and jean jacket, rhinestone-studded sunglasses holding back her auburn hair, she was stunning. Jealousy washed over Lee, a bitter wave.

"Over here!" called Charlotte, standing and waving. "Regan! We're over here!" Charlotte hugged Regan, and Lee stood awkwardly next to them, unable to speak. There was so much she wanted to say: *I'm sorry. I love you. You have everything I wanted. Please look up to me again.*

Lee glanced down at her own tiny miniskirt, suddenly embarrassed by her skimpy attire. Seeing Regan embrace her momhood made Lee's getup seem tawdry. What was she trying to prove? She closed her eyes and inhaled, summoning strength, remembering the way the Uber driver's gaze had lingered on her legs as she climbed out of his Honda Pilot. What else did she have to offer, besides her attractiveness?

"There you are," said Matt, approaching. To Lee's surprise, his hair was thinning—he was almost bald. He wore an expensive suit and loafers.

"Are you wearing loafers?" said Lee. She wasn't trying to be flirtatious, but it did sound that way.

Matt's eyes flashed, pleased. "I am," he said. "Do you like them?"

"I'm not the loafer-loving type," said Lee.

Matt put his arm around Regan and pulled her close. "Regan bought them for me," said Matt.

"Oh," said Regan. She seemed to flinch in his embrace. "You said you wanted . . ."

"They're fine," said Matt sharply. Lee blinked. His voice sounded exactly like their father's. My God, she thought, Matt's turned into a balding Winston. Was that why she had chosen him a million years ago? Some sick need to be with her father, to make a better ending to that story?

From the moment she had first seen Matt (walking down the hallway of Savannah Country Day as if he *owned* the place), Lee had been besotted. Matt—a scholarship kid, a running back, confident and well-spoken and utterly at ease in his own skin—was everything Lee wished she could be. Now, she felt a wash of fear. Regan did look pale. Was Matt unkind to her?

Regan looked at Lee, her gaze sad.

"You look beautiful," said Lee.

"Oh, please," said Regan. But she flushed, and as her cheeks reddened, Lee remembered Regan's evening performances for her family. She would make little tickets to her "song show," and they would all assemble on the back porch. Regan welcomed them, standing on the lawn in her nightgown. She took their tickets. And then she would sing in a clear and angelic voice. When she was finished, she'd look down, as she was now, growing flustered when they clapped.

Without thinking, Lee hugged her sister. Regan stiffened in her arms and pulled away. But she smelled the same: baby powder deodorant, strawberry shampoo.

9 / Charlotte

IN HER FIRST-CLASS SEAT, a plush blanket across her lap, a bowl of warm mixed nuts on the tray table in front of her, Charlotte gazed at her daughters. Lee (who had begun drinking wine and chatting with her seatmate, a young man with a beard, as soon as she boarded) was dead asleep, her mouth open. Regan gazed out the window, lost in thought. What, Charlotte wondered, was Regan dreaming about?

Charlotte knew it wasn't fair to feel a keen annoyance whenever she saw Regan in her showy, flowy clothing. Her daughter, wearing muumuus instead of going on a diet! It made Charlotte feel guilty, as if *she'd* done something wrong.

Over the years, Charlotte had resolved to be nicer to Regan, who was, after all, the only child who had remained near her. But Regan's servitude to Matt, her overparenting, and her drawstring pants made Charlotte's stomach ache. Charlotte had learned some things the hard way, but Regan didn't want to hear them. Regan thought Charlotte was silly, her opinions useless. Charlotte feared the same about herself, so being around someone who treated her like a child was painful.

Regan had known Charlotte at her worst—as a single mother, scrimping and saving, pandering to nouveau riche (and regular riche) clients. To Regan, Charlotte must have been a cautionary tale: See what can happen if your husband leaves you. You will end up alone. You will cry in front of your children. You will work hard, so hard, and fail. Now that Charlotte had regained a bit of dignity, she hated imagining what Regan thought of her, all the raw and broken moments Regan had seen.

And Regan hadn't even seen the worst thing!

The truth was that Charlotte envied her own daughter. Dismissing Regan allowed Charlotte not to examine her own shame, guilt, and jealousy.

Charlotte had not appreciated the sudden addition of Matt to her vacation. But he had paid his way, so how could she argue without causing a scene? It was kind of sweet, Charlotte supposed, but still, she was annoyed. Matt was a surgeon—maybe he would be called home for some orthopedic emergency. Charlotte could only hope (and send a quick prayer skyward). Hadn't Matt ruined enough already?

Or maybe her family's dissolution was Charlotte's fault—this was possible. She couldn't pinpoint any one thing she'd done wrong, but somehow her later years had become a mirror of her lonely childhood. How to remedy this—what actions to take or wounds to bandage—she wasn't sure. She hoped this trip would fill something, bring them together around her again. But on the flight to Athens, all she felt was dislocated.

Charlotte wished she were a pill popper. She closed her eyes, courting sleep but instead seeing her mother's face:

that pinch in the middle of Louisa's forehead, the way her lipstick bled into the crevices around her mouth. Her Parliament cigarettes ringed with ruby.

When her father was transferred to France, eight-year-old Charlotte was left behind in Washington, D.C., with her nanny. At ten, she was sent to boarding school. This was not seen as a punishment: it was the way things worked in their diplomatic circles. Her father, Richard, was twenty-eight years older than her mother. He was like a distant grandfather, and more than anything else, Charlotte ached for him to notice her.

Charlotte's mother had been the belle of the ball. Even when Charlotte was home on school holiday, Louisa (who had her own bedroom separate from her husband and breakfasted alone in bed every morning) was at her desk by 8:30 A.M. She worked on her correspondence until it was time to meet with the housekeeper, who supervised a staff of seventeen. The chef met with Louisa for fifteen minutes, and most days there was a luncheon. Louisa shopped and visited the hairdresser in the afternoons, then made absolutely sure to see Charlotte from 5:00 to 6:00 P.M. (Charlotte was usually in the bathtub. Her mother perched on the toilet and drank a sherry, gazing past Charlotte's pink shoulders and toward the window that opened onto the 8th arrondissement below.)

In the evenings, Charlotte's mother and father attended receptions, exhibitions, banquets, and long dinner parties. In her spare time, Louisa brushed up on her seven foreign languages (French, Italian, German, Swedish, Hungarian, Japanese, Chinese) or worked on her historical novel.

Charlotte tried to sleep alone. Often, when it was so late she was *sure* her nanny, Aimeé, was asleep, Charlotte would steal down the stairs to Aimeé's room, where she would curl up near enough to feel her nanny's warmth. Aimeé, a heavyset woman from a rural village, likely felt more out of place in Paris than Charlotte did. When Charlotte woke, she was tucked in tight, the sheets still smelling of Aimeé.

In 1960, when Charlotte was sixteen, she flew to Paris for summer holiday to find Aimeé missing. She was not in any of the three kitchens or the manicured gardens. In Charlotte's room, where her suitcases had been unpacked and her clothes put away, there was a note from her mother informing her that this summer she would be on her own.

> *Dearest Charlotte,*
> *I didn't want to tell you via post, but Aimeé has not been*
> *well and passed on last winter. She loved you very much,*
> *as you well know, and would want you to remember her*
> *with fondness and make her proud in your every thought*
> *and action. Daddy and I have a dinner we cannot miss*
> *this evening, but we are so very happy to have you home*
> *and I will see you tomorrow afternoon!*
>
> *With affection,*
> *Mother*

As usual, there was no discussion, no room for despair, no hope for comfort. In Charlotte's home, emotions were unsavory and unacknowledged. Strength, she had been taught, was found by relying on yourself, your steely ability to ignore complications. Louisa's favorite expression was "and furthermore." It meant: it is what it is. Move on. Don't speak of this again.

The view from Charlotte's childhood bedroom encompassed the wide Rue du Faubourg Saint-Honoré—pale, stately buildings with square windows and awnings like politely smoothed skirts. Cars moved slowly past expensive stores. Charlotte was too old to cry, so she stood motionless, watching. Waiting for something to happen. The shops closed and the night went quiet, light from window displays casting geometric shapes on the street. The sky turned scarlet, then black.

She unlatched her window quietly, pushed it open, and let the hot night touch her skin. Charlotte stepped from her room, moved across the roof to where it almost touched a tree, and leapt.

Could she have crashed, breaking her legs? Certainly. But she did not. Instead, she grabbed on to the tree and uneasily made her way down, maneuvering with effort from one branch to another until she reached the ground. There was a guard at the front gate, so she used the back. Within moments, she was on the street, and could go anywhere.

Charlotte strode along the Rue de Rivoli. She had no real plan, and ended up walking for almost an hour along the Seine, past the Pont Neuf—lit up and glowing, making the river sparkle—all the way to le Marais.

By this time, she was hungry and tired. She followed the sounds of laughter to Le Zinc, a café on the Avenue Ledru-Rollin. Through the window, she saw a table of people a few years older than she. Some of the men had beards; all of the women had long, messy hair. Everyone was smoking cigarettes, mouths stained with red wine. This was the moment. Would she run back home, climb into her bed, and wait for morning? Or did Charlotte have the courage to enter the café and approach a table?

She touched the door. A handsome man looked up and saw her. Had she ever been seen before? The man (the *boy*, really—he was so young then!) made his way toward Charlotte. His longish brown hair touched his collar. He had a wispy mustache.

Charlotte could still turn and run.

Through the glass, Charlotte watched Winston. He came closer. When he opened the door, she could smell cigarette smoke and a musky sour-booze fragrance—the scent (Charlotte thought) of a grown-up.

His lips were thin and chapped. He leaned so near that she thought he was going to kiss her. She felt stirred up almost to the point of hysteria. Terror rose in her chest, a sense that now, *finally*, her life was going to begin. Her face filled with blood. Winston opened his mouth, and was about to speak into the twinkling night when someone began shaking Charlotte, bringing her across time to the present.

"Mom," said Regan, her voice childlike with excitement. "Mom! We're here."

"What?" said Charlotte.

"We're in Athens!" said Regan. "We're here, Mom! In Athens, Greece!"

TWO

Athens, Greece

1 / Charlotte

AS CHARLOTTE'S GRECIAN TAXI rounded a corner, the *Splendido Marveloso* came into view. The ship was massive: thirteen stories high, over a thousand feet long, bone-white, wearing a waterslide like a gaudy hat. Charlotte squinted: it seemed that people wearing harnesses were bicycling around the perimeter of the ship. On a lower level, orange lifeboats awaited disaster.

"Wow," said Lee, who was sharing Charlotte's taxi to the Port of Piraeus while Matt took a nap in the hotel "day room" his travel agent had booked for him, and Regan and Cord went to find some food.

"It's jaw-dropping," said Charlotte.

"I just got an email from my agent," said Lee. "You are looking at Corpse Number Two, Episode Seven Hundred Fourteen, *Law & Order: Special Victims Unit.*"

"Wonderful, darling!" cried Charlotte. "Congratulations!" She was fairly sure Lee was lying, but decided to ignore this troublesome fact.

"We done," said the taxi driver. He heaved himself out of the cab, unlatched the trunk, and left Charlotte, Lee, and all the Perkinses' bags in the middle of a vast parking lot. The pavement literally steamed. Two men in orange shirts and black pants rushed over with carts. Lee snatched the boarding pass from Charlotte, who felt faint. The Greek sun was really something! Was this the sun Agamemnon had felt as he rushed into battle? Charlotte figured so. And like Agamemnon, Charlotte was ready to move forward into the unknown. . . .

Lee seemed to be flirting with the baggage handlers. Charlotte staggered toward a gray building labeled CRUISE TERMINAL B: THEMISTOCLES.

"Lee," said Charlotte, turning back to interrupt her daughter's latest tryst-in-progress. "Who was Themistocles? Do you remember?"

"Is the terminal," said one of the men in orange shirts.

"Terminal B," noted the other.

"Is that right?" said Lee, stroking her neck. Charlotte watched her with concern.

"Themistocles was a politician and general in ancient Greece," said a man with a clipboard, who seemed to have appeared out of nowhere. He was a tall drink of water. "His name means 'Glory of the Law.' He died in 459 B.C. at Magnesia on the Maeander," said the man.

Charlotte, Lee, and the baggage handlers mulled that over.

"I'm Bryson," said the man, putting his shoulders back. Charlotte peered at his clipboard. She saw a bulleted list, with the title *Possible Passenger Questions: GREECE*. Bryson's teeth were huge, so white they almost glowed. He wore a well-tailored shirt that gave just a hint of his muscled torso and then dropped straight down, unhampered by a beer belly, toward a beautiful bulge in his snug pants. She smiled at Bryson, thinking, Oh my, before turning to look at Lee, and thinking, Oh no. Lee's face was an open book—it always had been. And the book at this moment was titled *Hungry Eyes*.

"I'm your cruise director," said Bryson, holding out a big, glamorous hand, his nails perfectly oval-shaped, perhaps even buffed or covered with clear polish.

"I'm Lee," breathed Lee. And then—could it be true?— she licked her lips.

"Hello. I'm Charlotte," said Charlotte, attempting uselessly to tamp down the lust igniting between Lee and the cruise director. "I won the Become a Jetsetter contest. That's me."

Bryson turned to Charlotte and smiled as if he had no idea what she was talking about. The man had to be six-five. He was gorgeous, even better-looking than Lee's paramour (or former paramour?), Jason, who was now a bona fide TV star, though Charlotte couldn't fathom why anyone would want to watch a show about a grown-up with a pet robot.

Charlotte felt dizzy. As Lee and Bryson chatted away, Lee's face lit up with Greek sun and the possibility of new love. Charlotte sighed. Why was she never the one filled with joie de vivre?

"I feel a bit faint," said Charlotte.

"Do you need some water?" said Lee.

Charlotte lifted her chin. "What I *need*," she said, "is a cold glass of Chardonnay!"

2 / Cord

AS THEY WANDERED AROUND Athens, Regan's face grew pink, and Cord felt a weird, fatherly impulse to buy her some sunscreen, to rub it on her freckled cheeks the way he'd done when they were kids at the pool. Regan would insist Cord ride the waterslide with her, and despite his friends' teasing, he'd always agree, holding her hand on the ladder to the top, putting his arms around her as they hurtled down, trying to hit the water before her, so he could lift her up and she could breathe.

Cord swallowed, wanting to ignore the call he'd just received from his sister's best friend, Zoë. How could he tell his baby sister her husband was a monster?

"Are you okay?" said Regan.

"We should sit down," said Cord. He spotted a sign in Greek with a translation below: TAVERNA OPERATES IN TO THE GARDEN. "Oh, look!" he said. "A restaurant. That's what *taverna* means—I read that somewhere. Let's grab a bite."

"I should get back to the hotel," said Regan. "Matt booked us a room for the day."

"Please," said Cord. "I'm really hungry."

Regan paused, then shrugged her acquiescence. They

followed the arrow on the sign through a narrow passageway. A hidden garden was filled with empty wooden tables covered with sheets of white paper anchored by centerpieces of salt and pepper shakers, napkins, and toothpicks. Cord did not see a restaurant-type structure or any waiters, but he chose a table in a shady corner and they sat down. A butcher (he did appear to be the butcher—not only did he look like a butcher out of central casting, with the big belly and curly gray hair, but his apron was stained with blood) approached.

The man said something brusque in Greek. When Cord shook his head and tried to look amiably puzzled, the butcher said, "Lamb chops?" At least it sure sounded like "lamb chops."

"Lamb chops," agreed Cord. The man lumbered off, through the passageway and out of sight.

"Lamb chops?" said Regan. "We're going to eat lamb chops?"

"When in Athens . . ." said Cord, trying to be light. Regan shrugged.

"So," said Cord, making his tone suitably grave, "how are you?" He hoped this opening would allow her to tell him about the private investigator. Cord leaned forward, trying to look encouraging.

"I'm fine," said Regan.

"Are you sure?" asked Cord. He raised his eyebrows, willing her to confide in him. Oh, how he wanted to be someone's savior!

"Yes," said Regan, folding and refolding her napkin. "I'm sure."

The man returned with dishes piled high. Food had always helped ease Cord's anxiety: he lifted a hot chunk of bread (it seemed to have been grilled) and took a bite. It was delicious and dense, tasting of olive oil. He served himself salad. Every flavor burst in his mouth as if he'd never before tasted a real tomato or an inch-and-a-half-thick mouthful of feta. Cord thought for a moment of the pathetic "feta crumbles" he sometimes shook over his deli salad and felt mournful.

"So everything's . . . ?" he said.

"Fine," said Regan, who seemed to be concentrating on the vines encircling a trellis overhead. Cord realized this was going to be harder than he'd thought.

"I was wondering . . . how you and Matt were doing," said Cord.

"Why?" said Regan.

"No reason," said Cord. This was a lie. The truth was that Zoë had told Cord a private investigator had been tailing Matt, and had uncovered some shocking and sordid news.

"I sent the report to Regan," Zoë had said, "but she hasn't even responded. I keep calling her! She won't answer!" Zoë begged Cord to make sure Regan was okay.

"We're good," said Regan, spearing a piece of feta with her fork. "You know—it's marriage. Or I guess you don't know."

Cord watched her. She seemed subdued, but maybe this was just her personality now. Younger Regan had always been bubbly, so delighted by everything—birds, French fries, the moon. "Did you . . . um, get an email from Zoë?" he said.

"Zoë? Email?" said Regan. "No. Definitely not."

The man dropped off a platter of meat, then two plates of dips—one white yogurt and one pale green. "For bread," said the man, pointing to the basket. Cord nodded his thanks. He squeezed a lemon quarter over the meat, then lifted a chop. It seemed smaller than the steroid-fattened American chop, delicate. He took a bite, and almost moaned with pleasure as he tasted oregano and salt—yes! Salt!—combined with the better-than-American-lemon lemon and the rich, slightly gamy, melty, fat-studded lamb.

Cord looked at his baby sister, reached for her hand across the table. "Did you look at the report?" he said. "We can look at it together, Ray Ray."

She yanked her hand away and stood. "I don't know what you're talking about," she said, her voice steely and kind of mean. "Do you understand? I don't know what you're talking about and I don't want to hear about whatever you're talking about ever again."

Cord sighed. He was trying to move away from lies and subterfuge. He wanted this conversation to be different. He yearned to open up to Regan, to tell her about Giovanni, to strategize about how they'd break the news, together, to Charlotte. He wanted to help Regan make a new life without Matt.

"I'm going back to the hotel," said Regan.

"Regan! Okay. Okay, if that's what you want. We don't have to talk about this. But . . . I can help you, Regan. Don't you want me to help you?" She slid on her rhinestone sunglasses. The set of her mouth—and her desire to deny the truth about her marriage—made Cord sad and then furious. "What the hell, Regan?" he said. "This isn't you!"

"You don't even know me," said Regan. "You don't have any idea who I am anymore."

"Of course I do," said Cord. "Stop being dramatic."

He wanted her to smile, to shake her head. But Regan leaned close and said, "Back off. I mean it. You don't want anything to do with this, I promise you."

Cord was stunned. Were they in some sort of crime

drama? What on earth had happened to sweet baby Ray Ray? As she turned and strode off, he quickly grabbed a pork chop in each hand. To hell with his sister! He took one bite and then another. To hell with the Perkins drama! He was going to book a flight home to his Giovanni.

But first he was going to enjoy his delectable Athenian feast.

3 / Regan

SOMETIME IN THE MIDDLE of the night, Zoë had forwarded an email: the private investigator's report on Matt. The email had been titled CALL ME IT'S BAD. Regan had stared at the title for a moment, but she had not clicked.

Zoë had since called Regan twice, and Cord as well, it seemed. Regan felt panicked as her taxi pulled in front of the Acropolis Select Hotel. Matt was waiting for her, wearing new sunglasses. When had he bought new sunglasses? Regan rolled down the window and waved, trying to smile. Matt climbed into the car and they headed to the Port of Piraeus. Matt smelled like Old Spice deodorant. He greeted the driver, saying, *"Yassus."* Regan was surprised.

"What?" said Matt. "The least I could do was learn 'hello.'" He held up his phone, showing her a language app. "I've never been anywhere," he said. "This is a big deal for me."

It was true: they'd barely left Georgia in their years together. They had gone to Tybee Island for their honeymoon, to Atlanta once in a while for conventions. Before they'd had children, Regan had visited Cord in New York, but Matt had never had time to come along.

Now he seemed like his old self—kind, happy—and Regan's stomach ached with indecision. Her phone kept buzzing with missed calls from Zoë. Could she still change her mind and mend her relationship with Matt?

Regan was, and had been since childhood, a fixer. She was the mom you called when you needed someone to do car pool last minute. She could (and had) put together a kindergarten rodeo when the mother who was supposed to call Pony Rides of Coastal Georgia had run off with a Norwegian pilot she'd met online.

Regan could remember being woken by her father and mother fighting. She'd crept downstairs in her nightgown and made a platter of cheese and crackers. When she delivered it to the den, they turned to her with mottled, teary faces.

"Cheese and crackers!" she'd said. My God: she must have been seven years old.

Cheese and fucking crackers. But they had stopped fighting.

REGAN GAZED OUT THE window as they passed the massive Acropolis. As the myth went, Athena and Poseidon were battling for control of Athens when Poseidon struck the ground next to the Acropolis with his trident and created a salty spring. Athena knelt and planted an olive tree. King Cecrops declared Athena the winner, as her gift would provide food and oil for Athenians.

Regan, she decided, was an olive tree, rooted in the soil, flourishing despite the ravages of time and marital disappointment. She would rise above the fracas, protecting her girls from pain. She was strong enough to bear whatever attacks might come at her! She was like the goddamn giving tree!

One night, when Regan had brought *The Giving Tree* from the bookshelf, Flora had said she didn't want to hear that one anymore.

"Why not?" Regan asked.

"Because, Mommy," said Flora. "It's the saddest story in the world."

4 / Lee

LEE FOLLOWED THE SIGNS to her *Marveloso* cabin, her footsteps silent on the blue and green, wave-patterned carpet. As she walked along the hallway, which was lit with pleasant sconces, a popcorn smell faded and was replaced with a floral scent, though there were no actual flowers to be seen.

At last, she reached her room and dipped her card in the door lock, which flashed green and opened. Her cabin was the cutest 185 square feet in the world: there was a couch along one side opposite a sweet little desk, and a double bed by the window. The curtains were shut.

Across the bed was a large plastic cloth reading:

LUGGAGE MAT IS MY NAME

PROTECTING THE COMFY

BED IS MY GAME

Lee had her very own balcony, with two metal chairs and a view of the water and the Port of Piraeus. She felt sticky from the Athenian heat and decided to take a shower in the miniature bathroom.

With the water on her body, she tried to focus on her

breathing, the way she'd once done as a competitive swimmer. Lee had hated swim team at first, the chlorine in her eyes, the boring laps and strict coach, the overheated chemical air of the indoor pool. But as she grew stronger, she started to look forward to her nightly exercise.

Lee and her father would leave the house earlier than they needed to for weekend swim meets, stop for egg sandwiches, and eat them on a bench in Forsyth Park. Winston would buy the *Savannah Morning News*, and during the interminable competitions, he'd read in the bleachers, peering over his newspaper periodically to wink at Lee, sitting in her bathing suit and sweatpants below.

Lee's brain shut off as she concentrated on propulsion. When she began to study Transcendental Meditation in L.A. because a lot of big directors studied TM and she figured it couldn't hurt, Lee realized that swimming had already taught her how to meditate.

Focusing on her breath rather than her brain's messy and subjective thoughts seemed to be the key. Lee learned to pretend she was swimming even when she was on land. She'd slow her brain down, look around, stop time. This bled into feeling thankful, and gratitude helped ease the sadness she'd been born with—or maybe she'd been born blank, but for as long as she could remember, she'd been singed by a hopeless feeling. After Winston hung himself, Lee understood that she'd inherited his despair. She clung desperately to the belief that if she became famous, her glory would somehow fix what was broken inside her. She would rise above the blackness that had swallowed her father.

When she stepped out of the shower, Lee forgot to avert her eyes from the mirror. There she was: thirty-eight years old. Her calm disappeared. It wasn't the lines around her eyes—those could be addressed—and it wasn't the crepey texture of her neck.

No, it was the expression on her face. She looked grim, hunted. As if something was after her and she was losing ground. Wrapping a towel around herself, Lee sat down on her bed. She thought of Jason, who had made it, who was getting everything they'd talked about, all of it and more. Why hadn't she been able to say yes to a life with him— stability, a family?

Before he had dumped her, Jason had taken online quizzes on her behalf, telling Lee her racing brain and sense of hopelessness were symptoms of depression, probably manic depression. But who wouldn't be depressed in her position? Jason bought her books, told her about podcasts, and ordered nutritional supplements to treat her brain. But magnesium drinks weren't going to get her a job. Saint-John's-wort pills weren't going to change her dawning knowledge that nothing—not even fame—would bring her peace.

Without that hope, life seemed unbearable. And yet holding on to that hope was beginning to be unbearable as well. Lee sank down on her bed, and felt the sad fog envelop her. She needed to make herself get up. She closed her eyes.

5 / Charlotte

ALONE IN HER STATEROOM, Charlotte opened her suitcase, took out her erotic essay, found a safe in her closet, and locked the printout, her traveler's checks, and her passport inside. (Code 1960: the year she met the painter.)

She'd been shapeless that summer, a ghost to herself, but after the first night in Le Zinc, she understood what she wanted. It wasn't Winston, not by a long shot, but the cheap-red-wine world he was a part of: angry, attractive people who stayed up late and seemed to disdain her parents' bourgeois lifestyle. What a thrill it was to trade her desperation for disdain!

Within days, Charlotte felt as if the crew at the café were her family: Winston; his brother, Paul; three girls who'd hitchhiked from London for the summer; and assorted burgeoning writers, artists, and bohemian types. Charlotte was the youngest by a few years, but it hardly seemed to matter. She had money to pay their tabs, which was appreciated.

Paul (who died in a drunk-driving accident soon after Winston and Charlotte's wedding) was a poet. He wore a black flat-brimmed hat and smoked cigarillos, invited

Charlotte to come along on a picnic where they shared baguettes and wine and Paul wrote as the London girls stripped *naked* and danced. Even three sheets to the wind, Charlotte was shocked. (Winston brought her home early, walking her to the front door of the embassy like the buttoned-up man he was.)

It was a summer of burned dinners in cramped apartments, endless cigarettes, long hair parted in the middle and fastened at the nape of her neck, ballet flats, black dresses. Winston told her what to read and she read it: Sartre, Hemingway, Paul and Jane Bowles. Charlotte knew Winston was in love with her and didn't mind. She perfected the art of changing the subject.

One early evening, the waitress at Le Zinc approached their table with a bottle of absinthe on a silver tray. She placed a sugar cube on a slotted spoon and poured the green liqueur. She raised her eyebrows, setting the glass in front of Charlotte. In Charlotte's memory (though this could not be true), the room went dark, and a spotlight shone upon her.

"It's from him," said the waitress in a reverent voice, tilting her head. They all turned. In the corner of the café, a balding, gnarled man (he was almost eighty!) sat surrounded by an entourage.

The old man was bright-eyed, wearing a green scarf, staring straight at Charlotte. She encircled the absinthe with her fingers.

"For the love of God," said Winston. "Charlotte, do you know who that is?"

Charlotte couldn't bring herself to meet the man's gaze. She shook her head.

Winston spoke the man's name, looking concerned, impressed, scared.

"Oh," said Charlotte. "I believe I've heard of him." She raised the absinthe, met the stranger's gaze, and drank.

"Be careful, Charlotte," said Winston, putting his arm around her possessively.

"Who, me?" said Charlotte, breaking free.

THREE

Welcome Aboord

1 / Charlotte

A DUTIFUL CATHOLIC SINCE childhood, Charlotte attended mass every morning and had been worried about missing mass while cruising. Some cruise lines gave a free room to a Catholic priest who could perform services, but Charlotte had heard from her Bible Study group that these "rent-a-priests" were not always in good standing. Charlotte had consulted Father Thomas, who agreed that missing mass because of winning the Become a Jetsetter contest was a reasonable exception. She could enjoy the cruise, return home, go to confession, and Father Thomas would give her penance. She would be absolved and could receive Holy Communion again.

Still, Charlotte took a framed photo of Jesus and set it on top of the television in her stateroom. She unpacked her toiletries in the bathroom, which was no better or worse than the one at home. One of her church friends had sent Charlotte a link to an article called "After You Flush—Waste Disposal at Sea Is a Complicated Business," but Charlotte had declined to click on the link. Some things didn't need to be known and how cruise ships disposed of human effluvium was one of them.

There were plenty of clean (if thin) towels, and a cord could be stretched from one side of the bathroom to the other if one chose to wash their unmentionables in the sink. Charlotte hoped that her prize package included laundry, for Pete's sake.

A radio next to her bed was already switched on, and Frank Sinatra sang, "Fly me to the moon! Let me play among the stars."

Charlotte hummed as she unpacked. Although the absolutely *first thing* Charlotte's mother always did was empty her suitcases (or have them emptied: Louisa had never folded a cardigan in her life), Charlotte could feel her energy as a limited resource, and she wanted to sip some champagne. She quickly changed into a Talbots shift dress (Kelly green) and matching shoes; clipped on faux-gold, Ralph Lauren lion earrings; and applied lipstick, smoke-colored eye shadow, and a bit of mascara. A brush through her hair and a few pumps of hairspray (how she missed her clouds of Aqua Net, but one had to do what was right for the planet, not to mention those poor Australian children with a hole in their ozone layer) and Charlotte was ready to go.

She opened her cabin door and found herself face-to-face with a handsome man in uniform. "Oh!" said Charlotte, her hand flying to her chest.

"Good evening, madame," said the man. He was about Charlotte's age, with thick gray hair and a big smile. "I am Paros, your porter. I'm sorry to frighten you."

Charlotte wasn't the least bit frightened. She could smell Paros's manly, soapy smell. A longing welled inside her. She wanted to touch this man, to be touched.

"Please let me know if I can be of assistance," said Paros,

sweeping his arm up, as if presenting her with the narrow hallway.

"Oh, *my*," said Charlotte.

Paros looked at her, not past her, not above her head. His smile was kind and a bit sad. His face was leathered by years in the sun. His teeth were not the best. Still, Charlotte felt her heart quickening. Had she met this person before? She felt as if she should know him, as if she *did* know him.

"The night is yours, madame," said Paros.

2 / Cord

"DON'T GET ON THE SHIP," said Cord's sponsor, Handy.

"I know," said Cord, clutching his phone to his ear and staring at the gargantuan *Splendido Marveloso* moored in the Aegean Sea. He'd meant to go to the airport—he had! But something had made him tell the Uber guy to drive him away from Athens International and toward his inescapable, exhausting family. "What am I doing?" he said.

"You need to protect your sobriety," said Handy, his voice strong and certain, even bullying. "Get on a plane and come home. You're allowed to walk away. You don't have to take care of anyone but yourself. You're not alone, man. I'm here. Talk to me."

"Right," said Cord. "You're right." He could picture Handy, who had been famous as a child. Once in a while, as they sat with their Big Books open before them, sipping coffee, Cord caught a glimpse of the prepubescent star Handy had been, singing his catchphrase, *It'll all come out in the wash!* Handy wasn't exactly wise, and he was full of words that could be needlepointed on a pillow, but as far as Cord could tell, "working the program" meant listening, staying sober, and keeping your thoughts to yourself. Every other avenue had led to self-hatred and despair, so he was trying, he really was trying.

"Okay, so you're getting in a taxi? You need me to find you a flight?" said Handy. "You need me to meet you at JFK?"

"I'm not getting on the ship," said Cord. Yet he walked toward it, pulled by some mysterious force. A man in a white jumpsuit waved to him, beckoning Cord to hurry. There was a banner saying, WELCOME TO FUN!

"I'm not getting on the ship," repeated Cord, marching toward the banner. He couldn't just ditch his mother. How could he ruin Charlotte's last adventure?

"Good decision," said Handy. "You're doing the right thing. You need me to stay on the phone, man?"

"I'm good," said Cord.

He was going to board the ship. He'd have courteous conversations with Matt, whom Cord had never been crazy about, but whom he now detested. Regan would try to win back her man, and Cord would be forced to watch. He'd squire his mother to buffet dinners and the Twitters Comedy Club, gritting his teeth as she pointed out his possible wives. Cord would pretend he was proud of Lee, who had taken her talent and squandered it, who was shallow and vain. (To make matters worse, her shallowness and vanity were a bit like Cord's, so made him feel not just annoyed but culpable.)

Cord did understand what he was doing. But the thing about being an addict was that it *didn't even matter* that he understood what he was doing—that he'd done the same thing a hundred million times and every time it had come to ruin. It was reptilian: familiar, appealing, seemingly unavoidable. An alcoholic's chain of logic, excuse after excuse, zipping up a close-fitting suit of martyrdom: he had to board the ship, and in order to stay on the *Marveloso*, he was going to have to drink.

Hurray!

He could taste a fruity concoction already, something pink and heavy with rum. Ah, a shot! The fire on his tongue and a welling up from the pit of his stomach: instant ease and well-being! The pain of his multiple lives would disappear. He could buy into the myth that they were happy. For the hours he had booze in his system, Cord could forget what he owed Giovanni.

The porter was gesturing frantically now, waving both arms in the air like a nutjob at a Yankees game. "The ship!" yelled the porter. "The ship is closing! The ship is leaving! Hurry, please! You must run!"

If Cord stayed still—just didn't move a muscle—he would be okay. The ship of family dysfunction would set off into the Aegean and he'd be on solid ground. "Cord?" said Handy. "You there, man?"

"I'm losing you," said Cord.

"Okay, man, call me when you—"

"Can't hear you," said Cord. He pocketed his phone, picked up his bag, and began to sprint. A series of people in white jumpsuits with Splendido name tags welcomed Cord, checked his papers, took his bags, escorted him through a metal detector, and pointed him down a hallway. A large door was propped open, and outside it, a metal drawbridge led into the ship. For a moment, on the drawbridge suspended above the water, boyhood Cord rose up within him: *Wow! A ship!*

Boyhood Cord was weak, vulnerable. Cord stuffed him down.

He pressed on, into a mirrored hallway lined with portholes. He picked a direction at random and found himself inside a futuristic discotheque. The walls were seemingly made of glowing boulders, and the chairs looked like the ones aboard the *Starship Enterprise*—armless, blob-like. One entire wall was made of booze: rows and rows of backlit bottles of every shape and color. Cord's salivary glands woke up and began clamoring for grappa, Jäger-meister, crème de menthe.

Cord glimpsed a trivia contest in full swing: groups of people crouched around bar tables, scribbling with tiny pencils. A young blonde with a German accent, perched on a stool, read an answer into her microphone. "The color of a polar bear's skin? Is? In fact? BLACK!" she cried.

Some passengers cheered, but several looked crest-fallen. "I'm so sorry," an older man implored his wife. "I really did think it was pink."

"I know you did, honey," said his wife morosely, peering into her empty glass.

Cord spied a grand staircase and began to ascend it, try-ing not to mar the gleaming banisters by touching them with his sweaty hands. He had never seen so much chrome in his life! Everywhere, everywhere, there were sweeping expanses of metal, polished to reflect flashing lights so bright Cord hoped none of his fellow cruisers were prone to seizures.

Above the *Jetsons* disco, Cord wandered down a hall-way lined with the most awful artwork he had ever seen. An enormous painting of Michael Jackson and Ringo Starr riding tigers was placed next to one of a gorilla gazing into the eyes of an airborne owl. "Please, peruse," said a dark-haired woman who had materialized in front of him and slipped a glass of champagne into his hand. "This one," she said, her voice husky and accented. She gestured to a paint-ing of Robert De Niro wearing a white suit, brandishing a gun in front of a neon-colored lion. "Is special," she said. "Is a limited edition."

"It's so special," Cord agreed.

"Drink," said the woman. "Is a compliment."

Cord clutched the glass. Who would know if he brought it to his lips?

"Champagne auction, it takes place tomorrow," said the woman. "But for you, it takes place today."

"Uh," said Cord. He kind of did want the painting. Gio adored kitsch. They could hang it over their bed, or in the living room above the fireplace.

Later, he would wonder what it was that had made him buy the art—the woman? The peaceful, knowing lion? De Niro's "devil may care" expression? But in the moment, it felt like nothing. He handed the woman his Sail-N-Shop card. "I'll take it," he said.

After signing the papers that would commit him to almost a thousand dollars for a joke of a painting, Cord wandered along a dim hallway lit with sconces. He skirted a bizarre statue of a girl petting a giant egg, rushed past an entrance labeled SPORTSMAN'S BAR, and climbed down some stairs.

In the bowels of the ship, he discovered a strip mall with a gelato stand, a coffee bar, and a multitude of shops. Rows of overpriced things no one needed lay before him: watches, M&M's, Marveloso room diffusers, neon-colored sarongs. The ceiling was somehow covered with shining stars.

Were they *underneath the water*? Cord tried not to freak out.

Three clean-cut youngsters in uniform stood behind a precarious configuration of perfume and cologne bottles. They sprayed the pricey liquids liberally, but a cigar bar at the end of the mini-mall dominated Cord's olfactory input. "Free champagne and two-for-one Versace pour Homme eau de toilette natural spray?" asked one of the perfume team, a tall girl who'd gone to town with her green eye shadow.

"Why would I want two?" said Cord.

"I no speak English so much," said the girl, giggling fetchingly. She handed Cord another glass of champagne and spritzed, moving her arm in a dizzying figure eight. Cord sipped deeply, breathing in cigar smoke and European cologne.

The Marveloso truly was a marvel, a Xanadu dome of pleasure. Cord entered a room that could have been Liberace's ballroom, had Liberace installed ten stories of stairs inlaid with cut crystals and invited a few thousand frumpy guests to mill about his ballroom in bathing suits. There were maroon banquettes with glittering chandeliers above them. Potted palm trees rose from herringbone-patterned carpet. The walls looked to be made of marble, and fountains lit with neon strobes exploded every ten feet.

In the center of the room, a birdlike woman in a ball gown pounded on a grand piano. The woman's bony shoulder blades were a sight to behold as she gave the notes of "Memories" her absolute all, her head thrown back in ecstasy, giant beehive hairdo remaining, remarkably, intact.

"Smile, sir!" cried a guy with an elaborate camera around his neck. Dutifully, Cord smiled. A flash blinded him, and when his vision cleared, he saw the singer.

A man so massive he could have played linebacker for the Georgia Bulldogs, the tuxedo-clad singer employed a big set of lungs to fill the room with sound. "Touch me! It's so easy to leave me! All alone with the memory . . . of my days in the sun!" A cadre of women in flip-flops and oversize T-shirts, their hair still wet from the pool, swayed piano-side and sang along.

Cord approached a glass elevator, stepping in when the doors opened. It was the brightest space he'd ever inhabited, and when it started to rise quickly above Liberace's ballroom, he was honestly awestruck, staggering backward into two teenage boys holding soccer balls. "Watch it, old man," said one; the other said something in Italian and they laughed. Flushed with humiliation (was he an old man? Really?), Cord got off the elevator at the next stop, and found himself standing next to a jam-packed indoor pool. Four hot tubs were full to the brim.

"Two-for-one Nutella crêpe?" asked a man in a toque.

"Pardon?" said Cord. Something was happening above him; he glanced heavenward to see that a retractable roof was sliding open, exposing a purplish sky. "Whoa," said Cord.

"It's two-for-one Nutella crêpes," the guy next to Cord repeated. "You buy one but you actually get two." Was Cord disassociating? He felt as if he were on acid. The crêpe man was looking at him expectantly. A line had begun to form behind Cord, and a man with a ton of body hair wearing only a Speedo was standing too close. The crêpe man winked. Did Cord imagine it?

"Oh, sure," said Cord, handing over his ship card.

He walked through a set of double doors, emerging on the outdoor pool deck. People were everywhere: oiled up, carrying plates piled high with food, slurping drinks, dancing, reading, dead asleep (or—eek—dead?). A three-story waterslide snaked above him. Cord nibbled his warm, sweet crêpe. A DJ spun Salt-N-Pepa's classic "Push It," and Cord's hips started to sway to the beat. Despite himself, he murmured, "Oooh, baby, baby. Baby, baby."

Where was his luggage? Where was his family? Where was his dignity? Could he stay on this ship for the rest of his life?

Push it good. Push it real good!

From the football-field-size pool, jets shot into the air, then fell in arcs back into the turquoise water. Glass panels lined the edge of the ship, and beyond was the deep, mysterious sea.

Cord craned his neck to see three massive smokestacks belching plumes of exhaust into the evening sky. The lonely voice wanted to talk about climate change, about being a part of the solution and not the problem, about droughts and famines, refugees in the water, and the demise of humankind, but Cord didn't want to listen.

Beyond the "Aqua Zone" was the entrance to an insane buffet. There was mediocre food as far as the eye could see: burgers, pizza, fruit salad, chafing dishes filled with pastas, stews, and casseroles; cakes, pies, Jell-O molds, éclairs, slabs of meat being carved, and why were there framed drawings of Native Americans in headdresses behind the dessert station? Why the marzipan piano? Who cared? Honestly, seriously, *who cared?*

Cord grabbed a warm, clean plate (*don't think about germs, no, don't even think about salmonella*) and filled it, humming "Push It" and eating taquitos directly from the tray underneath the sign reading PLEASE USE SERVICE UTENSILS AT ALL INSTANCES.

Yo yo yo yo, baby pop—yeah, YOU! Come here, gimme me a kiss. Better make it fast, or else I'm gonna get pissed.

He ate a burger, ate some kind of noodle and salmon dish, finished off a slice of apple pie and a marzipan mouse. He just abandoned his empty plate and floated into a hallway, down some stairs, and into a packed Las Vegas casino.

The casino walls were painted with murals of other locales: Havana, Istanbul, Monte Carlo. Marble columns sprouted metal palm fronds and globular lights. It couldn't have been 8:00 P.M., but women in sequined gowns tossed chips, and tuxedoed staff spun roulette wheels. There were the ever-present grayish-skinned guys zombified before a row of slot machines.

"Free champagne and two-for-one cash money bingo?" purred an adorable fellow who emerged from nowhere (from Cord's wildest dreams?).

He would have one, just one drink, and then he would go back to the open-air Aqua Zone and watch the sky turn crimson, the clouds purple above the vast, astonishing ocean. It was so easy, after all the pain, and all the sober, sad, plodding work.

All he had to do was say yes.

3 / Regan

REGAN AND MATT HAD not had sex in over a year. It was excruciating to be alone together, jammed in a tiny cabin. Matt was sprawled on the bed, and Regan sat as far away as possible, brushing her hair at the vanity table. How much she'd once loved touching him! But now the thought of being physically close to her husband made her feel ill. Regan tried to remember the last time they had even been alone—it seemed as if the girls were always with them, or within earshot.

Matt turned to her. "Come here, honey," he said. "You're so far away."

Adrenaline throbbed in her veins as she steeled herself, moved toward the bed. Maybe this was how spies felt as they girded themselves to steal state secrets. Matt opened his arms. "Too many clothes," he said.

Regan pulled her silk top over her head and stood before her husband, the full glory of what he'd once called "the absolute best boobs in Georgia" on display. Her heart hammered in her chest. She hid the stretch marks on her stomach with her hands. The chilled cabin air was giving her goosebumps.

"Oh, my sweet one. I've missed you," said Matt.

She wanted to say, *I've been right here all along.* Was Matt saying that he missed sex, or that, seeing her now, he remembered everything they had to lose? She lowered herself to the bed, and it felt like the scariest thing she'd ever done to allow herself to be held.

"I've missed you, too," she lied.

Her life before Matt had been so painful and bare. It was as if she'd been living without skin, and he'd coated her in love. She had once thought it would ruin her to feel that way again. But now she was like a panther in the zoo, casing the enclosure night and day, alert for a chance to escape.

Regan knew what she had to do. She just needed to shut her mouth and open her body to the man who had turned her from a naïve idiot into whatever she was now—a predator, a woman who daydreamed of murder.

"Kiss me," said Matt. She could do it, and she did.

4 / Lee

WHEN LEE WAS THIRTEEN, Charlotte (with the help of a Catholic addiction counselor named Robby) had organized a Sunday afternoon intervention for Winston. Robby had told Lee to lead her father into the dining room, where everyone else was waiting. He explained that an element of surprise was useful: Winston wouldn't have time to mount defenses and could more easily be convinced to fly to rehab in upstate New York.

Lee knew her father drank too much. He was mean, perhaps abusive. But still, she wanted to win him, loved him mightily, and craved his approval. So as she knocked at the den door, rehearsing Robby's line ("We have a surprise in the dining room, Dad"), she hated Charlotte for making her betray her father.

"What?" said Winston. They weren't supposed to disturb him in the den.

"It's me," said Lee.

"Ah, Lee Lee," said Winston. "Come in."

She turned the knob. The shades were drawn and Winston sat in his leather recliner, a glass of scotch on the Oriental rug, a smoking cigarette in an ashtray. "What is it?" he said.

Her stomach roiled. She always felt revved up around Winston, ready to run. You never knew how he would hurt you. Lee had once written him a note that said, *If you love me, you will stop drinking.* She'd hidden it in his underwear drawer. It was all she had to threaten, and she'd innocently believed it was enough. It was not enough.

"We have a surprise for you in the dining room," said Lee.

He stood, sighing. He stubbed out his cigarette and lit another. "An intervention, I suppose?" he said.

Lee blanched.

"Even you," said Winston bitterly, shaking his head. "I wouldn't have thought even you."

"Dad, I . . ."

"Just skip it," he said. Winston picked up his glass, strode to the dining room, pushed the swinging door open. "Well, what do we have here?" he said.

Lee's siblings, along with Charlotte and Robby, sat at the dining room table. Lee joined them reluctantly. They addressed Winston as they had been trained: here's what your drinking has done to me; here's why you should go to St. Joseph's right now, after this meeting, it's all arranged; we love you. As each of them spoke, nine-year-old Regan crying so hard she could barely speak, Lee had thought, *Fuck this.* She saw the contempt in her father's eyes, and traitorously, Lee agreed with him: this blubbering, this vulnerability, was a joke.

When it was Lee's turn, she looked up from the carefully prepared script, a dot-matrix printout describing a litany of Winston's terrorizing behavior and drunk driving, and she said simply, "I love you, Dad." Charlotte reached over and took Lee's hand. Lee shook her off.

Winston looked at his family banded together in the naïve hope that they could change him. Without a word, he walked back to the dining room door, pushed it open, and exited. They heard the den door slam shut. Lee looked around the table at her ashen-faced mother, her young and pathetic siblings, and disappointed Robby. She understood that they were weak. Lee stood, and left the room.

WHEN SHE MOVED TO Los Angeles, Lee had thought she was free. But even on the other side of the country, she had felt responsible for Charlotte. And now here she was: surrounded by her family on a cruise ship, watching as the mandatory safety briefing morphed into a dance show.

"There's no such thing as too much fun!" crowed Cord, approaching and handing her a blue drink. Lee felt tears welling. Cord, her little brother. She wanted to bury her face in his chest and tell him everything. But she didn't know how to talk about failure. She didn't know how to ask for help.

"Hey," said Cord, who must have seen something in her face. "Are you okay?"

There had been a time when Cord would call Lee late at night, drunk and wanting to talk. She'd pour wine, settle herself into a chair by her bay window, and they'd commiserate, chatting for hours about not much at all. When had the calls stopped? Lee had been so caught up in her own life that she couldn't even remember. He'd told her, during one of the last calls, that his own drinking was scaring him. Lee had written it off—weren't they all

too hard on themselves? "Of course I'm okay," said Lee.
"Why?"

"You look sad," said Cord.

Lee bristled, immediately on the defensive. "And you
look drunk," she said.

He stepped back as if he'd been slapped. They were
always so hard on each other: Lee realized immediately
that she'd hurt him. It came naturally—it was the way
they'd always interacted. Lee burned a path forward, leaving Cord and Regan to follow in her scorched wake. She
was the one with the torch.

Cord swayed on his feet. Lee had thought that by not
caring, she would be safe. But what if she had stayed in the
dining room, after Winston had left? What if she had
squeezed Charlotte's hand back?

"I'm sorry," said Lee. "I'm so sorry, Cord."

Cord looked young, scattered lights from a disco ball
illuminating his face. "I am drunk," he said. "I can't seem to
stop. And you know what else? I'm gay." He looked down,
seemed unable to meet her eyes. Did he really think she'd
spurn him? Lee's insides melted. Her little brother was
vulnerable, open in a way that Lee would never allow herself to be. Even now, she wanted to shut this communica-
tion down, to walk away.

"I love you," said Lee. Of course, they all knew he was
gay. The only weird part was that he hadn't told them.
They saw each other so rarely, was how Lee had explained
it to herself.

"I need to tell Mom," said Cord.

Here it was—the space to tell someone how lost she
felt, how alone. A way to reach back through time and
gather him close. Maybe the answer had always been in
that dining room—that together, they would be okay.

Lee and Cord stared at each other. Lee felt dizzy, the edges of her vision growing black. She was very warm. She shook her head, unable to speak. But Cord remained still, believing in Lee more than she believed in herself, trusting she had something to offer him.

5 / Charlotte

IT WAS TIME FOR the captain's toast. Charlotte and her family stood in the Atrio, a three-story, mall-like space, staring at an enormous cylindrical screen, onto which moving images were projected, creating a column of color that tapered to a bar on the bottom floor, where adorable youngsters tossed cocktail shakers. The captain and his entourage—what were they called? Mates?—appeared on one of the Atrio staircases, illuminated by a spotlight.

The column, which had seemed filled with aquarium water and giant, multicolored fish when they arrived, began throbbing with light and images of corks popping from champagne bottles. It *was* bewitching, thought Charlotte, she'd give it that. If she had a giant pulsating column in her living room, maybe she'd be more easily distracted from her loneliness and decrepitude.

"Is it beautiful or tacky?" Charlotte wondered aloud.

"I think it's awesome," said Matt.

Charlotte surveyed him, the genial way he took in the insane Atrio. Matt reached for Regan's hand and Charlotte felt wistful.

It wasn't that she wished she were married, and certainly not to a man like Matt. He'd been a part of the family for so long that she almost considered Matt her own son, but while he was dull—a good match for Regan—Charlotte preferred a bit of spice. Matt was a bland pudding, and what Charlotte craved was a metaphorical hot jalapeño!

She longed to feel a man's erection pressing against the small of her back, hot breath at the nape of her neck. She wanted to feel skin against her skin. Charlotte blushed.

"Welcome," said the captain into a microphone, "to the *Splendido Marveloso*!" He wore a white suit and cap like Paros, her handsome porter, but the captain's chest was covered with ribbons. "There is a very special moment to happen at now."

A portly couple made their way past the elegant crew. The room quieted down, and the man fell to one knee. He spoke and the woman jumped up and down. "He says, *Will she be his wife?* and she says, *Yes, why not?*" said the captain.

The Atrio erupted in cheers, the column aswirl with gyrating triangles.

Charlotte sighed. Her own marriage proposal had been a dud. Back in Paris for her father's funeral, Charlotte had crossed paths with Winston, and after a week he had proposed, sliding a jeweler's box across a café table, saying, "I guess we belong together after all." Charlotte had opened the box and put on the ring, filled not with hope, but with resignation. She was tarnished goods, and this was all she could expect.

FOUR

Fun Day at Sea

1 / Charlotte

CORD WAS VERY DRUNK at dinner. Charlotte was disturbed. He kept repeating himself and saying, "Am I right or am I right?" Charlotte herself had never had a problem just stopping after a few glasses of wine. It was a matter of free will! But clearly some people couldn't keep it under control. Winston, for one.

Was it alcoholism that had changed Winston from the mild-mannered gentleman she'd first met in Paris into the cruel person he'd become, or had booze been a salve to him? Charlotte didn't know. She tried to believe that Winston's depression hadn't been her fault, and sometimes she succeeded.

Charlotte hurried through her "Marvelous Mediterranean meze platter" and declined dessert, wanting to return to her small, safe cabin and change into her nightgown.

"Mom! You've got to have a tiramisu!" protested Lee. "It's *free*," she hissed.

"Tiramisu for me and for you," said Cord. "Am I right or am I right?" His words were somehow both slurred and overenunciated. The way he was speaking reminded Charlotte so much of Winston that she was shaking as she touched the corners of her mouth with her napkin.

"In fact," said Charlotte, "you're wrong. I'm going to bed. Good night!" Cord barely glanced up. He was topping off everyone's wineglasses with great care, seemingly checking the levels to make sure they were even, then re-filling his own glass to the brim.

"Good night, Mom," said Regan. "Love you."

"Oh," said Charlotte, touched. "Well, I love you, too." For a moment, she considered staying for dessert.

"See you in the morning for towel-animal lessons in the Aqua Zone," said Lee.

"Wait, what?" said Regan.

"You heard me," said Lee, raising an eyebrow. "I said *towel-animal lessons.*"

Charlotte's children began giggling. Were they making fun of the cruise—of Charlotte? She blinked, trying not to be upset. She stood.

"I think it sounds fun," said Regan, grabbing a roll from the basket.

"Sure you do, hon," said Matt, patting Regan's hand. Lee and Matt laughed. Now it seemed they were being mean to Regan, who looked down at her butter plate.

"Who likes grappa around here?" said Cord, motioning to their waiter.

Charlotte turned to leave. Only Matt was kind enough to call after her, "Charlotte? Can you find your way back to the cabin? Do you need help?"

"I'm fine," she said, waving with forced gaiety and exiting the restaurant. She probably did need help, but was too embarrassed to admit it. Confronted with wide staircases and dazzling lights, Charlotte continued walking straight, but soon found herself completely lost inside an empty discotheque. She watched tiny rectangles of light move across the floor, trying to wrest her thoughts from Cord. It was unbearable to think that he was following his father's path. Charlotte almost turned back, believing she owed her son, or could help him in some way. Put him to bed. Scratch his back as she'd once done.

He used to come into her room, late at night. Next to snoring Winston and later alone, Charlotte would feel someone needing her—a mother's instinct—and she'd open her eyes to see Cord. He never shook her or made a sound, just sat cross-legged on the floor next to her side of the bed until she woke. He looked up at her, his pupils wide in the dark. His skinny legs in pajamas, his thick eyelashes. "I'm sorry, Mom," he'd whisper.

"Shhh," Charlotte would reply. She'd take him by the hand and lead him back to his room, settling him in, scratching his back, hoping he would fall asleep. He never did. When, finally, she'd stop scratching, holding her breath, he'd turn his head and open those fathomless eyes again.

He dared to say it only once: "Can you just stay?"

"Oh, no, honey," she'd replied quickly, instinctively. He never asked again. After a few more strokes along his back with her fingernails, she'd leave him in the dark to return to her own bed, where she lay awake until dawn, missing him—his warm body, his sweet, even breaths.

Why hadn't she stayed? It had seemed improper, or slovenly, or something. Weak. She'd been taught to remain solitary. Charlotte was proud of her ability to ignore and rise above her desires. Louisa had never stayed in Charlotte's bed, and that was for sure! But maybe, if she'd snuggled underneath Cord's navy comforter, Charlotte might have found a way back to the deep sleep she'd once had next to her nanny, Aimée. But she thought she was supposed to sleep in her own bed. Charlotte wasn't one to be needy, to burrow next to a child for comfort.

Now, Charlotte wanted to return to Cord, to take him by the hand and lead him back to his room, to tuck him in with a glass of water and two Advil on his bedside table. She would press her lips to his temple.

She did not turn back. Charlotte soldiered on, braving staircases (both crystal and non), elevators, passageways, room numbers that seemed to shape-shift as she passed them. At one point, deep within the ship, Charlotte opened a metal door to see men laundering sheets in clothes washers as big as cars. She stood, wobbly and blinking in the bright light, and watched as the men fed bedclothes into a machine and then gathered them when they spooled out, perfectly pressed. The room was uncomfortably warm and smelled of bleach and metal.

Finally, the elevator came and whisked her back up into the passenger area, which Charlotte never understood how she'd escaped in the first place. Again, she plodded down corridors—identical, dim, smelling of disinfectant and French fries. It seemed she was the only one on the ship. And then an apparition: her porter, Paros. He stood at the end of a long hallway. Was he real, or just a dream? "Mrs. Perkins?" said Paros.

She wanted to run toward him. To crash into him. To wrap her arms around him, allow him to lift her up, carry her soundlessly across the miles of carpet to her stateroom. There, they would order tiramisu and feed it to each other from long-handled spoons. He would hold her; she would allow herself to stay.

Charlotte had spent so long denying her desires—not

just sexual ones, but her longing to give voice to the desirous woman inside her. She plodded through her days—mass, grocery, dinner, bed—as if sleepwalking. If she acknowledged the flame of her need, Charlotte feared it would consume her.

"Mrs. Perkins," said Paros, "is that you?"

2 / Cord

CORD ROLLED OVER, HIS eyes hot coals in his head, his mouth a desert. One and a half years of sobriety, gone. He grabbed his iPhone from his bedside table and reset his Sobriety Calculator to zero. No, he told himself, to one. Day One, again.

His last Day One had been the morning after his 3rd Eyez visit, the trip that would determine his fate. If 3rd Eyez was a hit, he'd be wealthy and revered. If it tanked, he was ruined. *Ruined and alone*, said the lonely voice. It was always loudest after a binge, so forceful and authoritative that it was hard for Cord to tamp it down, to quiet it with logic. *Ruined and alone*, it repeated gloomily.

Cord had graduated from Princeton in 2001, at the end of the Internet boom. NYC Ventures, founded in 1998 by two members of Cord's eating club, Tiger Inn, was still flush with funds and Cord happily joined the firm, settling into an Upper West Side apartment where he bought furniture online and pretended to be straight (booze helped). It was all downhill from 2001 for VC in general and NYC Ventures in specific, but Cord still clung to his job even as the firm dwindled and his former buddies treated him with kid gloves after he was spotted at a gay pride parade. "Cord, are you gay?" asked Hammersmith over drinks at Dorian's.

Jacoby and Wyatt waited for Cord's response.

Cord, his gut seizing, nodded.

"Never would have thunk it," said Jacoby. He shrugged.

And furthermore, as Charlotte would say.

By hook or by crook, they'd kept NYC Ventures alive. In 2014, with only six employees left, they had raised a smallish fund. "We're looking for a *game changer*," said Jacoby (now balding, with three kids and an ex-wife in Rye).

Back at Princeton, one of Cord's best friends had been Georgie, a whippet-thin, pasty-faced girl from Florida. They'd bonded over late nights in the library, an unlikely duo: the closeted frat boy and the painfully shy genius. But they both loved nineties rap, microwave popcorn, and each other.

Georgie had dropped out of medical school after creating some complicated surgical instrument and cashing in. Lately, she'd been emailing Cord that she'd created a VR product that could "hijack your mind." Unlike the dumb headsets and battery packs everyone was messing around with, Georgie said her product, 3rd Eyez, could override the brain's ability to distinguish between real and virtual. It had something to do with lasers aimed at your eyeballs. "Seriously," said Georgie. "I can convince your brain that any world I make is real. And if we make the worlds fun enough, nobody's going to want to come out. The real world is old news at this point."

Terrifying implications aside, Cord saw dollar signs: videogames, teleconferencing, films . . . the hope of replacing all screens. 3rd Eyez did sound like it was making, as Georgie's marketing guys called it, "a disruption machine."

Because he was a friend of Georgie's, and because 3rd Eyez needed someone to lead their Series-A-round financing, Cord had been invited to Orlando to see the prototype. When Georgie got the flu and couldn't join her team in showing the product to Cord, Cord had given himself permission to empty his Sheraton hotel minibar. By the time he'd met the team for dinner at a steak joint, then added a few martinis to his bloodstream, Cord was flying high. He remembered sitting in the back of an engineer's car. There was a warehouse, a parking lot steaming with heat, a cooler of beers to enjoy while they checked out the machine.

Were there wires attached to his head? Electrodes? Cord remembered something about jungle animals coming to life in 3rd Eyez's conference room. An elephant? And then Michael Jordan and Babe Ruth hanging out, interacting with them. Something like walking through a Norwegian forest, touching icicles . . .

Then blackness. Cord woke up in a cold sweat at 3:24 A.M. in his Sheraton room, filled with nausea and the familiar crush of impending doom. He didn't remember the phone call he'd made, telling his NYC Ventures team to invest every last cent in 3rd Eyez. He didn't remember insisting *this was it*, the answer to their prayers. *I trust you, motherfucker!!!* Wyatt had texted at some point.

By the time Cord was sitting in a hastily located AA meeting, clutching a Styrofoam cup of coffee, shaking with regret and grief, the money had been wired. NYC Ventures led the Series A round, catapulting 3rd Eyez to viability.

They would find out within days that Cord had signed papers ensuring that 3rd Eyez didn't have to show anyone the product until the IPO. Cord had given them enough money to operate in secrecy.

"Man," said Jacoby, clapping Cord on the back when he returned to the office, "I just can't wait to see it."

Cord didn't say, *Neither can I.*

AND HERE HE WAS again. A new Day One. Why couldn't he stay sober? Why? Giovanni had known only sober Cord, Cord in Recovery. Gio had even once said, "You can have a bit of good wine once in a while, right?"

Cord held his head in his hands. Fear filled him. Dread pulsed inside his stomach. He was going to keep drinking, and he was going to lose Giovanni. Whatever he'd inherited from his father was going to kill him. He might as well stop fighting, open the minibar, and imbibe. He'd already checked out the selection: small bottles of everything from vodka to Malbec. Cord let the possibility of giving in fill him with shameful joy.

It wasn't as if he didn't know that the choice was real and quite possibly final. He could abandon himself to the booze or he could keep trying to stay true, to feel both the pain and the glory of ordinary, beautiful life. Cord stared at the tiny refrigerator.

3 / Regan

WHEN REGAN WOKE, SHE was alone in bed. Matt was sitting on the balcony, head bent over his phone. Regan's dreams had been harrowing. Inside them, she'd been back at the Come On Inn with Mr. Ragdale, her high school art teacher. He'd convinced her they were meant for each other. Or maybe she'd convinced herself.

The sour sheets, the smell of cheap cleaning fluids. Regan had known as the days wore on that running away with Alphonso had been a mistake. But she couldn't call Charlotte. Feeling as if she were soiled beyond redemption, Regan had called her sister's ex-boyfriend instead. And Matt had come for her, riding all the way to Statesboro on his motorcycle, banging on the flimsy motel door, confronting Mr. Ragdale, even poking him in the chest with an index finger, gathering Regan and her duffel bag of belongings.

The wind whipped her hair as she burrowed against Matt on the long ride home. He had been her savior. But that was a long time ago.

Regan didn't have to open the email from Zoë. What

was the point? She was furious that Zoë had called Cord. They all thought she was so dumb, that she had no plan, and was just going to float along like a goddamn cruise ship, letting everyone walk all over her.

They were wrong.

4 / Lee

LEE WOKE UP TO kisses along her neck and rolled into Luigi's sweet embrace. He was one of the captains, not the main one but still Italian, and had sent her a bottle of Cabernet at the Capitano Cocktail Lounge, where Lee and Cord had ended up after dinner. It was dimly lit, and Lee had had to squint when their waitress brought the wine and pointed to the table of men in uniform. Luigi had stood and bowed, blown her a kiss. He was a bit too old for her, but when he stopped by their table and asked if she'd like to walk along the Promenade, she'd smiled and said yes.

"Hey," Cord said, grasping her wrist as she stood. Lee looked at her brother, his drunken, pleading expression. "Lee Lee," said Cord. "Come on. Don't go. I haven't seen you in so long. We need to talk."

"Oh, Cord," said Lee. She looked at Luigi, waiting. "This is a cruise," she said. "I'm just having fun."

"Just having fun," said Cord morosely. "I get it, Lee Lee. I fucking get it. Adios."

Lee wanted to ignore Cord's words—write them off to his being drunk—but of course, he *did* get it. For a moment, Lee contemplated sitting back down and talking to her brother, confiding in Cord about her botched career, her confusion, telling Cord how their father's face had been blue when she found him hanging from the bathroom door. How she'd lifted him, wrapping her arms around his legs, and screamed. She'd stood in the bathroom holding him up for what seemed like hours. But Winston was already dead.

Cord looked bereft. But being with him reminded Lee of a time she wanted to forget. Cord and Regan didn't even know about Winston's suicide. Charlotte had told them their father died from a heart attack.

"I'm just having fun," Lee insisted both to her brother and to herself. Luigi put his arm around her waist.

Cord didn't answer, didn't look at her, just raised his hand to order another drink.

THE PROMENADE AT NIGHT was magnificent, so high it felt as if they were closer to the starry sky than to the sea. How could Lee help but submit to Luigi's embrace?

She'd thought the awkward but appealing moonlit kisses might lead her to his secret, fancy captain cabin, but he'd taken her to her room instead. The sex had been pleasurable—Luigi's unabashed thrill at her body was a huge turn-on—but then he'd gotten a call and had rushed off.

Luigi phoned late at night and asked if she'd like some dessert. She would, Lee told him. He arrived a few minutes later with a molten chocolate cake and coffees. Lee enjoyed both, then another round of lovemaking.

Afterward, he climbed from bed. Lee gazed up at the ceiling to avoid seeing his belly and wrinkled skin. "If I encounter you tonight," said Luigi, "I will be with my wife and my family. The next night, I am free for a visit, if you like."

"Your *wife*?" said Lee. Her head began to pound: she should have known.

"I told you, did I not?" said Luigi, standing and struggling into his pants.

"You did *not*," said Lee. She was surprised by her anger. The sight of Matt and Regan together had made Lee realize how fiercely she wanted something *real*, something she could count on. Yet here she was, discarded by a married man.

"I think I did so, yes," said Luigi.

Lee knew how to feign strength. She strode to the door and opened it wide. "Get out," she said, blinking back tears.

"Americans," said Luigi, shaking his head condescendingly.

Lee took his shirt and captain's hat and threw both into the hallway. Luigi sat on Lee's bed, his arms folded over his chest. "Bring me back my clothings," he said.

"GET OUT!" screamed Lee.

Luigi stood, and got out.

Lee collapsed on her bed and pulled out her phone. She scrolled—as she often did to alleviate loneliness—through Regan's pictures of her family with Matt. Somehow, the images produced not only envy but also a painful pleasure. It made Lee glad to look at photos of these well-loved girls as they moved through the world, a peace in their smiles unlike any Lee had ever known. What must it be like to feel safe?

Regan, holding a girl by each hand as they watched a Georgia sunset.

Lee wanted to be mothered.

Isabella, one front tooth missing.

Lee wanted to *be* a mother.

Regan, looking rumpled in the background, admiring the girls in pink leotards.

Lee would be a terrible mother.

Flora and Isabella, sharing a milkshake.

Lee's period was late.

5 / Charlotte

CHARLOTTE WAS APPLYING LIPSTICK when she heard a knock. She admired her Fun Day at Sea ensemble—a yellow shift dress with gold ballet flats—then turned and opened the door.

"Where shall I put your breakfast, ma'am?" said Paros, awkwardly balancing a tray with a carafe of coffee and covered dishes.

"Oh, Paros. Thank you for helping me get home last night. I'm so embarrassed. How could I get lost like that? Though the hallways do look very similar."

"The tray?" said Paros, looking strained. "Where would you . . . ?"

"Oh! I'm sorry. Anywhere is fine."

Paros laid the tray on her desk, then took a napkin and placed it with a flourish on her coffee table, setting a coffee cup upon the napkin. "How do you take your coffee?" he asked, lifting the carafe.

No one had asked Charlotte how she liked her coffee in . . . maybe ever. She made her own coffee every morning in her Mr. Coffee, adding one Splenda and a dollop of milk to her cup. After Winston died, she stopped moving the milk into a china creamer, just grabbed the carton, used it, then put it back in the fridge. Young Charlotte had presented sugar cubes with silver tongs, had arrayed the Splenda packets in a shallow bowl! Charlotte was both sorry for and proud of the woman she had been.

"A bit of milk and a Splenda, thank you," said Charlotte.

His brow furrowed. "I have a Sweet'N Low," he said. "Will that do?"

Will that do! What a hunk, thought Charlotte. A hunk—there was no other word! And there they were, in her cabin. What if he simply took her in his arms (oh my, they were hairy. She could see wiry gray and black hairs at the edge of his crisp shirt), dipped her toward the floor, as if in a movie, and touched his lips to hers? Charlotte covertly admired his strong shoulders. Heat rose in her chest. She *had* to stop reading her naughty novels!

"Mrs. Perkins?" said Paros. "Will Sweet'N Low do?"

"Sweet'N Low will be fine," she stammered.

As Paros prepared the coffee, Bryson's dulcet tones came over the loudspeaker: "Good morning, *Splendido Marveloso* passengers! Are you ready for a full day of FUN FUN FUN aboard the *Splendido Marveloso*? Did you hear me? I hope you heard me say FUN because today is going to be a FUN day at sea!"

Could one turn off the loudspeaker? Charlotte looked around the room for a switch. She couldn't even figure out where the thing was located.

"Let me start with the Poolside Fun," crowed Bryson. "At noon, there's an ice carving demonstration. At twelve-thirty—get ready, ladies and gents—it's the Very Hairy Chest Contest!"

Paros stepped into the hallway. "Paros!" cried Charlotte.

"Ma'am?" said Paros, turning.

Don't leave! was what she wanted to say. "Are you Italian?" said Charlotte.

"I am Greek," said Paros.

"From Athens?"

"I'm from Ikaria. It's an island."

Casting about for a way to keep the conversation going, Charlotte blurted, "Do you miss it?"

"Yes," said Paros. "Very much. Enjoy your breakfast, ma'am."

"I've never been to a Greek island. I'm really looking forward to it."

"Mrs. Perkins, have you ever had honey and yogurt for your breakfast?" said Paros.

"Please, call me Charlotte."

"If you like," said Paros.

"I do. And I'm a widow, by the way."

"My sympathies," said Paros. "My wife has also passed away."

They looked at each other for a moment. Could he possibly be interested in her? In moving close enough to touch? Charlotte berated herself—she was an old woman. She knew that no one saw her as an object of desire. Yet how she wished that Paros's formality was because he was at work, or unfamiliar with English. Or maybe—just maybe—nervous.

"Honey and yogurt?" said Paros. "Have you had honey and yogurt for breakfast?"

Charlotte knew he wasn't flirting. He couldn't be. Could he be? She felt giddy. "No," she said. "I don't believe I have. I'm a fan of English muffins for the most part."

Zip it! Charlotte admonished herself. *A fan of English muffins?*

"I can bring you Greek honey," said Paros. "My daughter makes it. It's darker than American honey. It tastes like honeydew and thyme."

"I'd love that," said Charlotte.

Paros nodded. "Ikaria," he said, without looking at her. "My island, it's near Turkey."

"Oh," said Charlotte. She tried to think of something more to add, a way of connecting, but Paros departed, the cabin door shutting behind him with a sound as final as the metal strike of scissors.

Charlotte sat down on her bed. If she were the type of person who dwelled, she would feel sorry for Paros and his colleagues, who were surely paid badly and housed in cramped, below-the-water cabins. But Charlotte was resolutely not a person who dwelled. How could she be?

Charlotte had once been someone who tried to get to the bottom of things. Winston, for example. She had continually tried to figure out what was wrong with him, attempting to anticipate what he might need or want so that she could keep him from sadness and, later, scotch. She had made his dinners with care, submitted to sex, woke early to shower and dress so that she could serve him breakfast with her face on.

But all that changed one Saturday morning. Charlotte was sitting at the kitchen counter in her tennis whites, doing the *New York Times* crossword puzzle. She'd dropped the younger kids at the Club and was waiting for Lee to wake up and pack her swimsuit. Winston had taken to falling asleep in the den, which was fine with Charlotte. She knew not to bother him until lunch, when he would like a turkey on rye with Grey Poupon mustard and Lay's potato chips.

Charlotte heard a scream. She looked up from five across ("Bobby Short's 'saloon,'" obviously "Café Carlyle"), her pencil still finishing the last "e." There was no other sound. Charlotte waited, then returned to her puzzle. (Five down: "A pilot's living room.") Her brain whirred, and she counted the spaces—yes! "Cockpit." She filled in the letters, then set down her pencil. She was still someone who investigated things, for a few more moments.

Charlotte climbed the stairs slowly. She paused at the top, ears straining, but heard nothing more. Had she imagined the shriek? "Lee?" she called quietly.

Lee's response was a wail of agony. Charlotte rushed toward the sound, which seemed to be coming from Lee's bathroom. Charlotte was wearing tennis socks with pompoms. Lee's room smelled of drugstore perfume. In her bathroom, Lee was standing on tiptoe, hugging Winston, whose face—

Why did he do it in Lee's bathroom?

How could she tell her friends?

What if Charlotte had looked for him before she took the kids to the Club?

How could he leave her alone?

What was she supposed to do now?

Oh, Winston, why?

YOU COULD KEEP ASKING questions, or you could stop. To survive, Charlotte did what she had to do. To this day, she could hardly look Lee in the eye. Only Lee knew how profoundly Charlotte had failed. Charlotte knew the truth weighed heavily on her oldest girl. She knew that Lee was breaking. The questions loomed: could Lee bear—

No. Charlotte swallowed. You could keep asking questions, or you could stop. Charlotte bowed her head and prayed, asking God to take care of Paros and Lee; Cord and Regan; her mother, father, and Minnie in heaven; and last, Charlotte herself. Then she stood, readying herself for a fun day at sea.

FIVE

Rhodes, Greece

1 / Charlotte

WHEN SHE OPENED HER curtains, Charlotte was amazed by the lively scene that had replaced the placid horizon. Pulling on her bathrobe, she stepped outside. Below the ship, a wide parking lot was lined with tour buses and taxis. Past a highway lay a medieval world: fortress walls, crenellated at the top, met deep blue sky. And was that a *turret*? Charlotte imagined a knight on his steed, cantering against the Greek breeze, brandishing a silver shield. And a dagger! Entering one of the dark passageways that led into . . . a moat? That the steed could leap over? A harem of lovely . . . princesses? A lawn-like battlefield? Charlotte definitely needed to brush up on medieval Europe. She went back into her room to find her coffee tray and a tiny, wrapped box.

Her heart beating fast, Charlotte opened the present and found a jar of honey. In the mirror above her dressing table, her expression was delighted, her cheeks rose-colored without any blusher.

Charlotte remembered her mother, how she never emerged from her room in the morning without a full face of makeup. When Charlotte was fifteen, Louisa had taken her to a beauty counter and bought Charlotte a bag of cosmetics. "Why do I need these?" Charlotte had asked on the way home, poking through the tissue paper to fondle jars of foundation and liquid rouge.

"Can you imagine what would happen if I stopped putting on my face?" asked Louisa. She barked, a sad laugh.

"What?" said Charlotte.

"Your father would find someone who hadn't let herself go," said Louisa.

"No, he wouldn't," said Charlotte.

Louisa stared out the window. "Let's not find out," she said.

Charlotte's parents had acted as if they were always on TV. They evaluated themselves and each other, speaking in fake voices. Charlotte's father called Louisa "darling," but they were rarely alone, and Charlotte never saw them embrace.

Maybe this was why Charlotte yearned for sex. It was messy and real. You couldn't be naked with another person and remain perfectly put together. Sure, your lover might leave you, might think you were ugly and wrinkled. But maybe that was the risk you had to take to connect to another. Was it too late for Charlotte to take the risk?

She slipped the jar of honey into her beach bag.

2 / Cord

CORD HAD READ THAT the medieval city of Rhodes had actual castles, Byzantine temples, knights' buildings, mosques,
stone-paved streets, and a *moat*. As they shuffled off the
ship into a parking lot filled with idling tour buses, he put
his hands on his hips and envisioned himself from above:
just a small dot on a crazy island between Athens and Turkey in the midst of the Aegean Sea. How far away his actual life seemed.

He put his arm around his mother and smiled as one of
the ship's ever-present photographers snapped a picture of
them behind a cardboard cutout of a life preserver with
RHODES, GREECE printed in (what else?) glowing orange. His
sisters crowded in, unable to resist a chance to preen: Lee
with her giant sunglasses and cosmetically enhanced lips
pouted in what she'd told Cord was called "duck face" and
Regan with an "oh, who me?" expression better suited to a
twelve-year-old. Cord's spirits sank; he was glad he'd had a
few mimosas to buffer the misery of being with his family.

"Look!" cried Regan. "A little trolley!"

There was, indeed, a tiny trolley in the parking lot, ac-
companied by a man who looked a great deal like Zorba

the Greek, if Zorba had worn a conductor's hat and held a sign advertising RHODES TOWN CITY TOUR 7 EUROS ONLY!

"Let's do it!" said Regan, grabbing Cord's arm. When he snatched it away instinctively, she looked stricken.

"Sorry," said Cord. "I just . . . we already have a tour arranged, so I thought . . ."

"It's fine," said Regan, her voice steely.

Matt the Philanderer had stayed on the ship for the day, telling them at breakfast that he had some work to catch up on. Cord wanted to punch him. He turned to Charlotte, who—despite her extremely bright beach outfit—looked small and a bit overwhelmed. "Mom?" he said. "Do you have the tickets?"

"Tickets?" said Charlotte.

Cord's stomach ached. He yearned to reach into his pocket for the tiny bottle of Jägermeister he'd stuck there for emergencies.

"*Yassus! Yassus!*" said a young woman, approaching them. "You are for the beach?"

"We are for the beach," said Charlotte proudly, gesturing to her monogrammed, terry-cloth cover-up (which matched her monogrammed visor and monogrammed beach bag).

Regan strode ahead of them toward the bus, followed by Charlotte. Cord turned to his older sister. "We need to talk about Regan," he blurted, desperate to share the bad news. "Zoë called me. There's some very bad news. About Matt."

"What?" said Lee.

"Zoë hired a private investigator. Regan won't even *look* at the report."

"Oh my God," said Lee. "Do you know what it says?"

"Yes!" said Cord. He told Lee, thrilled not to be alone

with the disgusting news. Cord had vague memories of Lee being not only his ally but his best friend. In the YMCA pool, swimming butterfly, or afterward, in her swim-team suit and gray sweatpants, she seemed invincible. A warrior. She protected Cord from Winston's wrath—she defended them all. One time, when Lee found Cord crying because Winston was making him join the flag football team with kids who bullied him, Lee stormed into the kitchen, where Winston was pouring himself a drink, and told him he should be ashamed. She actually said those words! And Winston said, "Give me a break, Lee Lee. That kid's going to need a *sport*."

"What he needs," Lee said, "is a father who supports him!" She'd been thirteen, the bravest girl in the world, her hair in a chlorine-smelling ponytail, her voice strident and strong. And Winston had relented! Cord, clutching brand-new football cleats in the hallway, was filled with profound relief when Winston rounded the corner and snatched the shoes from his grasp. "Forget it," he said. "Just forget it. I'll return these."

"How about telling him you love him?" Lee said, appearing behind him, her hands on her hips. Winston didn't answer, just went into his den and shut the door.

Cord looked at Lee. "Thank you," he said.

"I've got you," she said. He ran to Lee and she embraced him. "We're in this together," she whispered. "I'm here." Cord realized later that maybe this was what she'd wished someone would say to her. That Lee, as the eldest, had never felt she had anyone to watch out for her, so she became what she most needed.

But after Winston died of a sudden heart attack, Lee changed. She stopped coming home except to sleep. When Cord tried to enter her room to talk, she told him she was tired or busy. She bought a lock at the True Value hardware store and installed it on her bedroom door. Cord knew she was embarrassed by their cramped rental house. It dawned on him slowly that she wanted to flee her family, Cord included. She thought she was better than they were, above their paltry circumstances. It was as if talking to her low-rent siblings depleted her. This knowledge was crushing to Cord. By the time she left for California, she was a stranger. Even now, with Lee standing next to him, he missed her.

"What should we do?" said Cord.

"It isn't really any of our business," said Lee. Cord felt surprised—he thought Lee would figure everything out, save Regan. *Our business?* Were you allowed to not give a shit about your family like that? Cord didn't think so. He followed Lee onto the bus and sat next to Charlotte.

"Cord," said his mother, "what's going on?"

"Nothing, nothing," said Cord. He wanted everyone to be happy so much it hurt.

Charlotte pursed her lips. "You don't have to tell me twice," she said. And then she added, with cold jubilance, "I'm ready for some fun, fun fun."

"Three funs, Mom?"

Charlotte shrugged. "I deserve three funs," she said.

As they settled into their seats, Cord considered this proclamation. He was a person who felt he deserved no funs, and he wondered if it was because his mother felt she deserved three funs.

You get no funs, said the lonely voice. *You are the trampoline, not the gleeful jumper.*

"I don't want to be the trampoline," Cord whispered. "I want to be the gleeful jumper."

"What's that, dear?" said Charlotte.

"I'm very tired," said Cord.

"Oh, please," said Charlotte. "You think you're tired? At least you're not seventy-one years old and *alone*."

Cord bit his tongue so forcefully he drew blood.

THEY PASSED THROUGH A forty-foot-thick fortress wall and emerged in a medieval world: narrow streets lined with sandy-colored castles, minarets rising high. Tourists in sun hats marched like ants, pointing at towers and gazing in shop windows. Though he was the one in a bus, Cord felt superior as they veered out of Rhodes's Old Town, merging onto a highway.

The bus lumbered up a hill, and Cord took in the panorama of terra-cotta rooftops, bright green copses of trees, and faraway, scrubby hills. They turned a corner and the ocean appeared below. Cord could see two enormous cruise ships in the cobalt Mediterranean: an elegant Cunard and the cheesy *Splendido Marveloso* with its crimson snake of a waterslide.

Why weren't they going inside the castles? Who had chosen to go to a beach rather than contemplate an honest-to-God moat? Cord had the panicked feeling that he should be doing something differently, better . . . but then again, he could use a day in a beach chair. Work had been so stressful lately, as they watched their earnings dribble away and it became clear that the firm was utterly dependent on the 3rd Eyez investment.

Giovanni won't want you when the money's gone, said the lonely voice.

"Shut up," said Cord. He needed a few more drinks to silence the lonely voice.

"What?" said Lee.

"Sorry," said Cord. "I wasn't talking to . . ." He stopped

himself. Lee wouldn't understand the lonely voice. He'd thought, growing up, that his family was just better at ignoring the critics in their heads. But he had come to believe that Lee just didn't hear a lonely voice at all. Nor did Charlotte or solid Regan, the only one who'd made a family of her own. It was a strange reckoning to accept that his brain came with the lonely voice and others' didn't. Giovanni told Cord it made him deeper, more able to feel things, more incredible. He tried to believe Giovanni, whose low, rational words were taking the place of the lonely voice on good days. Handy told Cord he needed inner child work, EMDR, trauma therapy. Handy was probably right. But it was so much easier just to drink.

Outside the bus window, rows of bedraggled olive trees spilled down to the dazzling sea. They turned a corner and fruit groves came into view: bright yellow lemons among iridescent leaves. Cord gazed at the low stone houses and thought, *I should move to Greece and harvest olives.*

"I should move to Greece and make honey," said Charlotte.

"You mean olives," said Cord.

"No, Cord, I mean honey. Have you even *tried* Greek honey? *Real* Greek honey?"

"I'm not sure," said Cord.

"Ah," said Charlotte knowingly. "It tastes of thyme."

"Does it?" said Cord. His mother's cheeks were flushed. He shuddered, imagining she'd been reading some honey-drenched sex scene in one of the filthy books she and her pals trafficked in. Church ladies! They were some down-and-dirty gals.

"I've never had real Greek honey," said Regan forlornly.

Their bus driver spoke into a microphone. "*Rhodos,* she

means rose," he said. "My island makes many items for sale, including carpets, brandy, cigarettes, and soap."

"*Faaa*-scinating," said Charlotte.

Cord suddenly wished for Giovanni so much he felt dizzy. He wanted Giovanni to meet his eye when Charlotte said, "*Faaa*-scinating," to wink at Cord, making him feel loved and understood. Giovanni was so kind and untarnished. He would help care for Charlotte. He would laugh at her jokes, compliment her J. Crewish outfits. And she would adore him—his sweet asides, his belief in the kids he taught, his ironic sense of humor. Charlotte would fall for Giovanni entirely . . . if only she were someone else, or if Giovanni were a woman.

3 / Regan

AT TSAMPIKA BEACH, PERFECT azure waves lapped at white Greek sand. Next to Regan, Lee untied her bikini top and stretched, her impossibly symmetrical breasts glistening in the sun.

"Lee!" cried Charlotte. "Your top!"

"Oh, Mom," said Lee. "In Europe, people aren't so ashamed of their bodies." This was true, Regan realized. There were many leathery old breasts on display. (And leathery old penises, for that matter.)

Lee stood, then said, "I'm going for a dip!"

When they were kids, Regan was desperately jealous of her glamorous older sister. But now, watching Lee watching men watch her made Regan sad. When had Lee become pathetic? A slim guy stood up as Lee passed. She waded into the ocean and he followed like a shark smelling blood.

Regan had been aping her sister all her life, trying and failing at being a stunner. But Regan was realizing that she might be ready to put that burden down, to leave horny men's gazes to women like Lee, who seemed to want them.

Although most of her magazines and many of her

mom-friends seemed to believe otherwise, Regan knew in her gut that the person she needed to love and nurture was herself. Trying to keep her face unlined and her body teensy was a battle that would take all her might. Regan wanted to use her mind for other things—creating art, raising her girls, understanding what was happening in the world. God had given her a big bottom, strong thighs, a Rubenesque stomach. Her chest and pillowy arms were made for comforting, for loving. She could go to Orangetheory every day and drink only Shakeology drinks, but she wasn't going to look like Lee. That was the truth, and Regan was tired of pretending the truth didn't exist. Charlotte's staunch insistence on denying anything real was exhausting. Regan wanted to live another way.

She stood, her own bathing suit *on*, and walked along the beach. In the waves, she spotted an older Greek couple frolicking. The woman was deeply tanned, her hair mashed unattractively, her breasts long and veiny. The man's breasts, too, were paunchy and full, his round tummy gleaming in the sun. The woman was splashing water up into the air, and the couple danced as it rained back down on their shoulders. Regan smiled.

And then she ran into the sea.

4 / Lee

LEE SWAM UNDERNEATH CRAGGY cliffs toward a rock painted with the Greek flag. Her period hadn't come, but the cold water cleared her mind of worries. Tsampika was so different from the beaches in L.A., which had always struck Lee as pretty, sure, but lackluster. This beach had character. It looked exclusive. It was the kind of backdrop you saw in famous people's Instagram photos—you could simply *tell* it wasn't some low-class American shoreline.

And the man who approached her in the water wasn't American, either. His teeth were the giveaway—they were yellowed and a bit crooked; an American would have had them fixed. He was tall, his very tanned chest sleek as an otter's. Gazing back at the shoreline, Lee pretended she didn't see him.

"You're an actress, right?" said the man in a British or maybe Australian accent.

Lee pretended to be startled, letting her manicured hand flutter to her elongated neck. (She'd read somewhere that both swans and humans exposed their necks to attract the male gaze.) "I am," she murmured.

"I knew it. That movie about the bank robbery?"

Lee looked at him through her eyelash extensions. "No."

"The one in outer space, where you're wearing a silver suit and those fabulous moon boots?"

Lee laughed. "No," she said.

"I know! Wait . . . the TV show, the one where you're the coach of a Little League team, and one of the kids goes missing?"

"Yes," said Lee. "My God, that was ages ago."

"But those red shorts."

Lee laughed. *Run All the Way Home* had been one of her last big roles, though at the time, three years before, she'd thought it had been her *first* big role. How depressing. Almost as depressing as the news about Matt. Lee pushed Regan's problems out of her mind and turned to her new suitor.

"I'm retired," said Lee, trying out the words.

"Retired?" said the man. "Lucky girl."

"I'm finished with the rat race," said Lee airily. "I'm on to bigger and better things. L.A. is in the rearview mirror, if you know what I mean."

"Sure," said the man, looking puzzled but game. "So where do you live now?"

"I'm . . . in transition," said Lee.

He smiled. "I'm in London," he said, holding out his hand. "Pete," he said.

"Lee." She shook his hand.

"Race you," said Pete, and before she could respond, he lunged into the water and began swimming out toward a dock moored in the distance.

"Damn," muttered Lee, knowing her hair looked better dry and blown out. Still, it would feel good to get her blood pumping. She took a deep breath and went under.

LEE HAD QUIT THE swim team when she found a new dream: to be an actress. She'd tried out for *A Midsummer Night's Dream* on a whim, but was cast as Hermia, opposite Felix Henderson, the hottest thespian in her class. His floppy blond hair was irresistible, and as Lysander, he looked so unflinchingly into her eyes that Lee wondered if maybe he loved her in real life as well.

Spending time with her dad had grown stale. The intervention had made no difference. He'd say he was quitting drinking, but after a white-faced night or two, he'd be back at it. Lee hated his weakness for booze. It exposed him as fallible, and seeing him this way was so awful that she had to avert her gaze. Toward Felix. And his floppy hair.

The night she was cast, Lee announced the news during a chicken dinner she shared with her siblings and mother in the kitchen. This was the usual way of things: Charlotte would cook and share the "kids' dinner" in the kitchen while Winston drank alone in his den, and then she would prepare another meal for Winston and serve him in the dining room with full place settings, sitting down opposite him, cleaning up after him when he was done. Some nights, Winston brought his plate and utensils into the den, leaving Charlotte alone at the table. Lee could remember seeing Charlotte staring out the window of the dining room, her sad face illuminated by the candles she'd lit for her husband.

"So I'm quitting swimming," Lee had said. "It's at the same time as play rehearsals, so."

Charlotte put down her napkin. "Have you told your father?" she asked.

"No," said Lee.

There was a poignant silence. Winston sat just a few rooms away; they could hear the television from his den.

"He'll be disappointed," said Charlotte.

"But rehearsals are at the same time!"

"I understand, dear," said Charlotte. Helpless anger filled Lee: as usual, her mother was tossing her to sea without even a floatie of assistance, much less two floaties, which would hold her above the choppy waves of her father's drunken wrath.

"I'll come with you," said Regan, putting down her plate and utensils.

"You're not finished," said Charlotte. "And you haven't been excused."

"I'll come, too," said Cord, rising, reaching for Lee's hand. Charlotte pursed her lips and sawed at her chicken. She wouldn't argue with Prince Cord, thought Lee. This was a source of constant annoyance, and yet there he was, standing and waiting—he was *her* prince, too. He smiled. "Let's go," he said.

He was only twelve, yet he was so handsome, the bones of his face emerging from baby pudge. Winston rode him hard, wanting him to be a *man*, but Cord had a few close friends who balanced the scale. He'd found three pals who got his weird sense of humor; Lee would see them whispering and giggling in the seventh-grade hallway at Savannah Country Day. And seventh grade seemed simple to Lee, from her ninth-grade vantage point.

Fine, thought Lee. She could use the backup. She placed her hand in his. Regan rose to cover her other side, giving her a quick side squeeze. Regan! The sweetest little girl. She would be no help at all, but her hug was warm. United, they approached the den. Cord was the one who knocked.

Winston didn't stand from his leather chair, but turned toward them when they entered, his face a portrait of annoyance. He raised his eyebrows and waggled his face, a rageful gesture that said, "What idiocy now?"

Lee swallowed, then spoke. "I'm quitting swimming. I thought you should know."

He sat back in his seat, returned his attention to the television. Regan squeezed her hand. They waited. After a moment, he turned back to her. "You're too slow anyway," he said. He tapped a cigarette from his pack, lit it with a silver lighter. "Got your mother's thighs," he said.

Lee bit her lip. She left the den, pulling her siblings with her. They knew Winston wasn't done; they knew Charlotte offered no protection. By leaving Charlotte alone in the house, they were putting her at risk, but one thing their upbringing had taught them was that you had to take care of yourself.

Cord and Regan led Lee to the place in the rocks. They played Cave Family until the sun went down, never saying a word about Winston, or Lee's intermittent tears. Lee was too old for Cave Family, but she ate the invisible wild rabbit Cord brought home anyway, and played the stick game with Regan. Nobody came to look for them. The sun went down. When it began to lightly rain, they put themselves to bed.

Charlotte made Lee promise to never tell anyone—including her brother and sister—that Winston had not died of a heart attack. The fact that they had not saved him from suicide—had maybe driven him to it—was so shameful that Lee had not even told Matt. So while Winston's death was a reprieve of sorts for Cord and Regan, who bloomed without their father's dark presence, for Lee it was the start of her life as a fraud. She held it all—the fear, the sorrow, the pain of seeing her dead father. She couldn't stand to be around her siblings, and fled as soon as she was able. But the secret had eaten away at her. And no one would ever thank her for keeping it, of course—how could they know what she had done—was doing—to keep their world intact? And yet she yearned to tell them, the only ones who would understand.

A month after Lee quit swimming, and a few weeks before he hung himself, Winston tapped on her door, pushed it open without waiting for her reply. He was swaying a bit but not too drunk yet. "What?" she said. This insouciance with Winston was new to her; she tempered it with a "What do you need, Daddy?"

"How about swimming?" he said. "You're going to get fat if you just sit here every night."

"Dad! That's so rude." Lee cut a glance to the mirror above her dressing table. Was her jawline a bit rounder than usual? She wasn't sure.

"Stop looking at yourself," said Winston. "I'm saying I miss you. Let's go for a drive. Practice starts in thirty minutes."

"I told you I'm done with swimming," said Lee. "I'm going to be an actress, Dad."

"Is that right?" said Winston.

"Yes."

"Okay, then," said Winston. He stood in front of her for a moment, and then said, "God gave you those looks. Don't blow it."

When Winston killed himself, Lee knew it was her fault. He'd done it in her bathroom, after all. Why hadn't she gone for a drive with her father? He'd needed her and she had let him down.

She vowed to stay beautiful. She would not be abandoned again. She would become so famous that she would always be loved.

LEE BURST OUT OF Greek waves, her face hot. From the floating dock, the man waved. He looked a bit feral under the bright sunlight—skinny as a drug addict, his crooked teeth bared. Suddenly, Lee didn't want to swim to him. She treaded water, felt her blood thump through her body. "Yoo-hoo!" cried the man.

"Yoo-hoo," said Lee.

"Come to me, you gorgeous creature!" said Pete.

Lee didn't know how to say no.

5 / Charlotte

LULLED BY THE SOUND of the waves and the warmth of the sun, Charlotte fell deep into a dream of lying on a beach towel as the man on the cover of her book, *Taming Zeus*, rubbed tanning oil all over her body. When Cord shook her awake, she was immediately embarrassed, her body still pulsing with want.

"The first bus is leaving," said Cord. "I didn't want to wake you, but we're ready to go."

"Hmm," said Charlotte, pulling herself regretfully from the dream world where Zeus, holding a bottle of Bain de Soleil, remained. Lee, Cord, and a complete stranger stared down at Charlotte.

"I'm Pete," said the stranger in a British accent. Charlotte took in his bony physique and tattered swim trunks.

"Pleased to meet you," she said.

"So, Mom, are you ready?" said Lee. "If we go now, we can take a walk through old town Rhodes."

"It's actually Rhodes's Old Town," said Pete. "Not to be persnickety." He chortled, and Charlotte frowned.

"I never knew you to be interested in history, dear," she said.

"There's wicked shopping," said the stranger too eagerly. "Castle paperweights. Totes, tees, sarongs. Quite something, really. You feel like you're back in the Ottoman Empire, wandering through passageways, getting lost in it all. Like a sultan. Like you're Sultan Süleyman the Magnificent. And also, mugs."

Wandering through passageways getting lost in it all sounded downright frightening to Charlotte—she spent too much time already wondering if she was losing her mind. "Oh, I don't know," she said.

"Sometimes, I wish I were a sultan, to be honest," said the stranger.

"Who doesn't?" sighed Cord, who was holding a nearly empty beer bottle.

"I don't," said Charlotte. "And if it's all the same to you, I'm going to stay here and enjoy the beach." Lee and Cord exchanged a glance that they thought Charlotte wouldn't see, though her vision was still intact. "I'll be *fine*," said Charlotte.

"I don't know, Mom . . ." said Cord. "I feel like a jerk leaving without you."

"She'll be fine," said Lee. "Won't you, Mom?"

At least Lee had put her top on. Charlotte smiled sweetly and said, "Of course, darlings."

"Where's Regan?" said Lee. "That's our sister," she explained to leering Pete.

Charlotte scanned the beach. "I don't see her," she said. "Maybe she's taking a dip?"

"In her old-lady bathing suit?" said Lee.

"Be kind," said Cord.

"Sorry," said Lee.

Charlotte turned away from the disturbing spectacle of

Pete staring at Lee's chest. "Toodle-oo," she said, opening her book.

"I think I'll just stay with Mom," said Cord.

Charlotte ran the scenario through her head—Lee tottering on cobblestone streets with this skeevy fellow; Lee getting pregnant and needing to live with Charlotte forever. A squalling bastard child in her placid home. Named Pete, Jr.

Ugh!

"No, Cord," said Charlotte. "Please. I'm fine. Regan will turn up eventually."

"If you're sure, Mom," said Cord.

"I am utterly sure," said Charlotte. She added, trying to keep her tone light, "Just keep an eye on your sister!"

"Oh my God, Mom!" said Lee.

"I will," said Cord, leaning down to kiss Charlotte on the cheek. Why couldn't *he* find a dalliance? Maybe he'd meet some expert in Greek antiquities—a woman with tortoiseshell eyeglasses and a ponytail. Wearing a khaki jumpsuit, but in the evenings she'd change into a smart dress from Talbots and cook for Cord—lamb or whatever they ate here on Rhodes. Someone on the bus had mentioned octopus.

Was Cord gay? It was possible he was gay. But why wouldn't he have told her if he were gay? She did, okay, hope he was not gay. Pope Benedict XVI had said that gay marriage was "an offense against the truth of the human person, with serious harm to justice and peace." (Charlotte had looked it up.) But now there was a new pope, Pope Francis, who seemed more open-minded.

It would be hard to tell her church friends—and even worse, *Father Thomas*—if Cord was gay. The Bible said that being gay was "an abomination." Charlotte believed that the Bible said a lot of things, and maybe some of them were more allegorical than prescriptive, but "an abomination" was hard to put a positive spin on.

Charlotte wished Minnie were here beside her, though she knew what Minnie would say. "He's your son! You choose your son!" Charlotte thought of Father Thomas and his kind face. He had been there for her through these years . . . so many years, it felt, during which her children had abandoned her.

Father Thomas sat beside her when she needed comfort, and she loved his manly smell. If she didn't come to morning mass, he called to see if she was okay. There were days when, after mass, Charlotte didn't talk to anyone at all. The hours were endless, bleak, but there was the possibility that Father Thomas would stop by for coffee. People forgot Charlotte, assumed she was fine or busy or didn't feel lonely. But Father Thomas remembered. He treated her as a person, as the woman she still felt like inside, though she seemed invisible to everyone else.

Charlotte would not allow a gay son to cause her to be ostracized from church. How could she possibly choose between the faith that had sustained her and her own son? Charlotte loved Cord, but without Father Thomas, now that Minnie was gone, she would have nothing at all.

SIX

Valetta, Malta

1 / Charlotte

THE SATURDAY VIGIL MASS was odd. The priest couldn't use candles, so battery-powered tea lights cast a dull, dim light in the Tranquillo Conference Room. The priest pulled on plastic gloves before handling the host. A passenger wearing a zebra-striped pantsuit whispered to Charlotte, "He's wearing gloves because of the norovirus."

Charlotte nodded gravely.

The zebra-pantsuited woman leaned close enough for Charlotte to smell her perfume and body odor. She whispered, "The only reason they even *have* mass is for the Filipinos." She jerked her head toward a dozen or so men and women in folding chairs. "Can't run a ship galley without them," said the woman. Charlotte turned toward the makeshift altar and put her shoulders back, universal language (she hoped) for *please stop talking to me*. When mass was over, the woman stood at the same time as Charlotte. "Well, hello," she said, smiling. "I'm Jane-Ann and I'm from Oxford, Mississippi."

"Charlotte Perkins. I'm from Savannah."

"I *knew* you were a Southern gal," said Jane-Ann.

Charlotte did not ask how Jane-Ann knew. She didn't really think of herself as a "Southern gal," though she'd lived in Savannah for decades. Charlotte considered herself a woman of the world, a diplomat's daughter. She wished she could convey to Jane-Ann that they were not the same.

"Are you going to the co-cathedral?" asked Jane-Ann.

Charlotte had no idea what Jane-Ann was talking about, but didn't want the woman to think she was uninformed. "Hmm?" she said.

"St. John's Co-Cathedral? In Malta? It's supposed to be *beyond*."

"Hmm," repeated Charlotte, backing away. "Nice to meet you."

"You, too!" cried Jane-Ann. "It's refreshing to meet a real Catholic around here, unlike all the heathens upstairs at the morning buffet."

"Don't talk about my children that way!" said Charlotte. "I'm joking! Though they are at the morning buffet."

"Have you tried the marzipan animals?" said Jane-Ann.

Baffled again, Charlotte smiled noncommittally. She hurried back to her stateroom and ordered a turkey club sandwich, which was delivered by a female porter.

After her supper, Charlotte went out on her balcony and stared at the churning sea. The ship's lights were mirrored in the closest waves, but then the water became an enormous, dark blanket rolling out toward a navy sky.

Charlotte's essay was troubling her. The priest might be in the audience when she read it—or Jane-Ann! Charlotte balled her hands into fists. She wished she could call Minnie. She wished she could call anyone.

THE PAINTER & ME
By Charlotte Perkins

I was a beautiful girl when I first went to his castle. He was gnomelike, but in an attractive way. It's hard to explain, but I'll try. From a distance, you'd think, *Ugh*. He was short, with wispy old-man hair. He wore ridiculous clothing. Horizontal striped shirts matched with dingy plaid pants. And a beret. If you saw him coming toward you on a dim street in Aix, you'd think, *Oh dear, I better cross. That homeless elfin man looks drunk and I'm afraid he'll steal my pocketbook.*

He didn't care how he looked. This was one of the things I admired about him. It was also lucky for him, because his face . . . Well, his face was cragged, pinched with bovine intensity. His gaze was sort of frightening. You'd never meet his gaze and think, *What a kind person.* No. When he looked at you, it was as if he was consuming you. Like a tiger. He was sizing you up, deciding how to bring you down, and which piece of you to eat first.

He was SEX PERSONIFIED. He was sex personified as a gnome who shopped at T.J.Maxx.

He had said he wanted to draw me, so there I was, in the enormous dining room of his castle. My parents thought I was taking a day trip to see ruins. (As I told them this fabricated story, I pictured the painter's wrinkled face and did not feel I was wholly lying.) I looked at the Provençal floor tiles as he poured wine. They were octagonal, brick red. The painter was talking about himself.

"When I first came to this place, they asked me if

it was too vast and too severe. But I said it is not too vast, because I will fill it!"

"How interesting," I said, though he had not paused for my response. He went on:

"I said, 'It is not too severe, because I am a Spaniard, and I like sadness.' Ha ha!"

"Ha ha!" I agreed.

I was scared. I was a virgin, and I knew we were going to have sex. I had been taught that sex was absolutely wrong before marriage and would condemn me to Hell. Thus, I was curious. At this time, I didn't really believe in God or Hell. I was young, and I guess I didn't have a need to believe there was someone I could pray to, someone who was in charge of everything, even when it seemed that life was a cruel, random mystery.

God—before I needed Him—seemed so vague, and here was the painter, pulling me to him. He smelled like turpentine and dog hair, but I didn't see a dog.

In his blindingly white studio, we drank more wine. The room was absolutely magnificent, lined with dramatic crown moldings—flowers! Shells! Hounds! Men and women draped in togas! In the center of the studio, an elaborate mantelpiece at least twenty feet tall soared toward the ceiling. Instead of a hearth under the glamorous mantel, there was an empty space with a dirty cowbell inside.

This seems an apt metaphor.

We stood by the giant windows and I said I loved the view. I did love the view: rolling, blue-green mountains. The painter stood behind me and pressed against me. "Others have painted these mountains but now I own them," he said. I began to admit to myself that he was a bit of a braggart.

He gave me a linen robe, which didn't smell clean. He needed someone to do his laundry, it seemed, and I thought to myself, *I could do his laundry.* But I also thought I could set up an easel beside his, or do his accounting. I could hire someone to do his laundry. I changed into the robe in his bathroom and lay down on a settee.

He was no longer wearing his shirt, but he was growing more drunk and pontificating in earnest. Where had his shirt gone? I looked around the room but didn't see it. This bothered me.

He stopped talking and began to draw. He was drawing me, and I savored his gaze on my body. The sun from the open window was warm on my skin. A man—a famous man—drew me, paid attention to my bones and the skin over them. I was luminous.

He put down the pencil and approached. Inside his hideous pants, I saw his desire growing. He pulled the drawstring and stepped free, exposing very hairy thighs. They write in romance novels that "man members" are "throbbing" and you think, *Oh, honestly,* but his was. Seriously, it was.

It was throbbing for me.

He untied the sash on my robe. I didn't have to do anything. He parted the cloth and ran his rough and stubby fingers across my rib cage, to my breasts, my waist. He straddled me, guided his throbbing member into my most secret place. He pumped away, and I tried to feel something more than a vague concern that someone could see in through the window. The pain was sharp, somehow important. When he finished, I was a woman.

THE END

Addendum: *Nude on a Couch,* on permanent display in Barcelona, Spain, was painted shortly after our assignation. I am quite sure the nude on a couch is, in fact, *moi.*

2 / Cord

THE *MARVELOSO* HAD FOUR "regular" restaurants and six "specialty" ones. All passengers were assigned to a table for breakfast and dinner that was theirs alone. The Perkins family had Table 233 in Shells, an uneasy combo of Denny's diner and a Parisian whorehouse. It reminded Cord of a banquet hall where he'd once gone for a work seminar in New Jersey, back during his early days at the firm. The gold sconces, maroon wallpaper, great swaths of cream-colored cloth on the tables and windows—it all screamed, *Check me out, I'm luxurious!*

It occurred to Cord that Giovanni's mother, Rose, might love a cruise like this—maybe they could take her on one. Cord had to admit that he adored cruising, too. As much as he ridiculed the ship in his head, he loved being on it. Just wandering around taking in the bright lights, thumping music, and tasty snacks made him feel euphoric.

He had even indulged fantasies of surprising Gio with a balcony cabin on the Splendido Around the World cruise he'd seen advertised on the giant screen above the pool in the Aqua Zone. For a *full year*, passengers would travel from Europe to the Suez Canal; stopping in Egypt and

Dubai; then heading to India; over to Singapore; and up to Hong Kong; then to Australia and New Zealand, stopping in Samoa and Hawaii on the way to Los Angeles; then sailing south through Mexico and the Panama Canal; hitting Colombia's Cartagena; then Curaçao, Fort Lauderdale, and Bermuda; before sailing back across the Atlantic to Funchal. What even *was* Funchal? Could he wear a thick Splendido robe for a year? Cord imagined riding camels in Petra with Gio, dancing cheek to cheek in the Starlight Lounge. The daydream made him swoon with pleasure.

When it was dimly lit at evening time, Shells Restaurant seemed almost festive. But in the morning, Shells was revealed as the hungover party girl she was: a bit tattered, her napkins rumpled, her lavishments too much, too bright, too early. Even at the crack of dawn, the waitstaff were dressed in tuxedos.

"I'll have the . . . hmm . . . Maltese breakfast sampler. Why not?" said Charlotte. She handed her laminated menu to the waiter. "How do you even pronounce this?" she asked Cord, pointing to her Magical Malta Day Tour ticket.

Cord ordered an egg-white omelet, then scrutinized the word on his mother's ticket: *Marsaxlokk*. "Marshmallow-lox," he said. He lifted the carafe in the middle of the table and poured his mother a coffee, then filled his own cup.

"Where is everyone?" said Charlotte. "I need to talk to you all about my essay. There are some things you need to know."

"I haven't seen anyone since last night," said Cord. "I fell asleep right after dinner." In truth, he'd watched a movie and had WhatsApp sex with Giovanni, which had been surprisingly hot. Giovanni had been on his lunch break, and had brought his phone into the teachers' bathroom.

The event had been sordid, blurry, and very exciting. Afterward, Cord had fallen asleep without drinking anything from the minibar.

"Hmm," said Charlotte, vexed.

"What is it, Mom?" said Cord.

"I think I should tell you all together."

"Mom!" said Cord, teasing. "Do you have a secret?"

She looked flustered. "What?" she said. "No! Of course not!"

"Who's talking about secrets?" said Regan, approaching. Matt followed a few feet behind her, wearing a button-down shirt, pale pink shorts, and loafers. Cord felt a seething anger toward his brother-in-law, toward all the straight Southern men he'd known who thought the world was their oyster. Sometimes, he wondered what it would be like to be one of these men. On the outside, he looked like them, but under the skin, he knew he couldn't be more different.

"Now listen," said Charlotte, pulling out her tour tickets. "After a walking tour of Marshmallow-lox, a traditional fishing village, we go to the prehistoric temple of Hagar Qim, the Blue Grotto including underwater flora and fauna, and then we'll mingle with *locals* at a typical *whatever-this-word-is*, and see the place where some movie called *Black Eagle* starring Jean-Claude Van Damme was filmed. And then we see a Caravaggio painting in St. John's Co-Cathedral."

"Wow," said Cord. "That sounds . . ."

"Exhausting," admitted Charlotte.

Cord was relieved to hear his mother say so. "Why don't I run down to the Excursions Desk and see if we can change to a more low-key tour?" he said. "I mean, I want to see some of the sights, but maybe not *all* of the sites."

"Honey, would you?" said Charlotte. "I don't want to see all the sights, either! Just a few."

"Actually, there are crazy tunnels hidden underground here—war tunnels—wouldn't that be cool?" said Regan.

"We must see the co-cathedral," said Charlotte. "And then maybe a nice Maltese beach?"

"I didn't get any tours," said Matt. "I'm going to just relax by the pool."

"Matt," said Charlotte. "What are you talking about? We're in Europe. You can't just stay on the ship."

"I need a break, not an excursion," said Matt sharply.

Charlotte looked down, hurt. Regan pursed her lips but did not speak. Cord, fury coursing through him, met Regan's gaze. With her eyes, she pleaded for him to stay silent. "I'll be right back," said Cord, swallowing his ire.

There was a long line at the Excursions Desk. Cord searched on his phone and found a small operator out of Valetta named Kiko. He booked the Half-Day Delights of Malta tour, paying with his own card. Then he sat down in a bright orange chair to read the paper on his phone before heading back to Shells.

The story was fairly deep in the Business section of *The Wall Street Journal*. Cord would have missed it entirely had he not been so reluctant to return to his family. It was written as an op-ed, and the headline asked, "Is 3rd Eyez the New Theranos?"

"Oh, God," said Cord.

The story said that "anonymous sources" were reporting a "shake-up" inside 3rd Eyez, calling the company "secretive to a worrisome degree." Cord rubbed his forehead, anxious. An "insider" was quoted as saying, "Will 3rd Eyez change the way we see the world . . . or turn out to be just another overvalued scam? Only time will tell."

Disregarding the time difference, Cord called Georgie. "Cord," she said, "it's three in the . . ."

"Have you seen it?"

"Seen wha—"

"Third Eyez in *The Wall Street Journal*. I'll wait."

After a few moments, Georgie said, "Anonymous sources?"

"Yeah."

"I'm sorry," said Georgie. "I don't know who—"

Cord cut her off. "Is there anything I need to know?"

There was a long pause. "No?" said Georgie.

Cord's heart sank. "What is it?" he said.

"Nothing," said Georgie. "It's just . . . it's nothing."

"What's the shake-up?" said Cord.

"It's . . ."

"Tell me, G."

"I'm leaving Third Eyez," said Georgie. "I just . . . it's personal. It's not the product, Cord. I promise you. The product works. You saw it."

"Personal?"

Georgie sighed. "Well, here goes," she said, "I'm . . . well, I'm having a baby."

"Whoa," said Cord. He rubbed his eyes. "Okay. Wow."

"Don't sound so excited."

"I'm just . . . I'm stunned, G. Who's the dad?"

"No one you know."

"Wow," said Cord again. He smiled, shaking his head, then said, "I'm happy for you. That's amazing. A baby. When are you due?"

"January," said Georgie.

"January. Well, okay. But, G, will you let me know if there are any problems with Third Eyez? Promise?"

"I will. Cord, you know I will."

"My ass is on the line."

"I never told you to fund the whole thing," said Georgie. "That was your call, Cord. I was just letting you in."

Cord pressed his fingers to his temples. "Talk soon," he said.

"Yeah," said Georgie. Cord could practically see her in the oversize Garfield T-shirt she probably still slept in, her hair a mess.

"There's always Neptune," said Cord.

She laughed wearily. Cord couldn't even remember where the assurance came from—some line in an old movie—but they'd always said it to each other.

"Yup," said Georgie.

Cord called Wyatt next. Wyatt read the story sleepily, then said, "I'm on it."

"Okay. I'll check in later."

"Cord . . ." said Wyatt.

"What?"

"The technology. You've . . . there's something there . . . right?"

Cord paused, rubbing his eyes. "Third Eyez is going to change the world," he said.

"Okay."

"It is."

"Sure, I said okay," said Wyatt.

Cord hung up and stared into space for a moment. In front of him was the Excursions Desk; a woman in pink pants drinking a beer from a can; swirling carpet; and a glass staircase. But in his mind's eye, Cord saw his face in the mirror of his Orlando hotel bathroom the morning after the 3rd Eyez presentation: gray, skittish, freaked out.

Was there something there, inside the warehouse in Florida? Cord sure as hell hoped so. Uselessly, he tried to remember—what had he seen? He cast back into his memory again and again, like a fisherman running on faith.

But there was nothing.

3 / Regan

VIEWED FROM THE LIDO deck, the Grand Harbour was a medieval wonderland. This was Malta—a ninety-five-square-mile island between Africa and Europe, land of knights and secret World War II tunnels. The sky was pale blue, the sea a deeper blue, and in the middle, Malta was the color of honey. Like Rhodes, Malta was a scene from another time, as if modernity—with all its skyscrapers and McMansions and pollution and cellphones—had not yet happened.

"Well," said Matt. "I'll see you tonight."

"Sure," said Regan.

"What does that mean?" said Matt. "It's not enough that I have to hear it from your family?" Regan didn't respond, and he grabbed her shoulder. "Answer me," he said.

Regan turned around. With one good shove, Matt would go over the protective railing, breaking his legs, or maybe his neck. Her hands twitched. She smiled as sweetly as she was able. "I just wish you could come," she managed. "To Malta."

Matt watched her, his expression calculating. He wasn't

stupid, and she needed to remember that. "I'm sorry," he said.

"It's okay," said Regan. She made herself stay still. He would need to be the one to say goodbye.

"Well, have a good time," said Matt. He leaned down to kiss her on the cheek, and she allowed it.

As she joined the excursion line with her mother and brother (Lee had never shown up for breakfast), Regan tried to calm down. Her exchanges with Matt were so fraught—they left her shaken. They disembarked, and Regan spotted a short man holding a sign that said PERKINS. The man wore cargo shorts and a Yankees cap.

"Look! It's our guy!" said Cord.

"I'm not a fan of all those pockets," noted Charlotte. The way she immediately judged their guide based on his shorts infuriated Regan. It was so shallow!

"Welcome, welcome to Malta! I am Kiko," said the man as they approached.

"Nice to meet you. Very nice to meet you," said Cord, shaking Kiko's hand. Not for the first time, Regan wondered if Cord was gay. But he would have told her by now, wouldn't he? Still, she was not imagining it: Cord's eyes lingered on Kiko's lips. They were beautiful lips—plump and pink. They looked like they would be soft to kiss.

Regan watched Cord watch Kiko. She wasn't homophobic, but she didn't have any gay friends, either.

Regan could remember her father laying into Cord, as if Cord's inability to catch a baseball were a statement about Winston's own masculinity. Regan felt tenderness toward her brother. The difficulty she encountered as a bigger, voicey woman must have been increased a hundredfold for

Cord. No wonder he had ended up in New York. Maybe Regan should do the same.

"I am honored and pleased to show you my home. This is a magical island with so much history," said Kiko, interrupting Regan's thoughts. "Would anyone like to begin with a coffee or *pastizz* pastry?" he asked.

"I'd try a *pastizz*," said Cord. He'd slid on mirrored sunglasses, making his eyes impossible to read.

"Good, wonderful," said Kiko. He led them through a busy square to a food cart. Next to the cart, a man sold fish from a bucket to passing cars, haggling loudly. Kiko approached the cart, ordered, then handed Cord a pastry on a napkin. Cord tentatively bit and chewed. "This is . . . ?" he said.

"Peas and ricotta," said Kiko.

"Pungent," said Cord.

"And some more treats," said Kiko, handing Charlotte a brown paper bag. Where was Regan's treat? Regan approached her mother, hoping Charlotte would share.

"This one is *imqaret*, a date cake," said Kiko. "Next door is *kannoli*, you know this one?" They nodded. "We have then a Maltese honey ring, and lastly, almond torta."

"I couldn't," said Charlotte.

"You could," said Kiko. "Charlotte Perkins, you must."

"Well, if you say so," said Charlotte, selecting the almond torte. Regan, realizing no one was going to offer, reached in and chose a *kannoli*, biting into the sweet cookie.

"Come," said Kiko. He led them to a bench next to a wide stone stairway. "Down these stairs, you enter secret tunnels used in World War Two," said Kiko. "But, I'm sorry, the tunnels are closed on Monday."

"Damn," muttered Regan licking powdered sugar from

her lips. They walked along the water, and Kiko gestured to an enormous cannon, asking, "Have you ever seen a bigger cannon?"

"No," said Cord. "I have never seen a bigger cannon."

"Me neither," said Charlotte gamely.

"Because this is the *world's largest cannon!*" cried Kiko, throwing open his hands.

"Is it really?" said Charlotte. Kiko crossed strong arms over his chest and nodded. "That is something else," said Charlotte, opening her bag of treats and selecting another.

"The British constructed Rinella Battery between 1878 and 1886," said Kiko.

"Oh?" said Charlotte.

"It was built to house one gun weighing one hundred tons," said Kiko. "Also, a rifled muzzle-loading gun. There was once another battery to the west of the Grand Harbour, but this no longer exists."

"Isn't it hot?" said Charlotte. "I am very warm indeed." She unbuttoned her neon-yellow cardigan and took it off, rebuttoned it and positioned it around her shoulders, carefully arranging the arms across her chest. "It's very warm," she said again.

"Mom, do you want to sit down?" said Regan.

"Only two hundred-ton guns survive," said Kiko. "By arming Gibraltar *and* Malta, the British hoped to protect their route to India through the Mediterranean."

"I'm going to faint," said Charlotte matter-of-factly. "To be honest, these Maltese snacks are not agreeing with me."

"But wait!" cried Kiko. "In a few moments, there will be historical reenactors dressed as nineteenth-century British soldiers to provide a military show combining the live-firing of historic artillery and cavalry!"

Turning her back to Kiko, Charlotte limped to a bench

and sat down. Regan bit her lip, for once resisting her knee-jerk reaction to be the helpmeet.

"Another option is to skip the military reenactment," said Kiko. He ran a hand through his black hair, touched his goatee.

"A nice cool restaurant?" ventured Charlotte, eyes closed.

Kiko smiled. "I am the best chef in Malta."

"Are you?" said Cord. Flirtatiously! He said it flirtatiously!

"I will take you to my home. It is near a small village, and I make wine. We will cook and relax under my shady *gharghar* tree."

"That sounds very nice," said Charlotte weakly.

"I will go fetch my car quickly," said Kiko. "Please enjoy an air-conditioned touristic shop." Kiko led them inside a store called Woohoo Malta. "I'll be back in a moment," he said. Charlotte perked up a bit, scrutinizing dish towels with local recipes printed on them.

Regan spied a nail clipper with the Maltese flag printed on top. "I'm getting it," she said.

"A Maltese toenail clipper?" said Cord.

"It's for *me*," said Regan.

"Way to treat yourself."

"Please," said Regan. "Please, Cord, don't be mean."

Cord turned to her. Regan expected another cynical remark, but to her surprise, he took her in his arms. "I'm sorry, Ray Ray," he said, using the nickname he'd once had for her. Regan remembered, in his embrace, a much earlier hug. Her father was yelling outside a door, outside Cord's door. But Cord had locked the door and was protecting her, keeping her safe. Regan eased into her big brother, inhaling his smell. His *real*, dirt-and-butter smell, the one underneath his fancy cologne. How she loved him. And he would be there—she would have him—no matter what. Your "family of origin" (as her online therapist called them) could be toxic and strange, but they were yours: you could not escape them, for better or worse.

4 / Lee

LEE WOKE ON A DECK CHAIR. She wasn't sure which deck. Her last clear memory was ordering a double Chardonnay (oh, God) at the Red Rum Bar, and then there was a flash— could have been a dream—of holding a fluorescent drink in a plastic cup toward a starry sky. For about thirty seconds, her brain tried to convince her that coming to on a deck chair was somehow glamorous—a sign of her wild and freewheeling nature—but when she sat up and saw a man in uniform carefully sweep around her with his broom, she was disabused of the notion.

There was a night world on the ship. Roving teenagers who slept all day in the interior cabins their parents had paid for broke free, their faces glittering with makeup, their blooming bodies clad in leather and spandex; passengers shed their on-land personas and came alive under the disco balls and inside the flashing casinos; musicians, comedians, and dancers who worked on the ship were transformed by moonlight into superstars. There were people kissing in storage rooms, making love in roped-off corners. Lee had roamed the ship, marveling.

But daylight seemed to bake the allure from her midnight adventures. Morning sunbathers had given Lee a wide berth—her gold lamé dress made it clear she was a clubber gone to seed and not an early bird. Her head pounded. She hadn't had a hangover in years, and vowed she wouldn't have another. Her liver was too old to cleanse boozy toxins. And if she *was* pregnant, she was harming the baby. Was it possible? Was she pregnant? Lee thought of Jason, who sometimes ran her bubble baths, even lighting a lemongrass-scented candle and placing it in the soap dish. Once, they had made love in the tub and her hair had come too close to the candle, her ponytail briefly catching fire before Jason doused her in bathwater.

Lee's emotions were all over the place these days: she seemed to seesaw between the depths of despair and fireworks of elation. Now, she felt her happiness ebbing away, and knew that a deep misery awaited, the fog rolling in. When it lifted, everything seemed possible. Inside the fog, though, she wanted to die. It really was that bad. She felt so low she didn't think she could survive. She had taken too many sleeping pills once, when the fog had stayed for weeks. Jason had begged her to see a doctor, had even made her an appointment and driven her to the small office in West Hollywood.

"My father killed himself," Lee told the psychiatrist. "He hung himself when I was fourteen. I found him."

"How did that make you feel?" asked the doctor, a slight woman named Evelyn.

Lee tried to remember. "I don't know," she finally answered, truthfully.

"You don't know?" said Evelyn.

"I have no idea. I can see the bathroom, and I can see his body, but I can't remember how I felt."

Evelyn nodded, scribbling something on her pad.

"My boyfriend thinks I'm manic-depressive," said Lee.

"What do you think?" said Evelyn.

"I just feel numb," said Lee. "Numb and really tired."

Evelyn crossed her hands in her lap and waited. Lee squirmed. After ten minutes, she stood up. "No offense, but I just don't really have time for this," she said, as she opened the door to leave.

"I'll be here if you need me," said Evelyn. This turned out to be a lie. A year or so later, when the fog was thick and deep, when Jason had left Lee for Alexandria Fumillini and Lee was considering pills again, she summoned her strength and drove to the Spanish-style office park. She made her way to Evelyn's door. But there was a sign that said EASY ELECTROLYSIS. Lee tapped on the door anyway. It was locked.

So she got back into her Prius and called her mom, listened to Charlotte's chatter until the fog dissipated enough for Lee to feel safe. She flushed all her sleep medications, just in case.

LEE PEELED HERSELF OFF the *Marveloso* deck chair and limped toward the center of the ship. Once you were inside, it was usually clear where the elevator was, and once you were in the elevator, you could orient yourself, at least laterally. The ship was a massive network of hallways and splendiferous event spaces. If you were okay with wandering, you could always find your way home. (It was funny that Lee thought of her cabin as "home": it was the closest thing she'd had to one in a while.)

But seriously, thought Lee as she used the rail to hold herself up, lurching along the outer deck—what if she got a job on the ship? Maybe it wouldn't be so bad to join the

Velvet Vibe dance troupe, or to be the female version of Bryson, organizing eighties Rock-N-Glow parties, tossing the foam die and yelling trivia questions. She could replace (or augment) DJ Neon!

What this cruise needed, thought Lee, was a serious actor. Didn't these people ever get tired of the rah-rah dance routines? Lee hadn't been to any evening entertainment outside of a bar, but from what she saw on her cabin TV, the only performances in the Teatro Fabuloso were musical revues. How about Ibsen? Lee closed her eyes, allowing herself to remember her triumph as Nora in *A Doll's House* her senior year of high school. The school paper had called her "arresting."

Lee stopped under the SkyRide and closed her eyes, speaking the lines from memory. "We must come to a settlement, Torvald. During eight whole years . . . we have never exchanged one serious word about serious things."

Lee opened her eyes, blinking. The port city (what country was it?) was surrounded by fortress walls with tiny oblong windows. It was even more magnificent than Rhodes.

"During eight whole years," Lee repeated, the lines springing forth from her memory, "we have never exchanged *one* serious word about *serious* things."

What did that even mean? What, indeed, was a *serious thing*? A woman headed out into the night on her own, like Nora? The fog of despair that had swallowed Winston, that Lee was afraid was enveloping her again?

"Our home has been nothing but a playroom," said Lee, the words bubbling up from the depths of her . . . her soul! "I have been your doll-wife, just as at home I was Papa's doll-child."

A middle-aged jogger passed Lee, averting his eyes.

It was time to take a break from men, Lee decided. Like Nora, Lee had been serving men for . . . well, for her whole life. As a kid, she didn't know any better than to allow it; as an adult, she'd been courting it. Lee needed to figure out who she really was inside, in the place that had nothing to do with dewy skin and sculpted curves. She'd been given this trip to Europe, and she'd basically wasted it thus far, trying to seduce men, alienating her family, ignoring the cultural riches laid out before her. Here was a chance to do things differently. Lee vowed to try to open her mind to beauty. She'd been doing the same things for so long: auditioning, seducing, preening. What if she turned it around, and let the world try to win *her* for a change?

In her cabin, Lee took four Advil and called room service. After a half hour or so, the porter, Paros, brought her tray. He set it down on her miniature coffee table and Lee thanked him. He hesitated, then said, "Your mother was concerned. I can contact the Maltese guide, if you'd like."

"Hmm?" said Lee, staring hungrily at her French toast.

"Your family has begun their tour of Malta," said the porter.

"Malta?"

"Yes, ma'am," said the porter. "I can try to find your family's whereabouts in Valetta, if you'd like."

"Oh, no thank you," said Lee.

Paros nodded, seeming disappointed in Lee. He stood before her, his hands behind his back, like a judgmental penguin. When would men stop evaluating her? When would she stop caring about what their assessment would reveal?

She sighed. "Okay, okay," she said. "Maybe I will join them."

"Wonderful!" said Paros. "I will call you in a moment."

The porter seemed awfully solicitous, thought Lee, but she guessed that was the point of a porter. She ate her buttery French toast and crisp bacon, showered, and dressed for invisibility in her baggiest jogging shorts and a big Splendido T-shirt she'd gotten for free in her welcome basket.

The phone rang. "I have located your family," said Paros. "I will be at your cabin momentarily, with a map showing you how to find them. Or I can accompany you, if you'd like."

"That's really nice of you," said Lee.

"It's my job, Miss Perkins," said the porter.

"Actually, can I ask you something else?" said Lee.

"Of course."

"I'd like you to bring me a pregnancy test."

There was a pause, but the porter recovered. "Yes, ma'am," he said.

Lee hung up the phone and felt teary. It was something about the porter's fatherly concern. How she wished she could call her father, the version of Winston she had once believed existed, the one who would help her out of jams, who would always have her back. The father she deserved. But Lee understood that this man was a fantasy. Her real father had been a depressive alcoholic. He'd taught her that fighting the fog was a losing battle. Oh, how Lee wanted to prove him wrong, to show that she was stronger, that she would find joy.

Winston had been forty-seven when he fastened a necktie into a noose. She was thirty-eight now. Lee felt momentarily awed by her father: he had held on for nine more years.

Lee put her palm on her belly, looking at the magnificent Grand Harbour. There was a knock at the door, and she stood.

5 / Charlotte

KIKO BROUGHT CHARLOTTE AND her family to his farmhouse and welcomed them into his living room. It was *something* to enter one of these buildings—a cavernous space with exposed limestone walls, piles of books by cozy chairs, and a couch with a blanket Kiko said had been crocheted by his mother. It felt like being inside a well-appointed grotto, a respite from the punishing heat.

He brought cold cans of something called Kinnie from the kitchen. It was a weird soda, brewed (said Kiko) from bitter oranges and wormwood. Charlotte tasted it but shook her head. Kiko offered honey or cactus liqueur instead, gesturing to a bar cart in the corner, underneath a wooden guitar that had been hung on the wall as if it were a painting.

"I'm fine with water," said Charlotte. "Purified, please."

"I'm loving the Kinnie," said Cord amiably.

"Water for me, thank you," said Regan.

"What are you having?" asked Lee, who had joined them by the harbor. Paros had brought her directly to them, having contacted Kiko himself. What a peach! Lee had arrived looking pale and ill, but handsome Kiko, it seemed, had roused her. When they'd met, Kiko had gazed at Lee as if she were the bodily manifestation of a lifetime of dreams. Sex was in the air in Malta, Charlotte thought, admiring Paros's buns in his starched white pants as he strode back to the ship.

"I'll have the cactus liqueur," said Kiko, smiling. "Come, try. It's called Zeppi's *bajtra*. I have a fresh bottle in the kitchen. Follow me."

"I'll wait here, but thanks," said Lee. It was refreshing to see her checking out the art on the walls instead of the man in attendance. Lee had always had an eye; she'd once told Charlotte that her couch would look better along the south wall of the living room, and to Charlotte's surprise, Lee had been absolutely right.

"Is it too early for liquor?" said Regan.

"When in Malta," said Cord, standing to look at Kiko's bookshelf. "Love this one," he said, pulling out a copy of some tome called *Infinite Jest*.

"I love that one," said Kiko, reemerging with a platter of warm bread and cucumber-and-cheese salad. "What a wise person."

"Yes," said Cord. "He was. But tortured, as well."

Kiko looked at Cord. "So I've read," he said. "He had depression. A disease we don't talk about here."

"We don't talk about it much, either," said Lee. She looked pointedly at Charlotte.

"I'm not depressed!" said Charlotte.

"No one said you were," said Lee.

"Then why are you looking at me?" said Charlotte, feeling annoyed. Leave it to her children to ruin a sunny picnic! Before Lee could answer, she said, "I always say, *Look on the bright side.* It's a much better way to live," she said. "Don't you think, Kiko?"

"Not everyone can be bright, Mom," said Lee.

"I don't have any idea what you're going on about," said Charlotte, though of course she probably knew more about depression than any of them. After Winston's suicide, she'd read many, many books—trying to understand, seeking a way to forgive herself. The books said it was a disease, that Charlotte couldn't have saved Winston no matter what she'd done. Charlotte wanted to believe what she read. But she had never stopped blaming herself.

"Let's take the food to the garden?" said Kiko.

"Yes, let's!" cried Charlotte. The patio was shaded, somehow cool in the middle of the day. Kiko set a table with linen napkins and put out chilled bottles of pink Gellewza wine. "It tastes like strawberries," he said. "Come, Charlotte," he added, handing her a long-stemmed glass.

She sipped. It was sweet and just the right amount of rancid. She tried to focus on the taste of the wine, to yank her brain from thoughts of Winston, how his face had looked almost peaceful in death, how terror had caused Lee's limbs to tremble for days. How, when Charlotte found her in the bathroom, Lee's lips were pulled back in a silent scream, exposing both rows of her even teeth. She'd been fourteen. The muscles in her swimmer's arms had bulged as she held his body off the ground, but no strength could change what Winston had done.

Kiko brought pastries, rabbit stew, beef with olives, and fresh stonefish seared with herbs and served with lemon. They feasted, surrounded by Aleppo pine trees.

At one point, Charlotte watched as Lee emerged from Kiko's tiny bathroom, drying her hands. Lee looked so young as she gazed around at the garden. She looked like the girl she'd been a million years ago, a happy toddler who danced ahead of Charlotte when they went for walks in Forsyth Park.

Charlotte felt a wave of concern and love for her first-born. When Kiko came to Lee's side, pointing out a bird called a "wall creeper," Charlotte was surprised to see Lee step away from him politely but firmly.

Despite Lee's newly demure persona (or perhaps because of it), Kiko seemed utterly smitten. Lee did look lovely without all her makeup and hairspray, her curves hidden beneath a gauche cruise-ship T-shirt.

Regan, on the other hand, acted as if she were a graduate student prepping for an exam. She asked a lot of questions about the various occupiers of Malta, and Kiko answered animatedly. Charlotte's head spun: Malta had been occupied by the Phoenicians, the Carthaginians, the Romans, the Vandals, the Goths, Romans redux, the Arabs, the Normans . . . at this point in history, Charlotte spaced out, but when she started listening again, Kiko was talking about the Knights of Malta. "The Turks forced them out of Rhodes, and so they came here," he said.

"Rhodes!" cried Charlotte. "We were just there." It gave her immense pleasure to utter this statement. "Ah, Rhodes," she added, a wistful aside she hoped to repeat frequently.

"I love Rhodes," said Kiko. "Did you visit the Palace of the Grand Master?"

"No . . ." admitted Charlotte.

"The Acropolis of Lindos?"

"Um . . ." said Charlotte.

"Did you go to the beach?" asked Kiko, smiling.

"It was an awesome beach," said Lee.

Kiko laughed. "You'll have to return," he said. "Sometimes you need to stand in the footsteps of history, and sometimes, a day at the beach."

Regan was holding a pencil and a little notebook she must have bought somewhere. "And after the Knights of Malta?" she queried.

"Apologies. Okay. Then France was in charge," said Kiko, "and then Great Britain, until 1964, when we became independent. So you see, we're a very important place."

"Amazing," said Regan.

"We have three hundred and sixty churches," said Kiko. "How about it? Would you like to see one? St. John's Co-Cathedral has two Caravaggio paintings! A quick trip, and then I return you to the port?"

Charlotte picked up her glass, but thought of Father Thomas. How could she tell him she'd chosen pink wine over a famous cathedral? He had made her promise to invite him over for lunch and show him every one of her pictures. "You could make a slide show," he'd suggested, his large hands gesturing. "I bet I could find one of those slide-wheel projectors in the basement. We could make European-themed hors d'oeuvres!"

Sometimes, Charlotte thought that perhaps Father Thomas was even lonelier than she.

Sighing, she set down the Gellewza. As if Father Thomas could hear her, she pronounced, "We'd love to tour the cathedral."

Kiko drove them back to Valetta in his VW convertible. Charlotte could feel sea-scented wind in her hair (and made a note to tell Father Thomas this very detail. Sea-scented wind!).

The cathedral looked simple from the outside, with two bell towers, but the interior was so beautiful that Charlotte felt as if her brain were overheating. Baroque,

Charlotte could appreciate, but this church was, as her granddaughters would say, *bonkers*. Every surface of the limestone walls was carved, painted, or gilded. Every inch inspired closer attention. It was the definition of glorious. But all this glory—it was almost a bit much. "Look at the floor," whispered Kiko.

How could she *not* look at the floor? Marble angels and skeletons were inlaid below her feet. "We are standing on over four hundred tombs," said Kiko. "They tell a story, the story of the inevitability of death, and the rapture of the afterlife."

Charlotte was silent, overwhelmed. Lee came and stood next to her. "What do you think?" she asked.

"It's so sad," said Charlotte. She couldn't bear the thought that she wouldn't feel rapture in the precious years she had left, that she'd have to wait until she was dead.

"But hopeful, too," said Lee, putting her arm around her mother. "Rapture sounds good to me."

It felt wonderful to have Lee next to her. Later, when she went over every moment that led Lee to perch on her balcony high above the ocean, Charlotte would curse herself for not saying something else in this moment. What if she had said, "There's rapture right here" or "Lee, I love you."

What if she had said, "Please don't leave me"?

But no, Charlotte had said, "Rapture does sound nice, I suppose." She wasn't thinking. She'd had no idea. She'd simply wanted to say something, while her daughter was listening.

SEVEN

Sicily, Italy

1 / Charlotte

CHARLOTTE HAD VISITED ITALY with her parents when she was small, but all she could remember about the entire trip was standing in a chilly bathroom beside her mother. Louisa (in Charlotte's memory) turned to her and said, "I was not crying. Now go and give your father a kiss."

Charlotte remembered leaving the bathroom, running through a dim restaurant, flying toward her father, who wore a suit and did not look up.

And now, more than sixty years later, she woke again in Italy. Well, near Italy, anyway. In Italian *waters*. Ah, *bellissimo*!

"I am here with a coffee," said Paros, from the hallway.

Charlotte froze, frantically teasing her sleep-flattened hair in the mirror, rummaging uselessly in the drawer for a brush. "Um . . . ?" she said.

"I'll leave it here and come back later for the tray, Mrs. Perkins."

Charlotte exhaled. "Thank you!" she called. When she'd heard his footsteps fade, Charlotte brought the pot of coffee and a raspberry Danish (what a wonderful surprise!) to her balcony, felt the Italian breeze on her face. She reached for what she thought was the bill, but saw a handwritten note instead:

> *Homer wrote in the Odyssey that a many-headed mon-*
> *ster (SCYLLA) guarded the entrance to the Strait of*
> *Messina and ate sailors who tried to approach . . . and*
> *that the whirlpool CHARYBDIS waited for vessels . . .*
> *Luckily the Splendido Marveloso has already safely*
> *docked. I love the view of Sicily and the Calabrian coast*
> *and I hope you have a wonderful day.*
>
> *Yours,*
> *PAROS*

Charlotte gripped the note. She wanted sex, it was true, but Paros's attentions were exposing a deeper need: she yearned for love. She had spent her mornings alone—or with imaginary lovers—for so long. She had not allowed herself to imagine the deep satisfaction of reaching out in the night to touch a warm body next to her own.

Charlotte sipped her coffee and gazed at the rocky coastline, the deep green hills, clouds like smoke. How lonely it was to have no witness to her life. No one to guard her passage into slumber, no one to know that she had made it through the night.

2 / Cord

HOW COULD THIS BE Cord's first trip to Italy, the worldwide mecca for fashionable, carb-eating gays? It was a crime that he wasn't here with Giovanni. Instead, Cord was with his mother and sisters, boarding a motor coach helmed by a very enthusiastic woman named Diana. *"Buon giorno!"* she cried, as soon as they and about a dozen other cruise ship passengers were seated. *"Buon giorno!* This, it means hello in Italian. Can-a everybody hear-a me?"

She spoke into a microphone with the volume turned way up: everyone could hear her.

"Isn't this *exciting?*" whispered Charlotte, who sat behind Cord and Regan, popping over the seat like a Lilly Pulitzer–clad jack-in-the-box.

"Thrilling," said Cord. He was freshly showered and bleary-eyed. The night before, he had stayed up playing Texas Hold'em, drinking cappuccinos until his hands shook. He'd missed the Friends of Bill W meeting (code for Alcoholics Anonymous—Bill W had founded the program) and his scheduled call with Handy. He had been sober for two days and counting but had scarcely slept, his mind catastrophizing and trying to find a path from where he was now to a wedding ceremony in his mom's backyard.

"The beaches, as you see, are small storms," said Diana. At least, Cord thought she'd said storms. Maybe stones? "Etna down there is the wine," said Diana. "Lava rocks, and then the sand-a. Sicily, it is so beautiful! And now you know."

Diana sat down.

"What do we know?" said Cord. "I missed something." Regan, who had been drawing in her notebook, looked similarly bewildered. "What are you writing?" asked Cord.

"Do you really want to know?" Her timidity was heartbreaking. What had Matt—or motherhood—done to his sister, the girl who had made him eat Ethiopian food in Harlem, who had gotten up and gyrated with the belly dancers after a bit of honey wine?

"Yes, Ray Ray! I want to know."

"Well, Malta was all about bones, in a way. Those skeletons in the church. All the violent attempts to take over, to erase the past . . . but you can't erase bones. You can't even burn them fully, or it's hard to. So I guess I'm thinking about that, and hearing about the volcanoes here, what they buried, what remained . . ." She stared into a middle distance, seeing something Cord could only imagine.

"That's fascinating," said Cord. She turned to him, seeming shocked to hear him take her thoughts seriously. She watched him quizzically, as if he were about to make fun of her. "It is. Really interesting," he said, happy to surprise her by being kind, but also sad that she seemed desperate for such mild attentions.

She shrugged, flushed. "I'm going to start thinking about my art again," she said softly.

Regan had once been a pink-haired student creating

stunning collages—her large-scale images of genteel white Southern women made out of cut-up photos of slaves were brutal and brave. Cord didn't know how to remind her of that student without making her feel embarrassed— didn't know how to bring up the private investigator's shocking photos again, since Regan had so firmly shut that door—so he was silent.

Matt had stayed onboard, and despite the appalling fact that he was a grown man who didn't want to set foot in Italy, being on her own seemed to suit Regan. Maybe she'd still become a great artist, flowering in her later years.

Cord blanched. If Regan was in her later years, then so was he. While Cord was happy enough with his career, there was so much more he wanted to do. Marrying Giovanni seemed like the beginning of a fuller life; he was thankful to be so thrilled about what lay ahead. He just needed to stay sober. That was all. Cord knew that if he kept drinking, it would all slip away.

"Honestly, it's just nice to have some space to think about all this again," said Regan earnestly.

"Yeah," said Cord. He turned to her. "Regan," he said, "are you sure you don't want to talk about Zoë's email?"

"I'm sure," said Regan. "Please. Just let it be."

"But, Regan, he's . . ."

She fixed him with a stare. "Cord," she said, so quietly he almost couldn't hear. "Please. Trust me."

Trust her? Cord was confused. He'd always thought of Regan as a . . . well, kind of a sap. A doormat. It had never occurred to him for a second that she might be in control of her life. "But," he said, "don't you need my help?"

She laughed—she actually laughed! "No," she said. "But thanks. Thank you."

"Another town-a," said Diana, standing again, her expression animated, her lipstick newly applied. "Very famous for the American people. They make-a the movie. Which movie? Al Pacino and the Godfather movie! Francis Ford Coppola, he comes here. You see some small towns and they are here. For example, Corleone? When he tastes wine? It is here. There is also *Godfather Two*."

The view outside the bus was lovely: brushy hills, farmhouses, and sweeping views down to the ocean. The bus entered a tunnel, but this did not stop Diana. "Now you know how we eat here. We eat the appetizer, and the pasta," she said, her face shifting in shadows. "Pasta, pasta, pasta! We eat-a the pasta!" Diana yelled, in the dark of the bus.

A man in a Jimi Hendrix T-shirt said, "Yeah, baby!"

Light spilled over them. "Now, Taormina!" said Diana. "Tonight, at the ancient theater, is Robert Plant. I will go. My husband, he pays, so I don't know. I buy just something to eat and he does everything. It is right. I cook."

"Oh, darn," murmured Charlotte, poking Cord. "I bet you hoped she was single!" Cord winced, then saw that Lee was listening. She raised her eyebrows.

Tell her! mouthed Lee.

Cord turned away, pretending not to understand.

"I make-a the meatball-a," Diana added. The man in the Jimi Hendrix T-shirt cheered again.

"Now I have to introduce you to our mama. Mount Etna!" said Diana, pointing out the window at an enormous mountain, steel-colored against the turquoise sky.

"Mount Etna," said Charlotte reverentially. Cord gazed out the window at the slumbering volcano. Regan was sketching Mount Etna with a *Splendido* pen.

"The first two extinguished cones-a on the left-a. Part of the touristic stations was destroyed by the lava flow." Diana pulled out laminated photos. "Nobody is listening?" she said, peering over her audience, who seemed largely to be asleep. Cord tried to meet her eyes and look engaged. He wasn't sure why he felt it was his job to keep Diana from feeling slighted, but he did.

"You only care about the cooking, right?" she said, disappointed despite Cord's best efforts. "*Va bene*. If you don't know something, you ask-a. Now look," she said. "Outside the window, some pine trees, coriander. More trees-a. Vegetation. Typical vegetation."

Diana sat down.

"Vegetation," whispered Charlotte, nodding, peering out the window. Regan wrote *Vegetation* in her notebook.

They exited the highway and turned down a street bordered on either side by high, whitewashed walls. They passed what seemed to be a burned-out, vacant church with one of its three bells missing. Finally, the bus parked and Diana stood. "Here is *il giardino di Villa Romeo*!" she said. "Villa, what do you call a villa?"

"House?" called Cord obsequiously.

"No, I don't think so," said Diana. "Anyway, we disgorge."

LEE AND CORD LEANED against a limestone wall. Cord touched the gritty surface. Blinding light, the smell of smoke, a feral cat watching them from a distance. "Italy!" said Lee, squeezing his arm.

"Italy," he said, kissing the top of her head, which smelled like mint. He whispered into her hair, "Stop giving me such a hard time."

"But seriously," said Lee.

"It's not your deal," said Cord.

"Isn't it killing you?" asked Lee. "Pretending to be someone you're not?"

Cord looked at her. He sighed. "Yes," he said, "it is."

"So tell her," said Lee.

"You say it like it's easy," said Cord.

"I know it's not," said Lee. "Believe me."

"Why do we feel so responsible for her?" said Cord. "She's supposed to be the adult. But I . . ."

"I feel like I have to take care of her," said Lee.

"You, too?"

Lee smiled sadly and nodded. He took her hand. "I love you," said Cord. "You're maybe the only one who knows me."

"Cord—" Lee began.

He cut her off. "After you left, I waited by the phone every night," he said, realizing he sounded like a petulant child, but unable to stop himself.

Lee's eyes widened. "That was twenty years ago, Cord."

"You told me you'd call every night." Cord remembered sitting next to their big button phone in his pajamas. But it never rang. "You went to California," he said, "and that was that. You didn't even come back for Christmas."

Lee sighed, staring into a middle distance. "I thought if I made a clean break . . . you guys would have a chance."

"A chance? What does that mean?" said Cord. "A chance of what?"

"I just wanted . . ." said Lee. She looked away from him, biting her lip.

"A chance of *what*?"

"A chance to be okay," said Lee. The anger in her voice took Cord by surprise.

"I don't understand," he said.

"I know," said Lee. "I know you don't." She looked at him imploringly, her eyes clear and watery. "You don't understand. That's the point."

"So explain it to me," said Cord.

Lee shook her head. "Forget it," she said. "I shouldn't have said anything."

"I'm not going to forget it," said Cord, growing incensed himself. "If you have some excuse . . . some way you want to justify why you ditched us to become a fucking movie star, then please, tell me what it is."

"I didn't ditch you," said Lee. "Calm down."

"You did ditch me," said Cord, close to tears. He felt like an abandoned boy again. "You did ditch me," he repeated.

Cord remembered the day Lee had boarded a plane to go to college. During the drive back from the airport, sitting next to Regan in the backseat of Charlotte's VW Rabbit, Cord had sipped his McDonald's orange soda, cold through a plastic straw. Charlotte always got lost. She sometimes forgot to buy dinner. Once in a while, the power company cut the electricity. Lee had always been the one to find the bills and pay them, to make the lights come back on. Without Lee, Cord had realized, he was the one in charge. The world outside the car window seemed suddenly huge and fraught with possible disasters.

"Cord," said Lee now. "There were . . . there *are* things you don't understand."

"Spare me," said Cord. "Just spare me your theatrics, Lee."

"Okay," said Lee. "You're right. I should have called. I'm sorry."

She looked immeasurably sad. Cord knew something had been pried open—he had pried it open—but suddenly all he wanted was to shut it again. "And furthermore," he said: a joke, a plea.

"And furthermore," said Lee.

3 / Regan

"*BUON GIORNO!* WELCOME TO my family home!" cried a man in a polo shirt wearing sunglasses and a red cap. Two black Labrador dogs rushed toward Regan as she and her family entered a courtyard surrounded by palm trees.

The villa owner led them into his gardens, talking about his rainwater collection system, the "artifacts such as this olive press carved from a single piece of lava," the pepper trees, aloes, prickly pears, persimmons, chestnuts, and apricots. Regan sighed as he showed them an aquamarine pool hidden behind the gardens. All this beauty—this sparkling pool, these gardens—existed beyond her tiny Savannah life.

"Come-a to the kitchen!" called Diana. "It is time for Sicilian cooking school!"

In the villa's kitchen, Diana tossed eggplant caponata with red peppers. "Now, I set aside to fester," she said, placing the bowl on a steel-top table. In the cramped, blue-tiled kitchen, she handed out vegetable peelers and explained how to create long, silky ribbons of zucchini, which would be tossed in olive oil, lemon juice, and mint to create *carpaccio di zucchine*.

Cord was an eager student, grabbing a vegetable peeler and getting to work. Lee and Charlotte stood on either side of the schlump in the Jimi Hendrix T-shirt, who had found a bottle of unlabeled red wine and was struggling to pull its cork with a rusty wine opener.

Regan, realizing that she herself was festering in the hot kitchen, situated next to a fierce stove on which two pots of boiling water sent plumes of steam into the air, headed for the wooden doors of the farmhouse.

"Regan!" cried Lee. "Where are you going?"

Where was she going? God only knew. In the courtyard, Regan sank into a chair. The sun felt nice on her scalp, and she noticed the scent of sage coming from somewhere, with a faint edge of lemon. She took a deep breath and looked at the ancient patio stones. The villa owner came outside, opened a pack of cigarettes. "Is it a bother?" he asked.

It was a bother, but of course Regan said, "Oh, no."

The man didn't pull out a phone or chat. He lit his cigarette and smoked it. The silence weighed on Regan. Her mind churned, trying to think of what to say, then berating herself for not knowing what to say. "Oh, dogs," she blurted out. "I just love dogs." She did not, in fact, love dogs. Regan actually disliked them—their dirty mouths and the way they went right for your crotch.

"Eh," said the man. He shrugged and looked the other way.

Regan smiled. "Eh." She was going to have to use that one. What would her days be like, pondered Regan, if she were the sort of person who answered inane statements by saying, "Eh"? What a cool, stress-free existence, to disconnect from other humans, to not give one hoo-ha about what they thought.

Regan stood. It was time to say *eh*. "I'm going to need a taxi," she told the man. He turned to her, raised an eyebrow. "All I do is make food," said Regan. "Breakfast, lunch, dinner. I don't know who signed up for a cooking class on vacation, but I didn't come all the way to Sicily to stand in a hot kitchen and get lectured by Diana!" She crossed her arms over her chest.

"You want taxi?" said the man.

"You're goddamn right I want a taxi," said Regan.

4 / Lee

LEE WATCHED HER CLOSETED brother, her lonely sister, her mother, who was growing old. Pain seemed to radiate from them, and Lee felt it enter her bloodstream. She wanted to lie down and sleep. At the same time, she was ravenous. Ever since Kiko's incredible picnic lunch—that bread! Hot from the little AGA stove in his sweet kitchen in the house he'd grown up in!—it was as if a switch had been turned on. Lee felt as if she'd been starving for years and now couldn't get enough.

Her mind frightened her. How could she be a mother when she felt so unmoored, her emotions all over the map? And what of her giant appetite—did it mean she was pregnant? Paros had bought her a test in Valetta, delivered it to her room in a subtle brown paper bag, but Lee had been too frightened to even open the box. If she didn't know she was pregnant, she didn't have to make any decisions. Lee was good at compartmentalizing: it was what had kept her heading hopefully to auditions even as her prospects dimmed.

Did she want to be pregnant? Lee didn't know. She wasn't skilled at understanding what she wanted. She could tell you what everyone in the cooking class thought of her, but she truly didn't have any idea what she desired. When she tried to ask herself, there was a trembling silence.

Lee's phone buzzed, and she glanced down. There was a text message from a number she didn't recognize. Lee frowned and opened it.

Dear Lee, I cannot stop thinking about you. Do you believe in true love? Yours, KIKO

He had asked for her number as they waited in line to board the *Marveloso* and she had spoken it aloud, not thinking he'd ever call. He was handsome, and she had felt so safe in his cave house. But did she believe in true love? No, she did not. Lee typed back:

I'm sorry but I don't.

SHE WANDERED AROUND THE old Sicilian farmhouse, trailed by the two shaggy dogs that lived there. There was a giant hearth stacked with wood: Lee could almost imagine chilly winter nights on the overstuffed couch, reading by firelight, snuggled up with . . . Kiko.

Lee frowned. She wanted to strengthen her bonds with her family, get the courage to pee on the stick, and figure out a new career path. She needed to find a way to feel more stable. Daydreaming about a Maltese tour guide did not further any of these objectives. Yet she gazed at the fireplace anyway. Did Kiko like snuggling by the fire?

Her phone buzzed again, and she read:

Let me convince you?
Air Malta Flight 63
6:10 p.m. departure
From Rome, Fiumicino—Leonardo da Vinci Intl. (FCO)

To Malta Intl. (MLA)
1h 25m, Nonstop
This ticket is purchased in your name. Yours, KIKO

THEY WOULD BE IN Rome in two days. What an adventure, to fly back to Malta! Lee put her phone away, feeling buoyed by Kiko's invitation. At table, she breathed in the delectable smells, and served herself heaping portions of garlicky spaghetti, breaded chicken with roasted grapes, and spicy caponata. Regan had taken an early taxi back to the port, so Lee ate two slices of coconut cream cake.

On the bus back to the *Marveloso*, Lee wrote Kiko back: *Maybe.*

5 / Charlotte

THE SHIP HORN SOUNDED, and from their table in Shells Restaurant, the Perkins family watched as the mighty *Marveloso* engines churned Sicilian waters, pulling away from the island and heading across the Tyrrhenian Sea to Naples.

"I keep thinking about Malta," said Lee, her chin in her hand.

"You mean Kiko?" said Regan.

Lee smiled shyly. "He was nice," she said. "But I feel like I need to take a break from guys. I need to figure out my own self, honestly."

"A break?" said Charlotte. "What about Jason?"

Lee sighed, placing her hands on either side of her plate. "I guess I might as well just tell you," she said. "Jason dumped me for the girl on *Me & My Robot*. Alexandria Fumillini."

"The girl who *owns* him on the show?" said Cord.

Lee nodded.

"I'm so sorry," said Regan. "He's like her . . . pet."

"That about sums up the situation," said Lee, shaking her head. Cord put his hand on hers. "And while I'm talking," said Lee, her words speeding up. "I might as well tell you this, too. My career's over. I haven't booked a job since the Tampax commercial. I was lying about a big, new project. I was lying about *Law & Order: Special Victims Unit*."

They were silent. Charlotte felt nervous, saying emphatically to try to smooth things over, "You were *excellent* in that Tampax commercial."

Lee looked at her sadly. "Thanks, Mom," she said.

"Things don't always work out," said Regan.

"Yup," said Lee. She exhaled. "It feels good just to tell you guys," she said. "So I don't know what's next. I don't. I need to figure out what the heck I want, I guess."

"I wish I had," said Regan.

"Regan!" cried Charlotte. "What does that mean? And where's Matt?"

"Yeah," said Cord, sipping a Perrier. "Where's ol' Matt?"

"You're always making fun of me," said Regan. "I don't *know* where Matt is. He's not in our cabin. I can't find him anywhere!"

"Calm *down*," said Charlotte, glancing around to see if anyone was watching. She could hear her mother's voice in her ear: *Do not cause a scene and humiliate yourself.* Her brain skittered helplessly, searching for words that would erase Regan's unpleasant outburst. Charlotte had taught her children to look on the bright side! Or at least to be cheery in public spaces.

"I'm not making fun of you," said Cord.

"You *are*," said Regan. "You don't even know you're doing it. Everybody thinks my life is a joke!"

"You're hysterical, dear," said Charlotte, patting Regan's hand. "Keep it down, now."

"I AM NOT HYSTERICAL!" cried Regan.

"Regan!" cried Charlotte, aghast.

The Perkins Family Meltdown was interrupted by the

entrance of the Fun Times Dance Squad. The lead singer held a microphone and wore red sequined pants. He stood by the salad bar and waited for the dancers to assume position. Music began to play from unseen speakers, a hush fell over Shells Restaurant, and the singer brought the microphone to his lips. He threw his head back. "You're simply the best!" he sang. "Better than all the rest!"

The waitstaff joined the dancers, creating a herky-jerky show. The singer intoned, "Stand up! Everybody stand up! It's time for the Dinner Napkin Twirl!"

Rule-followers to the end, the Perkinses stood.

"Simply the best!" sang Lee, hoisting her napkin. "Better than all the rest!" It occurred to Charlotte that Lee might belong on a cruise ship.

Cord looked ill, his hand raised at half-mast. Regan mournfully mouthed the lyrics. The lights in Shells dimmed, strobes flashing on and off.

"Ooooh, you're the best!" the ship's performers sang as they paraded around the circular tables nimbly. "I'm stuck on your heart, baby!"

The Fun Times Dance Squad finished the Tina Turner tune with panache, falling to their knees and crying out, "You're the best!"

The music faded and Charlotte sank, spent, into her seat. She picked up her menu. "Regan," said Cord. "I'm really sorry you think I'm making fun of you. I think you're amazing. I really do."

"What?" said Regan.

Cord nodded.

"You know what feels great," said Lee. "Is telling the truth." She was staring at Cord for some reason, really staring. "We all love you, Cord," she said.

"What are you talking about, Lee?" said Charlotte. "Of course we love Cord!" But her body knew: her stomach seized.

"Yeah," said Regan. "What are you talking about?"

"Cord?" said Lee.

"What?" said Cord.

"Don't you think everyone should *tell the truth*?" said Lee.

Cord made a weird, strangled sound. "Is something the matter?" said Charlotte. Lee's words made her very nervous. Speaking of *truth*, Charlotte needed to tell her children about her pornographic essay before she read it aloud in the Teatro Fabuloso.

"Is someone sick?" said Charlotte. "What's going on?"

"I'm not sick," said Cord. "But honestly? Lee? I'd appreciate you shutting the fuck up, is what I'd appreciate."

"Cord!" Charlotte felt as if she'd been struck.

"Actually, I feel sick," said Cord, standing up. "I'm going to bed. I'll see you guys in the morning." He strode out of Shells, and there was silence. Charlotte's gut churned, but she knew how to spackle over confusion and pain. She'd been doing it all her life. "Will you look at this bread?" she said, her voice high and strained in her ears. "Look at this bread! It's so delicious!"

"Yeah," said Regan. "Yum."

Lee looked deflated. Whatever she'd been doing, it had failed.

"Well, hello there!" said Matt, appearing tableside in a fresh shirt, his face sunburned and relaxed. "How was Sicily?" He sat down and gave Regan a showy kiss on the cheek.

"Where have you been, Matt?" said Regan evenly.

"I've been in the room *all day*," said Matt, grinning. "Very refreshing," he added. His lie sat, an extra loaf in the middle of the table.

Lee observed her first love as if he were a strange exhibit at the zoo. "Oh, Matt," she said. "What's happened to you?"

"What does that mean?" said Matt.

"Let's eat some bread," said Charlotte, forcefully. No one moved. "Lee!" cried Charlotte. "Regan! Eat some delicious bread!"

"*I'll* eat some delicious bread," said Matt.

EIGHT

Naples, Italy

1 / Charlotte

CHARLOTTE WAS SO UPSET about her family's dysfunction that she could barely sit through the Michael Jackson musical revue. Cord had told her how much he'd been looking forward to the show, but though she called his cabin and even went to knock on his door, he did not reappear. So much for the idea that he couldn't absent himself on a ship!

As they entered the theater, Regan made sure to seat herself between Charlotte and Lee, leaving Lee next to Matt on her other side and Charlotte next to a fat man wearing a Yankees baseball cap *to the theater*. Charlotte had known that "cruisers" (as they called themselves on the Internet) weren't the most refined—the vast majority of their web conversations were about how to smuggle booze onboard—but honestly, a baseball cap? Charlotte flared her nostrils in distaste and scooched herself as far as possible toward Regan.

As the lights dimmed and the stage exploded to life, Matt appeared to be having a fine time, shaking his shoulders to "Billie Jean," oohing and aahing as a lithe woman in a red zippered jacket hurled herself around a gold cage–

like apparatus that hovered midair. But it was hard for Charlotte to enjoy herself with her baby girl, Regan, so clearly distraught. Regan's face was impassive, but Charlotte could see her hands balled into fists in her lap.

A man in a tuxedo and a lovely woman in white took the stage and began singing a slow song called "You Are Not Alone." Regan appeared to be transfixed, her face a mask of pain. Lee sang along, her voice low and lovely. The baseball cap man brought a hoagie sandwich from a bag and unwrapped it, taking a bite. As the smell of meatballs reached her, Charlotte was horrified and also hungry. Cord was gone.

Charlotte sighed audibly, but no one seemed to hear her. The show went on. The *Splendido Marveloso* moved through the night, engines buzzing, heading for Naples. For a moment, Charlotte wished she had never come on this cruise. She ached for Godiva, a plate of Triscuits, a few slices of plain old American cheddar. Her children, it seemed, were irredeemably messed up. It was her fault, and furthermore.

2 / Cord

THE VIEW FROM CORD'S balcony was gritty: a row of red-brick buildings, trucks idling in a parking lot, a hill stretching toward a smoggy horizon. A few dinghies were anchored along the Molo Beverello dock. To the right, he could see passengers walking off the ship already, filing toward the blocky blue Stazione Marittima, the passageway to the city of Naples.

Cord felt a primal thrill. He wanted to run into the city—grab a slice or three of pizza, shove that crisp crust and hot cheese into his mouth—he could taste it—kiss a stranger on one of these dirty streets with his oily lips. He was aroused just thinking of it.

He had slept well because he had taken three Benadryl tablets. He didn't have any Ambien, and thank God he'd asked the porter to clear out his minibar, because when he'd returned to his cabin the night before, he would have started unscrewing those tiny caps. Being with his family was making him anguished. That was the word—anguish. There was nothing to do. There was nothing that could be fixed. He just wanted not to feel the anguish. That was all.

He should have called Handy, or found a meeting onboard. But he took bright pink pills and lay in bed and waited and fortunately, sleep came.

As the sun rose, Cord felt shaky but okay. He just needed to get through four more days—Naples, Rome, Florence, and Marseilles—and then they would dock in Barcelona and he could go home. A small, true voice in his brain said, *You can't do this. Get off the ship or tell her who you are and accept what comes.*

He told the voice to shut the fuck up.

FILLED WITH APPREHENSION, CORD returned to his family's table at Shells for breakfast. Regan looked puffy-faced and miserable sitting next to her husband's empty chair; Charlotte looked peaked but game; and Lee looked about sixteen years old with no makeup and her hair pulled into a high ponytail. No one said a word about the previous night's dinnertime theatrics.

"Good morning," said Cord.

"Oh, hello, dear!" said Charlotte. "How did you sleep? Well? I slept well. I slept beautifully. And now we're in Naples! Can you believe it? I can't believe it. Can you?"

"I can't believe it," said Cord. He hated to see her trying so hard! It brought to mind the days after their father's heart attack, when Charlotte continued to make dinner for Winston and get dolled up, as if he might somehow rise from the dead. Cord thought of the night when he saw his mother pause before setting out Winston's plate on the table. She stood by the cabinet, as if frozen. And then she put the plate back.

Cord leaned down to give Charlotte a hug. "It's the

birthplace of pizza, Cord!" she chirped. "Did you know that? The birthplace of pizza!"

"Is that right?" said Cord.

"Yes!"

Cord sat down, attempting to plaster on his "Holiday Cord" face. "What bus tour awaits us today?" he asked.

"Lee, I'm going to ask you a question," said Regan. "Okay? And I just need you to be honest."

Lee looked up, her cheeks coloring. "Be honest about what?" she asked, her voice a bit high. Cord's radar went off: Lee was definitely acting suspicious.

"Matt didn't come back to our cabin last night," said Regan, her voice low, resigned. "Was he with you?"

"What?" said Lee. "Oh my God, what are you talking about?"

"Regan, what's the matter with you?" said Charlotte. "Seasick," she whispered to Cord. Cord closed his eyes and took a deep breath.

"What's the matter with Lee, is the question," said Regan evenly.

"Jesus," said Lee, examining her laminated menu with great concentration. "I'm going to just forget you said that."

"I'm not hungry," said Regan, putting her napkin on her plate and standing. "I'll see you guys on the excursion line at ten." She walked out of Shells, and the table was momentarily quiet.

"*I'm having an omelet!*" cried Charlotte.

"We should talk about Regan and Matt," said Cord. "Obviously, she needs our help."

"*I love omelets!*" Charlotte insisted. Cord gripped his thighs with his hands. Ah, his mother. She smelled of Chanel No. 5. Her love was so heavy. As a child, he'd yearned for her to take care of him, and as an adult, he'd felt he had to deny who he was to keep from breaking her. But he was fragile, too! Though he wanted to run from the table, Cord didn't move. He was going to have to have just one limoncello to get through the day. Just one, and maybe two.

3 / Regan

A YOUNG WOMAN IN a tight red tank top was talking about how old her family's olive press was. It was very old. Regan touched the giant limestone circle, which rolled around a big tub to squash the olives. She'd never wondered where olive oil came from. People asked insipid questions:

How many times a year do you press the olives?
What do you do with the olive fruit after extracting the oil?
Can I buy some of your olive oil?
Do you live here at the farm?
Exactly how many years has this exact stone been in use?
Could I press olive oil in my apartment?

And on and on. Did people really care about the answers to these questions, or were they all just trying to impress the woman in the tank top? Or impress one another?

Regan tried to focus on the mechanics of an olive press, but her mind wandered. Had Matt received the telegram? Where had he spent the night? After the Michael Jackson musical revue, he'd gone to the Galaxy Bar "for a nightcap" and he'd never returned to their cabin. For the first time in years, she didn't know what he was having for breakfast.

Regan felt angry, sure, but also sorrowful. She hadn't realized how sad it would feel to burn her life down. She'd
imagined feeling triumphant.

Regan vividly remembered her childhood days in a
rental apartment with a bathroom off the dining room.
She could visualize Lee, her hair wrapped up in one towel,
her body in another, standing by Charlotte's china cabinet,
yammering into the wall phone. She could see Cord, his
long legs sprawled out in his cramped room, comic books
surrounding him, Depeche Mode blasting from his boom
box. Somehow she'd labeled those days a humiliation.
She'd based her choices—her giant house, her daughters'
schools, her constant attention to family life—on erecting
a wall between her grim childhood and her bright future.
But she was beginning to see that the camaraderie with her
brother and sister, the yummy microwaved dinners, the
way they'd crowd around the small TV to watch *Family
Feud*, yelling out answers—in some ways, those days had
been wonderful. She promised herself now: *it will be okay*.

Matt must have received the telegram. He'd be getting
ready to go. And as soon as that domino fell, Regan was
going to need money.

After the olive press demonstration, their group was
seated before an outdoor stage. A piece of driftwood had
been painted with the words FURMAGG E MILLICENT. The
crowd buzzed in anticipation.

On one side of the stage was a stove with a huge metal
tub of water coming to a boil. Four bowls were arranged on
the table, as well as a display of bottled oils and honeys.
Dried peppers, onions, and three stuffed cows were suspended from the driftwood. Two heavyset women appeared, one in a yellow T-shirt and the other in a shapeless,

sleeveless housedress. An American kid in a fedora began videotaping.

"Welcome to the making of the cheese!" cried the woman in yellow. The older woman (Millicent?) began stirring the pot on the stove. "This on the side, it is not boiling water, but boiling whey, ya?" said the woman in yellow. "And believe me, this is really hot now. When the whey boils, raise up on top of it another type of cheese, like white cream that she have to skim off."

The older woman plunged her arms into one of the bowls on the table, and her cohort detailed the process of mixing in the curds, of kneading and the hours it took to create a braided round. "You can have a nice picture with Millicent if you just wait," she said. "She doesn't speak English, but . . . get your cameras ready."

Obediently, everyone raised their phones. Millicent lifted her fresh cheese out of the bowl, her face sweet and ruddy.

"You ready? Now Millicent has something she say to you."

Millicent said, "Cheese!"

At the cheese tasting afterward, a young man brought around trays of limoncello. The liquid tasted like medicinal cleaning fluid, but Regan's shoulders unfurled, just a bit. Regan saw Cord staring at her drink. His desirous gaze made her worried. "Cord, are you okay?" she asked.

"Fine," he said, standing and striding toward the farm animal petting area. Lee stood and followed him. Pigs rushed toward the siblings, grunting.

"This really is delicious," noted Charlotte. Regan longed to join her siblings, but she stayed next to Charlotte. She looked at her mother, both frail and mean. It was time.

"Mom," she said.

"Mmm?" said Charlotte, not looking up from the cheese platter.

"I'm going to need money," said Regan, balling her fists in her lap.

"Mmm?" said Charlotte, lifting her gaze.

"Matt has, um," said Regan. Charlotte was looking fully at her now. "I guess it's pretty clear that Matt and I are having trouble," said Regan. "I think . . . well, we might not make it. I might . . . be on my own. The girls and I will need help. Financial help. I need a lawyer, for one thing. Right away."

Regan waited for her mother to speak, to make her feel disgraced. She swallowed.

But Charlotte's face grew soft. When she spoke, her tone was sympathetic, even kind. "I've been careful with my savings and I get a pension now," said Charlotte. "I can help, sweetheart."

Regan felt relief flood through her limbs. She hugged her mother hard. "Mommy," she said.

"That's enough," said Charlotte, but Regan continued to squeeze her, and Charlotte did not pull away.

4 / Lee

MATT HAD, IN FACT, visited Lee's room the evening before. He'd shown up two hours after the musical revue, just as Lee was settling into bed in pajamas with the *Splendido Evening Newsletter*. (Lee had charged a pajama set to her mother's account: it seemed impossible to begin a new, more serious life clad in the filmy negligees of her old one.) "Oh," she'd said, when she opened her door to find Matt, his face flushed. "What is it, Matt? What are you doing here?"

"I don't know," he had answered miserably. "Lee, I honestly don't know. Something's wrong with me. With us. I don't know how to fix it, and I just want to go home."

"Are you drunk?"

"Not really," said Matt.

"Matt . . . ," said Lee, blocking the doorway.

"She doesn't love me anymore," said Matt. "She has all this pottery. So much pottery from the mall."

Lee shook her head, dismayed and confused.

"Remember the Hilton Head Island Holiday Inn, Lee?" he said. "I would have married you. I would have!"

"I know," said Lee. It had been the summer after their

junior year. Matt had surprised her with a room on the beach for her birthday. (It had taken him months of working at the Piggly Wiggly bagging groceries to pay for it.) Lee's period had been a few days late, so they'd bought a pregnancy test at a Walgreens on Palmetto Bay Road. When it had been negative, they'd celebrated with wine coolers and carefully condomed sex. Lee sighed, wanting to tell Matt she might be pregnant now—wanting to tell anyone—but deciding against it.

"I think about it sometimes," said Matt. "How it might have been."

"Jesus," said Lee. "Matt, really?"

"Really," said Matt. "I meant what I said at the wedding, Lee. I wanted it to be you."

"It was your *rehearsal dinner*," said Lee. "What did you want me to do?"

"I wanted you to stop me," said Matt.

"It's too late now," said Lee.

"I know," said Matt.

"So you're cheating on her?"

He exhaled. "Yes," he said.

"But your daughters . . ."

Matt looked up, and a flash of something like anger lit his expression. "You don't have any idea," he said. "I came on this fucking trip to try to find some love again. To try to see if there was . . . anything between us. But it's over," he said. "I didn't want this! But Janet . . . I met Janet. She's a single mom. And she needs me, Lee. I'm all she's got. I love her—I don't know what else to say. I hate myself about how it all happened, but I love Janet, and Regan and I are done."

"I can't believe what I'm hearing," said Lee. "This just makes me so sad."

"Me, too," said Matt. "But she's going to be okay. Regan's going to be okay. I promise."

"Baby Ray Ray," said Lee, shaking her head. She wished she could protect her sister, keep the pain of Matt's affair from her somehow.

"I thought I'd saved her," said Matt. "I thought I could take care of her. But she . . . it's like she's a ghost inside. She acts all loving . . . like we always have perfect dinners or whatever, but it's a mirage . . . everything always looks fine but you try to . . . touch her, reach her . . . and it's just air."

Lee thought of her sister, the lovely mother she had become. She was confused by the distance between Matt's version of Regan and what Lee had seen. To Lee, Regan seemed deep and vibrant. Sure, Regan was conflicted—even worried (and with good reason)—but she was so realized, so grown-up, alive. "You're wrong," Lee said.

"I was so lonely," said Matt, not seeming to hear Lee. "I thought I was going crazy. But then I met Janet," he said. "I fell in love. It happens. What am I supposed to do?"

"What you have with Regan . . . it's a lot of people's dream come true," said Lee.

"I'm not a failure," said Matt. "I just fell in love. Real love. And I can't give that up, Lee. I just can't."

Lee remembered telling Matt she was moving to Los Angeles. He had been furious, desperate. "You need someone who wants what you want," Lee had told him, her mind bright with visions of her California future. He'd wrapped her in his arms, clutched at her.

Now, Lee remembered that Regan had been there, too. At the edge of her bedroom door, a flash of auburn hair. The sound of footsteps down the stairs, but when Lee went to the hallway, she found a platter of cheese and crackers.

My God. Had Lee somehow known that Regan would put Matt back together after she left? Had she subconsciously set it up, so she could run? "Matt, look!" she'd said. "Cheese and crackers."

"Regan's so wonderful," Matt had said, picking up a Ritz.

5 / Charlotte

THE RUINED CITY OF Pompeii was hot and horrifying. Charlotte walked along uneven streets that had once been a community. Regan's admission that her marriage was falling apart was weighing heavily on Charlotte. How sad that Regan would have to live as Charlotte herself had: alone, frightened, unloved. She could imagine how upset Louisa would have been to witness her granddaughter's broken family. Charlotte had called her mother in hysteria after finding Winston's body and cried, "Mom! It's Winston! He's . . . he hung himself!"

Louisa had responded, "Don't move. Don't tell anybody anything." She arrived at the house as the paramedics carried Winston out. "A heart attack," she said. "Tell everyone it was a heart attack." Charlotte had rushed to her mother for a hug, but Louisa had stepped back, searching Charlotte's face, asking, "What did you do?"

Oh, so many things! She had spent the years since Winston's departure cataloging them: she let herself go, she tried to make him sober, she let the kids "run the show," she didn't keep them quiet enough, or servile enough, or maybe she should have been less obvious about how much she hated sex with her bloated, boozy husband. She'd let herself be deflowered early by an old man *and she'd sort of liked it*. She was no prize. She'd always been plain.

Here she was, nearly seventy-two, and still she heard Louisa's and Winston's criticisms. And to add insult to injury, Charlotte would have to watch her own daughter's sad story unfold. Her mind spun, imagining Regan crying on her lemon-colored couch; Regan waitressing at Denny's; Flora and Isabella humiliated on a public school playground, wearing that awful purple mascara that had heralded Regan's own demise into troubled teendom.

Their guide, a tall man named Massimiliano, held a pole with a placard that read SPLENDIDO 27. Among hundreds of people and dozens of guides with poles, Charlotte struggled to keep number 27 in sight. There were pillars and brick walls. There was an amphitheater where, my heavens, the sun was strong.

"I am so hot," said Lee.

"For the love of God, just keep moving," said Cord.

"I could use a cold drink," said Lee. "Or a bag of ice to dump on my head."

Massimiliano seemed able to walk backward, not pass out from heatstroke, and keep up a lecture simultaneously: Mount Vesuvius had erupted in A.D. 79, burying this Roman city under volcanic ash. The ash, said Massimiliano, "poured across the land like a flood."

Ugh. Charlotte held on to Lee's hand and struggled to keep up.

"The city was captured in a darkness like the black of closed and unlighted rooms. That is a quotation. Can you imagine this? Try to imagine this."

Charlotte didn't want to try to imagine this.

"Two thousand people died and the city—this city—was abandoned."

Massimiliano, mercifully, led them inside a building. It was still stifling, but at least there was a respite from direct sunlight. Charlotte leaned against a wall and closed her eyes. "In 1748," said Massimiliano, "explorers rediscovered this place. Pompeii was intact! Skeletons and buildings and paintings and tools can teach us about what it was like in this place before the eruption that ended human life here."

Minnie would have loved Pompeii. She'd been a history buff, always watching late-night documentaries and telling Charlotte about them whether Charlotte was interested or not. Oh, how Charlotte missed Minnie now, her dull stories and grating laughter. It was still a shock that Minnie was just gone, that Charlotte would never, ever, see her again. And then the selfish part: was Charlotte next?

Massimiliano led them through the rooms of the house and back outside. They stopped at a street corner and Massimiliano explained there was a big line waiting to see a stone penis that had been carved in the road to show the way to an ancient brothel. "We will have to wait here approximately forty-five minutes to see the penis," he explained. "Some people, they take a selfie with the penis."

"Oh, my," said Charlotte.

"No, thanks," said Cord.

Regan looked conflicted, but Lee said, "No! No penis selfies."

"We move on," said Massimiliano, seemingly relieved.

On their way to the exit, their tour guide stopped by a display case of ceramic pots. "Do you want to hear what it was like for them, the ones who did not flee in time?" he asked. His voice was eager—it was clear he wanted to perform. When no one responded, Massimiliano pointed to a stone figure among the pots. "You see it is a human," he said.

"Where?" said Charlotte, narrowing her eyes. "Oh," she said, making out the mummified figure, knees to chest, head down. If you didn't look closely, you wouldn't see the man. You would think he was a vase.

"Fuckety fuck," said Cord.

"Language, Cord," said Charlotte wearily.

"When the sky went dark," said Massimiliano, warming to his topic, "you would have grabbed your valuables from your house. And your children. And your wife. You tried to get out, toward the sea, where you hoped a boat would save you. But the dark—and earthquakes—would make it hard to find your way. Buildings began to collapse. Frightened, you decide to stay still. You hope it will be over, and the sun will rise again."

Clearly, Massimiliano had had theatrical training. He projected his voice over the crowds. They were spellbound, the heat of the day forgotten.

"You crouch down and pull your children close to you. You pray to God and you wait. Like this man, you see?" Massimiliano pointed to the figure.

Charlotte felt tears behind her eyes.

"But then the massive pyroclastic surge came at dawn," said Massimiliano darkly. "You are made into the fetal shape as you die. Your cadaver spasms so you are like a baby again. And the rain comes, turning the pyroclastic flow into cement, which preserves your body as so."

There was a moment of hushed reverence. Regan

pressed herself to her mother's side. Lee moved close to Regan. Cord encircled them all in his arms. The Perkins family stared at the form of a man who had been dead for two thousand years. It was hot. Charlotte could smell underarms. Life was so precious and so short.

NINE

Rome, Italy

1 / Charlotte

CHARLOTTE WOKE EARLY. HER sheets were warm and smelled faintly of detergent. She lay still for a moment, just savoring. It was finally starting to happen, thought Charlotte. Her children were coming back to her. She was *needed* again—by Regan especially, but also by Cord and Lee. It felt so good to be asked for help! Her purpose on earth, she was beginning to understand, was taking care of her kids, now and always.

Still, and to be honest, she felt a twinge of regret that she wasn't going to have another romance of her own. Someone just for Charlotte, who loved her to her bones. Who would think she was beautiful even though she was old, hold her tight if she was afraid. Someone who would counter the dark march toward death with the hot flash of sex, an explosion of limbs intertwined. Charlotte wanted to wake and find a pot of hot coffee ready—a morning when she could just take a mug from the cabinet and pour.

Minnie had insisted the idea of a "one true love" was a falsehood created by smutty writers trying to sell books and men scheming to keep women vacuuming quietly instead of changing the world. It wasn't that Minnie was a *lesbian* (though who knew?) but that she was pragmatic. After her husband died, Minnie was done with romantic love.

"Once you give up on finding Mr. Right," she'd implored Charlotte, on one of their daily walks around the lagoons, "you can find yourself. Inside." (Here she struck her rib cage with a fist. Beside them, a crepe myrtle bloomed.) "Do you know what I mean?"

"Sure, I guess," Charlotte said. "But I can't help what I *want*, can I?"

In Minnie's view, of course you could.

How ironic, thought Charlotte, that Minnie didn't live to see Charlotte accept her dour pronouncement. "Okay," she said now. "I give up. It's time, Min. I've got the kids, and that's a lot. I've got Father Thomas to talk to. You're right." She could almost see Minnie in her aqua golf visor, nodding with a self-satisfied expression.

Charlotte rose and parted her curtains. It was too dark to see much as they approached the port. Taking in the gray, blocky buildings, Charlotte felt sorry for the inhabitants of Civitavecchia, overrun each day by tourists who (like the Perkins family) would trample through on their way to glittering Rome.

She pulled the curtains firmly closed and made a concerted effort to focus on happiness. Was that the feeling inside her rib cage? It was a skittery excitement, like drinking too much coffee before heading downstairs on Christmas morning. Maybe her children would move back in with her! That was probably pushing it, but watching the nightly news with Cord and Lee as Regan prepared cheese and crackers . . . well, that was a lovely image.

Charlotte showered, ran a brush through her hair. It

was only when she looked in the mirror that she realized she was singing aloud. She'd thought the song—Tony Bennett's "Song of the Jet Set"—was inside her head.

"Shining Rio, there you lie," crooned Charlotte. "City of sun, of sea, and sky!"

2 / Cord

CORD HAD BEEN DREAMING about sleeping in a bathtub made of velvet when his phone rang. He sat up, completely disoriented, the weird urine-perfume smell of his cruise ship cabin bringing him back to reality. His brain was fogged with pills and bourbon. His phone buzzed again. They must have been close enough to shore to pick up a signal. "Hello?" he said.

"It's me," said Giovanni.

"Hi, you," said Cord. He got out of bed in his underwear and stepped onto his balcony, where he could see faraway twinkling lights against a dark expanse of sea. "What time is it?" he said, taking a deep breath, tasting salt and ocean water.

"Listen, Cord, this is important," said Gio.

"I'm listening," said Cord. He marveled at his utter lack of panic, his bloodstream full of depressants silencing the lonely voice for the moment. Oh, it was going to come back, and with a vengeance. But for now, Cord enjoyed the blessed quiet.

"Did you tell your mom about me? Does your family know?" said Gio. His voice was breathless, excited.

"Yes, of course," Cord lied without hesitation. God, it was easy to lie! He'd forgotten how simple life could be. The engine of the ship thrummed beneath him like a snoring animal.

"Did you say *yes*?" said Giovanni.

"They can't wait to meet you," said Cord, pulling a cigarette he'd bought at the Galaxy Bar from his robe pocket.

"Charlotte can't wait to meet me?" said Giovanni.

"That's what I said," said Cord, using a matchbook from Shells to light up. The smoke entered his lungs and made him even more languid.

"So they know," said Giovanni, with wonderment. "They know who you are."

"Yup," said Cord.

"Do you want to talk about it?"

"Nope."

"Rome today, right?"

"Yes," said Cord, sitting down in his deck chair, resting his feet on the glass partition that kept him from falling overboard. "I believe our tour is called 'Panoramic Rome by Motor Coach.' We drive by all the glories of the city, pause for photos, then motor on."

"You don't even get out of the bus?" screeched Giovanni.

"I don't believe so, no," sighed Cord.

"Oh, dear," said Giovanni.

"Well, Mom's old," said Cord. "We'll do it again someday, you and me."

"Promise?" said Giovanni. "Promise me Rome?"

"You promise *me* Rome," said Cord. "I promise you everything."

"I love you," said Giovanni.

"And how I love you," said Cord. This, at least, was true.

"I've got to go," said Giovanni, a note of something—glee?—in his tone.

"Where?" said Cord. "Where are you going?"

"I'll never tell!" said Giovanni, sounding shockingly like Charlotte. "Have a good day in Rome, my love!"

"You as well," said Cord. "Little goofball."

HE SAT ON THE balcony for a while, watching as the ship approached port. As much as he made fun of the bus tours, the drink specials, the whole "cruising" experience, there was something deeply moving about approaching land from the sea. Cord felt connected to the explorers and soldiers who had done the same. How much more terrifying and exciting their lives had been!

He just wished his two worlds didn't have to collide. And did they? Did they really? How hard would it be to just keep things divided? With a boozy brain, it seemed possible.

CHARLOTTE WAS UNUSUALLY CHEERY at breakfast. "I'm just so happy," she said. "All my babies, all right here around this table!"

"Oh, Mom," said Regan, leaning over to envelop Charlotte in a hug. She wore a baseball cap, rumpled sundress, and Teva sandals. Cord narrowed his eyes and looked—really looked—at his sister. Her nose was reddish, her eyes sunk deep in their sockets. She wasn't well, he could see. He was flooded with worry. Where was Matt?

Charlotte struggled to free herself from Regan's overlong embrace. She met Cord's eye for a moment, winking. The wink said, "How silly is Regan?" as if Cord shared his mother's view that Regan was silly, that a broken marriage was a joke. He didn't share this view! He was terrified for his sister, heartbroken that her husband was a liar, concerned for his nieces. He wanted to throw Regan over his shoulder and spirit her away, whisk her through museums and order her exotic foods and restore her to the Regan she'd once been, long ago. He wanted to fix her, to fix everything. Instead, he picked up a *pain au chocolat* and shoved it in his mouth.

Lee was tapping at her phone. She'd traded in her leather pants and tube tops for a weirdly demure dress with a Peter Pan collar. Cord's stomach burned. This was the most time he had spent with his family since childhood. My Lord, he was sick of them.

Cord took his mother's arm as they filed off the ship, stopping to pose for a photo behind the fake life preserver proclaiming FUN IN CIVITAVECCHIA! Would his mother purchase this photo from the Fun Store on Level Three? Would Cord gaze at it someday, when she was gone? Would this be the photo he took to OfficeMax to blow up and set next to her coffin, or urn or whatever?

He shook off his maudlin thoughts and strode forward, putting on his sunglasses and scanning the throng of men selling random crap and holding signs for various day tours.

"They should be right here," said Charlotte. "The sign should say 'Perkins,' or 'Panoramic Rome' or something."

"I don't see anyone," said Regan, squinting.

"Cord!" cried a familiar voice.

Cord turned, and his blood went cold.

3 / Regan

REGAN KNEW ABOUT SECRETS, and how. But even she was stunned when a skinny young man in a linen suit and Vuarnet sunglasses rushed toward her openmouthed brother and wrapped Cord in his arms. The young man closed his eyes and pressed his face to Cord's chest, his expression blissful. And then he grabbed Cord's hand and faced them. "Well, hi!" he said gleefully. "I guess you've been wondering who stole your brother's heart. *C'est moi!*"

There was, of course, the possibility that this young man was deranged. But it was all clicking into place: Cord's endless single life, the way he kept himself at a remove from them, his abrupt departures from Savannah holiday weekends. In some part of herself, Regan had always known.

"What's going on?" asked Charlotte, her voice high and wheezy. "Can somebody tell me what's going on?" Her hand fluttered to her rib cage.

"Cord?" said the young man, continuing to grip Cord's hand. There was a hopeful expression on the man's face. He looked like he could be Italian, with dark hair and a five-o'clock shadow in the morning, but his accent was American.

"Giovanni," whispered Cord. He seemed utterly terrified.

Regan had not known her brother this way in a long time—she was reminded suddenly of the afternoon he'd returned from a pheasant hunt with their father. "Shot one right between the eyes," Winston had said proudly. When Winston turned to pour a drink, her brother's expression changed. Cord tried to hide how the day had broken him, but Regan saw. And now she understood that her seemingly strong brother still needed her. And Regan loved knowing what to do.

She strode toward Giovanni and held out her hand. "I'm Regan," she said.

"Regan! I feel like I already know you," said Giovanni.

"And I'm Lee," said Lee, following Regan's lead, shaking the young man's hand.

"Of course you are," said Giovanni. "I follow you on Insta and Snap."

"Where is the Panoramic Motor Coach Tour of Rome?" said Charlotte.

"It just seemed *depressing*," said Giovanni. "You know? I thought, Let's really see *Roma*! Get nitty-gritty. And so I booked us a golf cart!"

It was obvious the young man was nervous. He reminded Regan of her daughter Flora before a choir show.

"What are we waiting for?" said Lee, putting her shoulders back. Regan tried to meet her eyes, but she stared resolutely ahead. Regan wished she and Lee could return to the days when their love for each other was simple. Regan had once thought Lee would take care of her forever. How nice it had been to believe that, even if it had turned out to be a lie.

"Well, okay!" said the young man.

"I do *not* understand what's going on around here," said Charlotte.

"Believe me, I know the feeling," said Giovanni. "By the way, I love your hat."

"This?" said Charlotte, touching the brim. "Oh, it's just a *chapeau* I picked up in Athens."

"Now *that* was a glamorous sentence if ever I heard one," said Giovanni.

Charlotte gave him a dazed smile. "Oh, well," she said.

"So we take this bus to the golf cart," said Giovanni excitedly. "And then we'll go to the Trevi Fountain, the Spanish Steps, the Pantheon . . . pizza in Campo de' Fiori . . . we'll pop by the Villa Borghese . . . we can get gelato . . ."

"I love gelato," said Regan, trying to sound reassuring.

"I thought about trying to get tickets to the Vatican," nattered Giovanni. "But I wasn't sure, with just one day, that we could . . ."

Cord turned to Giovanni. "It's fine," he said.

"Aren't you surprised?" said Giovanni.

"It's fine," Cord repeated, as if to himself. The driver helped Charlotte aboard, and Lee followed. Regan climbed on the bus. Charlotte opened a map of Rome and focused intently. Through the window, Regan watched her brother. He seemed younger, flushed as he spoke to Giovanni. And right there in the middle of the parking lot, Giovanni reached out and touched Cord's cheek with his fingertips. Cord leaned into the touch.

"Oh," said Regan. She knew love when she saw it. She wanted to be happy for Cord. But what she felt, as a searing pain in her rib cage, was envy.

———

REGAN'S MARRIAGE WAS DONE. She had returned from Pompeii the day before to find Matt packed and ready to leave. Regan opened their cabin door and he stood, cleared his throat. His expression reminded her of the times she'd seen him break bad news to a family about the way a surgery had gone. "Regan," he said. "We need to talk."

Regan sat down on the bed. She was warm from the day and her feet ached, but she wasn't going to take off her shoes. She put her shoulders back. "Why is your suitcase out?" she asked, gesturing to his American Tourister.

"I'm in love with someone else," said Matt. His voice was assured, rehearsed, cold.

"Oh," said Regan. She'd known it was coming, but still, it stung.

"I didn't want this to happen," said Matt. "I didn't. But it did happen. I love her."

"Who is she?" said Regan.

"She's a teacher. Her name is Janet."

"Janet," said Regan.

"I tried. I tried so hard, Regan." He stood straight, his voice lowering to a pleading tone. "I thought maybe this trip would fix us, but I . . . it just seems like prolonging things now. I want to do the right thing here."

"What about me . . . and the girls?" said Regan. Matt knelt by the bed and pulled Regan into his arms. She didn't struggle.

"I'll always take care of you, Ray Ray," he said. She closed her eyes and held her breath. *Let me go*, she thought. *Please.* "I'm so sorry," said Matt.

He would need to be the savior in his own mind, Regan

knew. She had to be careful. "I know you'll take care of us," she said.

"I will," he said. "I promise. Always." Regan kept her head down and exhaled slowly. Her heart was a metronome. "You should stay," said Matt. "You enjoy the cruise with your family. But I'm going to fly back. She . . . she needs me to come home. I need to go, before the ship leaves port. But I . . . I wanted to tell you in person." Matt rose, approached the door. "I'm so sorry," he said, and then he left.

Regan found her phone in her purse and called Zoë, who answered on the first ring, though it was midmorning in Atlanta, and she was surely at work. "Thank goodness," Zoë said.

"It's me," said Regan.

"Did you see the report?" said Zoë.

"I'm going to need a lawyer," said Regan. "A good one."

"I have a guy," said Zoë.

"I knew you would," said Regan.

"You're going to be okay," said Zoë.

Regan nodded, but didn't speak.

"I love you," said Zoë.

"I know," said Regan.

Before heading to dinner, Regan called the lawyer Zoë had recommended. She left a message, and then she emailed him the private investigator's report. Sitting at her computer, Regan saw that Matt had thrown the telegram into the trash can under the desk. She almost pulled it out to look it over, but why?

She already knew what it said.

4 / Lee

THE AIR IN ROME was scorching. Lee shaded her eyes and spied an extralong golf cart heading toward them. It was piloted by a man with enormous muscles and a large gold chain around his neck.

When he reached them, the man halted the cart. His eyes were hidden by aviator sunglasses. "I am Donte," he said. "Hop aboard for the adventure your lifetime."

"Oooh, I'm so excited!" said Giovanni. He slid inside the cart, and patted the seat next to him. "Charlotte?" he said, "I saved you a seat!"

"Good heavens," said Charlotte. She was trying to be aloof, but Giovanni's clear delight was infectious. "Is this safe?" she asked.

"I'll hold your hand," said Giovanni. "Don't be scared."

"I'm *not* scared," pronounced Charlotte, though she did accept Giovanni's hand as she stepped into the cart.

"This is basically a dream come true, right?" said Giovanni. "I mean, you love golf carts, and everyone loves Rome!"

"I wouldn't say I *love* golf carts," said Charlotte. "They're convenient and don't use too much gasoline."

"And the wind through your hair!" trilled Giovanni. "Don't forget the wind through your hair!"

"Well," she admitted, "yes, that is a nice feeling."

"E voilà!" said Giovanni, pulling a six-pack of cans of sparkling wine from his satchel, each with a tiny straw. He opened Charlotte's, inserted the straw, and handed it to her. "I want to be your favorite," he said. He turned around, his smile bright and absolutely winning. "I want to be everyone's favorite," he said. Lee saw Giovanni search their faces, seeming confused by the Perkinses' muted reaction to his onslaught of cheerfulness. Giovanni turned to Cord, who was staring at his shoes.

"Please, grip tight and we go," said Donte.

"It's hot all right," said Lee, putting her lips on her tiny straw, but then remembering.

"The cooling breezes, they begin," said Donte, and with a jolt, they were off.

AS THEY BUMPED ALONG in the golf cart, nearly missing tourists and turning sharply to pass the Colosseum, Circus Maximus, and then the Arch of Constantine and Aventine Hill, Lee touched her stomach through her new sundress. It was still perfectly taut, but she knew that would change. If she kept the baby. Was she going to keep the baby?

Everywhere Lee turned, a building more jaw-dropping than the ones she'd already seen came into view. She wished fiercely that she had taken an art history class at Chico State. But even with no idea what the buildings *meant*, or when they were built and *why*, she felt a visceral joy craning her neck and taking them in. Lee had never realized how hideous most of the world was until Rome.

Beside Lee, Regan was quiet. They'd once been close, a

million years ago. But the tables had turned from the days when Regan worshipped her sister: now Lee had a lot to learn from Regan, who knew how to be a mother. Lee watched her sister, taking in her baseball cap and breezy sundress. Regan looked comfortable in her own skin. Maybe Matt had been right—she was the strongest one of them all.

This realization made Lee feel insecure. She'd always assumed she herself was the leader of their pack of three. But no matter what happened to Regan, she would have Flora and Isabella on either side of her. What did Lee have?

Regan turned to Lee, interrupting her reverie. "What do you think?" said Regan.

"You mean . . . about Matt?" said Lee, pleasantly surprised to be asked for her advice. She considered what to say, how to impart wisdom to her little sister. "Well—" she began.

"No," said Regan, cutting her off. "Not *Matt*. What do you think of *Rome*?"

"Oh!" said Lee, embarrassed. Of course Regan wouldn't turn to Lee for help. They really didn't have a relationship anymore. Lee and her sister were like strangers, jammed together on a golf cart. "It's gorgeous," said Lee, recovering. She brushed her hair off her bare shoulders. "I feel like Sophia Loren," she said, slipping her fake persona on easily.

Regan smiled vaguely. Her brow furrowed a bit, and Lee was saddened to see that her sister was looking at her with both kindness and pity.

THEIR GUIDE DIDN'T SAY much, just drove the cart at a breakneck speed, whipping his gaze back and forth to capture everything with the GoPro camera he had strapped

around his head. Was he going to sell them this video foot-
age later? Who would want to watch the whirling feed of
heavenly structures? Actually, maybe Lee.

She loved Giovanni already. Although Cord had seemed
to think his coming-out was a big shock, Lee had known
her brother was gay since she could remember. She'd
watched *Will & Grace*, after all. He'd never had a boyfriend, not in Savannah, but then he'd never had a true
girlfriend, either. He was always the generic popular boy.

Cord had referred to the situation only once. Lee had
come home late and her drunken father had yelled at her
for a while. After he'd finally stopped, Lee had gone to bed
crying, and Cord had come into her room. He climbed into
her bed and scratched her back under the covers. It was a
tremendous comfort, and Lee's sobs quieted.

She was almost asleep when she heard Cord whisper,
"Imagine what he'd do to me."

THEY PULLED INTO A square called Campo de' Fiori. "*Fiori*,
it mean flowers," explained Donte. "Here was the execu-
tions." He pointed to a statue of a hooded, somber man.
"That guy," he said. "His name Giordano Bruno. Burned
here at the stake. Also, nice snacks for purchase. See you
one hour."

His elucidation complete, Donte walked off, entering
one of the restaurants lining the square.

"Weeeeell . . ." said Giovanni, his eyes twinkling, "*that*
was something!"

Lee wanted to laugh. She wanted to link arms with this
sweet guy and lean into him, befriend him. She waited for
Cord to make it possible. But he looked into the middle
distance, frowning. "Do you want to . . ." said Giovanni.

"Do I want to *what?*" said Cord coldly. His Winston-esque tone turned Lee's stomach.

"See you in an hour," she said, hopping off the cart and following her mother into the maze of covered stalls. There were tables of beautiful vegetables: giant eggplants, tomatoes as red as blood, lush green beans, and the ripest strawberries Lee had ever seen. Charlotte was admiring tiny bottles of grappa lined up underneath a row of ham legs. She looked up as Lee approached.

"Honey!" said Charlotte. "Do you think they'd let me on the ship with a bit of grappa?"

"Mom," said Lee. "What do you think about Giovanni?"

"Hm?" said Charlotte. "Oh, and *look*! Olive oil!" She held up a bottle of viscous liquid. Lee sighed. Her mother had been doing this all her life—blithely pretending not to hear what Lee was saying; making Lee feel like she was the crazy one. It was unbearable.

Lee turned from Charlotte, skirted the market, joined the line outside a pizza shop called Forno Campo de' Fiori. When it was her turn, she pointed to a square of thin-crust pizza and a man in a little white cap slid it into waxed paper. Lee handed him a bill and he said something with gusto and handed her a bit of change.

Outside the window, Lee could see Giovanni and Cord. Cord was *still* looking at the ground and Giovanni was yelling at him passionately. Regan sat by a majestic fountain on the other side of the square, her face lifted to the sun.

Lee unwrapped her pizza and took a bite. The hot crust and salty toppings were divine: she got right back in line to order another square. She breathed in the scent of dough baking, of fresh oregano and mozzarella.

If she got in a taxi, Lee would be at the airport in an hour, and in Malta by evening. Or she could get back in the golf cart with her family. She could give in to new romance or to motherhood; she could refuse them both.

Her phone buzzed and she peered at it, wondering if Kiko had sent another love note. But it was a text from her agent, Francine.

> Lee, BIG NEWS. New reality show wants you to audition for a role. Call me ASAP. Am emailing 150-question personality test. Also need video by tomorrow. Where are you?

Lee reached the front of the line. "Yes?" said a man in white, swiping the back of his hand over his forehead. He held a pencil and waited. "Lady, what you want?" he said.

5 / Charlotte

EVERYONE SEEMED CRANKY AFTER LUNCH. Cord's friend, Giovanni, gave Charlotte a dry peck on the cheek and whispered, "This wasn't how it was supposed to end," before jogging away into the shimmering city streets; Lee was distracted; Regan was quiet; Cord was ashen-faced and morose; and Donte drove the golf cart with wild abandon, whirling them past the glorious Trevi Fountain and the Pantheon (Charlotte tried to ask him to stop—she'd always wanted to go inside the Pantheon—but he didn't even slow) before returning them to the parking lot across the street from the Colosseum.

"Now you do the tour," said Donte, pointing to a sweaty young woman holding a tour flag. "Have your nice day," he concluded, adding, "Your video emailed shortly. Ciao."

Well! Charlotte had hoped a lunchtime nip of grappa would make the day more pleasant, but it seemed to have the opposite effect. Her niggling worries about who Giovanni was and what was going on with Cord did not fade with Giovanni's abrupt departure. Instead, they coalesced into a solid, cold fact: Cord was gay. He loved men, or in any case, one man. Giovanni. Charlotte felt a heavy dread, imagining what her church friends would think. If she embraced her son, Charlotte knew, she would lose Father Thomas, who was so kind. Father Thomas had brought her a bouquet of hydrangeas once, just because.

Louisa had loved Charlotte only when she was good. But when she screwed up, Louisa's love vanished. Charlotte didn't want to pass on the bleak feeling that came when a parent loved you only some of the time.

What a disappointment, Louisa had said, when Charlotte had told her about the famous painter. Charlotte had been seeking comfort, but Louisa offered only shame.

CHARLOTTE CLIMBED QUICKLY FROM the golf cart, grabbing Regan's arm. To distract herself, she focused intensely on the Colosseum tour leader. The guide gave them each a little headset, pointed them toward the large group they seemed to be a part of, and directed them, en masse, across the busy Piazza del Colosseo.

Charlotte focused on the ancient arena. My God, the building was magnificent.

She had just inserted her little earpieces (they reminded her uncomfortably of hearing aids . . . which she didn't need!) when the girl's voice came booming through: *Welcome to the underground tour of the Roman Colosseum!*

It was so hot, hotter than Charlotte had imagined was possible.

Follow me! said the voice in Charlotte's ear, *as we travel back in time! Imagine, please, tens of thousands of Romans waiting with bated breath to see the show right here. Gladiators fighting panthers, hippopotami, crocodiles, and even . . . a LION!*

Lee and Cord seemed to have disappeared. Charlotte

tried to remain upright as Regan admired the cunning wooden contraption that had been used to ferry lions to the arena. (It was a facsimile, said their guide, wherever she was, in their ears.) They plodded through dark and creepy hallways into the Colosseum dungeon.

Here, in the dungeon, said the voice, *is where the gladiators awaited their fate! Imagine how it might have felt to be a gladiator about to enter the arena, knowing this breath might be your last . . .*

"Yikes," said Regan, meeting Charlotte's eyes and grinning.

"What's funny?" said Charlotte. Regan's face fell. They kept moving, climbing up and passing under an enormous arch to enter the arena.

Now we are walking through the Porta Libitinaria . . . or Gate of Death! cried the guide. *Imagine fifty thousand people cheering. Imagine facing an army of tigers, or other armed gladiators. Will you survive?*

From across the vast space, Charlotte saw her son. He spotted her, raised his arm, waved. His face was open. "Mom!" he called, loping toward her. "Mom!"

What a disappointment.

Charlotte knew she should go to her son, embrace him. But his need was too like her own—naked, endless, weak.

Charlotte pretended she hadn't seen him. She turned away, heading back into the labyrinthine hallways. She walked quickly, the packed earth hard under her ballet flats. She went left and then right, becoming lost in the Colosseum, wanting only to find a way out.

TEN

Florence, Italy

1 / Charlotte

IN CHARLOTTE'S DREAMS, SHE was young again. Someone had given her a surprise gift—a silver package—but she had misplaced it in an enormous castle. She was chilly, wearing a pink flannel bathrobe she'd thrown away a decade before. She searched the kitchen, the basement, the attic, and many dusty bedrooms. She wanted to unwrap the present.

Charlotte opened her eyes. It took her a moment to realize that there was no wrapped box. It was 2:00 A.M. Charlotte had taken the bus from Rome back to the ship with Regan. Had Lee and Cord returned to the *Marveloso*, or were they still in Italy? Charlotte had lain down for a nap, and must have slept straight through dinner.

Alone in the middle of the night, Charlotte began to worry. She was due to read "The Painter & Me" aloud in the Teatro Fabuloso the following evening. Her children still had no idea what the essay was about. Not one had asked. Maybe they assumed it was about Winston, or them.

Part of Charlotte was terrified at the thought of standing in a spotlight and exposing herself, but another part was ready for her children to hear her secrets. Or, okay, her one secret, sordid as it was. Maybe they would *see* her, just for a moment.

Charlotte had, to be fair, worked hard to keep her children from knowing her. It was perhaps the signature accomplishment of her life, how airtight the construction of her false self had been. She'd known neighborhood mothers who'd gone off the rails: leaving husbands for handymen or other people's husbands; spending ruinous amounts of money; and (in one case) absconding to Puerto Vallarta, Mexico. Charlotte had clung to her pious persona like a lifeboat. Perhaps she'd even come to believe it was real.

But Charlotte could imagine a shadow self. A woman who would move toward a kiss. A Charlotte who invited lovers in, who opened her body to them without fear, abandoned herself to pleasure. A woman who believed herself worthy of love.

Lying in her nest of Splendido blankets, Charlotte remembered her wedding day. It had been six months since her father's death had exposed the bad investments that left them paupers. Winston waited beside the priest, crisply dressed, looking at her expectantly. She didn't feel much of a connection to him. Yet there she was, wearing an ivory dress.

Why did Winston marry Charlotte? She annoyed him on a daily basis; many of her habits seemed to grate on him like sandpaper. Charlotte knew their relationship was based on people they'd once seen in each other. To Winston, Charlotte was a trophy, a prize that even a famous artist had desired. Winning her made him believe that a thrilling life was possible even as he soldiered on at his father's law firm. Charlotte watched Winston's hopes dim as the years passed. She wasn't magic, couldn't deliver him from the alcoholism and depression that had been in him all along.

Charlotte had been badly burned when the painter and then her mother spurned her. She had wanted to feel safe, and giving up on romance seemed like the price for safety. Winston had money, of course, though not very much. Marrying him had given Charlotte and Louisa a path forward.

On her wedding day, Charlotte wore new shoes that chafed at her right ankle. It hurt as she walked down the aisle. She'd had an angry blister for weeks, and a new husband who told her to stop complaining.

Charlotte tossed and turned. There was so much space in the bed. Was this her fate—to be alone at night, and invisible during the day?

The boat rocked slowly, almost imperceptibly, and Charlotte realized that she had never really known what it felt like to be someone's true love. She tried to fall asleep again, to go back inside her dream. She wanted to find the silver gift, tear the paper off, and see what lay inside.

2 / Cord

CORD MISSED HIS MOTHER. He missed his tight little tucked-in bed in his musty, fusty cabin on the cheesy monstrosity that was the *Splendido Marveloso*. For a moment, gazing at the Fontana dei Quattro Fiumi, the fountain's noise rushing in his ears, his head and heart aching, Cord realized that he'd probably miss the megaliner for the rest of his life. Once you'd known the comfort of cruising, life on land was jagged and difficult indeed. There was no Paros, no breakfast tray, no carb-o-licious buffet on the lido deck with a bottomless carafe of coffee. Cord had exiled himself from the Promised Land.

He stretched. Cord had walked around the Eternal City for hours searching for Giovanni. Each time he rounded a corner, stumbling upon another historic treasure, he'd imagined their reunion: Cord's tearful apology, Gio's forgiving embrace. It would be a sweeping black-and-white film of a reunion!

Except Cord never found Giovanni. Maybe he'd gone back to New York. He wasn't answering his phone or posting anything anywhere. Giovanni's face, when he'd confronted Cord next to the golf cart, was filled with rage and pain. "You have serious problems," Giovanni had said.

"Help me," Cord had said.

Giovanni crossed his arms over his chest. "I thought this thing with your mom was something you had to do," he said. "But now I get it. It's who you are."

"It's not what I want," Cord managed. "It's not who I want to be."

"Goodbye, Cord," said Giovanni, before walking away, then picking up his pace, turning a corner, and disappearing.

"Don't leave me!" cried Cord.

But Gio was gone.

Cord couldn't leave Rome, not like this. Countless glittering bars beckoned. He could get drunk. He could meet up with the ship at its next destination (Florence, wasn't it?) or even go home and deal with the 3rd Eyez mess he'd created. Across from him, lights played upon the majestic fountain, illuminating a young couple madly making out.

Cord pulled out his phone and stared at it. God, he wanted to jam it back in his pocket, resume his fruitless search. But he'd already gone down every avenue he could imagine to make things right. And none had worked. He was, as they said in the rooms, his own worst enemy. He needed help. Beaten down and unable to think of any other option, Cord dialed Handy.

"Ah," said Handy, answering on the first ring. "It's you, man."

"Yeah," said Cord. "It's me."

"Are you drinking?"

"No."

"I'm glad."

"Not today. Not right now at this minute."

"That's good."

"But I did drink. I fucked up."

"It's okay, man," said Handy. "We're alcoholics. It's what we do."

Cord heaved a long, shuddering sigh.

"Where are you?" said Handy.

"I'm in Rome. I'm sitting in front of a big fountain. I don't know where to go, and I don't know how to make things right."

"Yup," said Handy.

"What does that mean?" said Cord angrily.

"It means, I hear you."

"I'm sorry," said Cord, rubbing his eyes.

"You don't have to be sorry."

"But I am," said Cord. "I'm so sorry."

"You know what I'm going to say?" said Handy, after a pause.

"Yeah." Cord laughed sadly.

"What?"

"Go to a meeting."

"Right. What else?" said Handy.

"Accept the things I cannot change."

"Good one. And . . . ?"

Cord tipped his head to look at the navy sky. "You're going to tell me to wait for God to tell me what to do."

"How've you been doing on your own, man?" said Handy.

"Not so well."

"Yup," said Handy again. Cord's fury ebbed, and he began to laugh. "Gio came to surprise me," he said. "Handy, he hired a golf cart. To drive my mom around Rome. And I just—I don't know. I blacked out or something."

"You were drunk?"

"No," said Cord. "Sober as a mouse or whatever they say."

"A church mouse," said Handy.

"Yeah. But I just went comatose. In the golf cart." Laughter bubbled up, and Cord giggled. "Gio told me to go to hell," he said. "My family didn't know what was going on. My mom . . ."

"But what about you?"

"Huh?"

"What about you?" said Handy.

Cord stopped laughing. A Japanese couple having dinner at an outdoor café was staring at him. He didn't care. "You know what I want," said Cord bitterly.

"I sure do," said Handy.

They were silent. Cord felt glad not to be alone. "Thanks," he said. "You get it, I know that. That's a lot."

"You need me to come on over there to Italy?" said Handy. "Drag you to a meeting?"

"I can do it," said Cord.

"Do it, then," said Handy. "Call me afterward."

"Okay," said Cord.

"One day at a time, man."

"I hate that fucking saying."

"Yup," said Handy.

"Handy?" said Cord.

"I'm here," said Handy.

"Can you not hang up yet?" Cord sounded like a baby, like a goddamn baby, and though he was a bit ashamed, it felt good to ask for what he needed.

"I'm right here," said Handy.

3 / Regan

NO ONE BUT REGAN showed up for the Wonders of Florence tour. She sat by herself on the bus from Livorno, peeking out the window as the bus stopped at the Cathedral of Santa Maria del Fiore. The cathedral was begun in 1296 in the Gothic style and sprawled over almost ninety thousand square feet. Regan stepped back to take it in: the wedding cake exterior of the basilica was fitted with marble panels in pink and green, bordered in white. *Beauty*—the word sprang into Regan's mind.

Throughout high school, Regan had kept giant scrapbooks. She'd filled them with sketches, musings, Polaroid photos, and ticket stubs. Sometimes locks of hair and even (once) a bloody Band-Aid to remember the night she fell at a Green Day concert and scraped her elbow. Regan believed she was making something beautiful—even something *important*—from the detritus of her days.

In early marriage and after the girls were born, she'd continued her projects, adding recipes and receipts, using the girls' finger paints and crayons, spending sleep-deprived midnight hours at work, then sitting cross-legged on the floor of the playroom while the girls created their own art. Why had she stopped? Regan remembered needing a new scrapbook and just never getting to the store to buy one. Her brain gradually filled with grocery lists, car pool times, paint swatches for the den. Regan's art seemed less important than her family's constant needs.

Their guide was a bespectacled blond man with a clipboard. He talked for a while about Il Duomo, the dome, which was 375 feet tall. It was made of brick, said their guide (Regan squinted to make out the name on his tag—NICO), and was a miracle of physics. Its creator, Filippo Brunelleschi, had studied the Romans' construction of the Pantheon as he figured out how to create the dome without using a wooden skeleton. Instead, he proposed placing the brickwork in herringbone patterns between a framework of stone beams.

So it wasn't all about beauty, thought Regan. It was also about math and showmanship. Regan felt a familiar thirst, staring at the marble façade of the church, wanting to understand more. She asked Nico how the patterns and stone beams actually worked, drinking in his explanation as he moved his hands through the air, sketching interlocking shapes.

Regan thought of her peaceful morning hours at Monet's Playhouse. Of course, this architectural marvel was nothing like painting ceramic figurines, but the process— a vision and its eventual execution or abandonment—was the same, wasn't it?

Nico briefed them as they drove toward the Ponte Vecchio: it was a medieval stone closed-spandrel arch bridge with three segments. While the shops along the bridge had originally housed butchers and gold merchants, they now sold jewelry and tourist knickknacks. "Please, I implore you," said Nico. "Do not buy a lock. We have to remove the locks weekly. They are a hazard."

As the bridge came into view, Nico pulled out a boom box. "Puccini mentions the bridge in 'O Mio Babbino Caro,' " he said. "Please, be silent and enjoy."

He pressed Play. A soprano sang, her voice rising with the music, and although Regan didn't understand the Italian words, the song pierced her. When the bus stopped, passengers began shoving past her to get to the shops, and Regan was surprised to feel a hand on her shoulder. She looked up, into the kind eyes of Nico. He was so young.

"You understand," he said.

Regan nodded. She did understand.

THEY WERE GIVEN A few hours to wander, and told where to meet the bus to head back to the port. Regan walked along the cobblestones, peering idly at gold jewelry. The searing voice of the opera singer kept coming back to her, making her feel melancholy. She plodded forward, wishing she weren't alone.

And then she saw him, as if conjured from her hopes. Crossing a square that was loud with zooming Vespas and shouting locals, Regan recognized the back of his head. He was haggling with a vendor in fluent Italian, holding up a bottle of balsamic vinegar. Regan approached him, suddenly shy.

He finished his conversation, took the vinegar, and turned. "Regan!" he cried.

"Giovanni," said Regan. "What are you doing here?"

"Oh my God," said Giovanni, taking her arm and walking purposefully. "I'm so embarrassed I could die. I took a week off and spent all my savings. I booked a room on your stupid cruise ship. I boarded the dog at Hotel Bark Ave! I thought this was going to be the best week of my life."

"Wait," said Regan, "you're on the ship?"

"Pathetic, right?" said Giovanni, running a hand through his lustrous hair. "But what am I going to do, throw away the ticket? No, ma'am. I danced at that revolting disco all night long. I drowned my sorrows in bottom-shelf tequila. I'm ashamed to tell you that I almost made out with DJ Neon."

Regan couldn't help but laugh. "I'm not laughing at you," she said.

"You are, but whatever," said Giovanni. "Let's lunch."

They slipped into a restaurant with high ceilings and pale blue walls. Giovanni spoke to the woman at the hostess stand and she seated them. Every other table was full and the din was incredible. Regan didn't see another American in the place, which seemed a miracle and made her feel like an insider.

"Mind if I order?" said Giovanni.

"Please," said Regan. "I love everything."

"The woman of my dreams," said Giovanni. He ordered in Italian from a young brunette with her hair in a ponytail, her arms laden with plates.

When he had finished speaking, the woman nodded and said, *"Si, prego."*

"I know I should be looking at monumental works of art," said Giovanni, "but I lived here for my junior year in college, so I've seen them. And I'm too hungover."

The waitress returned with a carafe of wine, two glasses, and a blue-and-white bowl filled with pasta. *"Pomodoro e basilico e tagliatelle fiori di zucca e scamorza,"* she said.

"Oh my God," said Regan, tasting the noodles. "This is incredible."

"Pumpkin flowers," said Giovanni, pointing with his fork. "And can you taste that milky, caramelly cheese on the *tagliatelle?* That's *scamorza.*"

"*Scamorza,*" repeated Regan.

"So," said Giovanni, "where's your husband?"

"Oh . . ." said Regan. Giovanni looked sympathetic, waiting for her to continue. "It's not a pretty subject," said Regan.

Giovanni nodded, his wineglass aloft. "Go on," he said.

"Let's just enjoy lunch," said Regan.

"Spill it," said Giovanni. Regan grinned—he was so different from her family. It had been a long time since she had confided in anyone other than Zoë. But once she began talking, it was hard to stop. She told Giovanni everything, from turning down art school until the moment Matt admitted he was in love with someone else and was leaving her.

"I'm so sorry," said Giovanni. "What a bastard."

"Can I tell you a secret?" said Regan.

"Please," said Giovanni.

Regan took a sip of wine, remembering the night she first saw Janet—vibrant, young, red-haired Janet. Regan and Matt had brought the girls for dinner at one of their favorite restaurants, the Bonna Bella Yacht Club. (Regan loved the crab fritters.) They approached by water, pulling their boat to the restaurant's communal dock. As they climbed the wooden stairs to the Bonna Bella entrance, Regan spied a group of young teachers from Savannah Country Day enjoying happy hour on the outdoor deck. Regan sat down with Flora and Isabella at a nearby table, and Matt went to get drinks at the bar. As the girls drew with crayons, Regan heard Matt's laughter, a rich, delighted sound she hadn't heard in a while.

"Daddy's talking to Miss Janet," said Flora. "Her red hair is like Ariel's red hair."

The waitress came to take their order and Regan stood to get Matt's attention. Matt was leaning against the bar, his beer in one hand, Regan's glass of wine in the other. Regan watched her husband's expression as he spoke animatedly to an adorable young woman wearing a yellow sundress. He looked delighted, happy, even nice.

"Miss Janet teaches kindergarten but her husband died," said Isabella.

"Oh, no," said Regan.

Matt laughed again, a sound that had once made Regan feel at home but now filled her with dread. Janet seemed to be thrilled with whatever Matt was saying, though, and an idea bloomed in Regan's imagination, a plan unfurling, a golden road out.

Regan looked at Flora and Isabella and imagined waking in a home without his cutting voice, without his watching, without Matt. They could stay in pajamas all day, and eat cereal for lunch. Hope filled Regan, warm and bright.

It was only later that she recognized Lee had done the same to Regan, maybe without even knowing she was doing it, placing her squarely in Matt's path, hoping he would be distracted as Lee escaped.

That night, as she drove the boat home on the Skidaway River, leaving Matt to "have some fun" at Bonna Bella, Regan pointed out an osprey to the girls. "See?" she said. "It's the mom, right there, in her nest."

"I see it," said Isabella.

"I see the baby birds!" said Flora.

Regan slowed the boat. The air was humid, smelling of marsh. They watched as the mother osprey surveyed the river and the sky, then took flight.

———

GIOVANNI LISTENED TO HER story, putting his hand over his mouth as she concluded. "Wow," he said. "Just . . . wow, Regan. So you set up your own husband's affair? It's like *Dangerous Liaisons* in suburban Savannah!"

"It wasn't even my idea to hire a private detective, though I'm sure the pictures will come in handy during the settlement."

"I'm impressed," said Giovanni. He drained his glass and shouted something that made the waitress bring more wine and bowls of truffle ravioli. "So what are you going to do now?"

"I honestly don't know," said Regan. "I haven't really ever applied for a job."

"That is rough," said Giovanni. Regan paused, realizing how amazing it was that Giovanni didn't seem to need to give her an answer, or even help her in any way. It *was* rough, but she would sort it out. In Gio's position, she'd feel as if she had to solve everything.

"What about you?" said Regan, lifting her fork, resolving to just listen.

"Sometimes it's best to move on," said Giovanni, shaking his head. "Cord's going to get it together or he's not going to get it together. I know that sounds cold."

"Yeah," said Regan, thinking of Cord as a boy, of the way his eyes had flashed when Winston yelled. But Cord never yelled back. He just looked down. He just took it. "Our father . . ." said Regan.

"Save it," said Giovanni, holding up his hand. "He's thirty-six years old."

The waitress appeared with a third serving. *"Fusilli alla contadina e ai peperoni,"* she said. Regan was beginning to feel uncomfortably full, her face flushed. She topped off her glass of wine, and ate.

"Look," said Giovanni. "I know you guys had a hard childhood—really hard—but that's over now. We all have problems. Get therapy, take meds, I don't know. But for him to still be in the closet . . . that's just some shame I don't know how to handle."

Regan nodded.

"I thought I could make him better. But I tried. And it seems like I can't." He shook his head, suddenly mournful. "I don't want to give up," he said. "I don't want to give up on him."

Regan took Giovanni's hands in her own. She wanted to say, "Never give up." She wanted to say, "Hang on to love, no matter what." She wanted to say, "In sickness and in health." But the truth was, she didn't believe those words. Not anymore.

"He's an incredible man," she said.

"I know," said Giovanni. "What do you think I should do?"

"He's just so wonderful," said Regan. "I love him so much." It was hardly an answer, but it was the truth.

"I love him, too," said Giovanni sadly.

BY THE TIME THEY'D had coffees and paid, the *piazza* (somehow, tipsy, Regan knew what it was called) had become vibrant. Afternoon light bathed the city in a soft glow, and Regan was enamored with the smell of gasoline and garlic that seemed to permeate the air. Giovanni led her to the Arno and they held hands and looked at the water.

"We should get back on the bus," said Giovanni.

"I don't want to go," said Regan. They walked along

cobblestone streets, Regan feeling languid and fabulous. When she saw a stationery store, she paused. There, in the window, she saw a large notebook bound in deep brown leather. In the back of the store, she saw a man lowering a sheet of paper into what looked like a vat of paint. "Look, he's marbling," said Regan. She had tried the technique of mixing paint and glue, then dipping paper to create riotous patterns.

"Come on, now," said Giovanni.

"No," said Regan. She put her hand on the brass door-knob. The man in the shop lifted the paper upward and Regan saw its blue-and-green print, exquisite fans of color resembling peacock plumages. In her pocket, she could feel the receipt from lunch. She would draw the Arno, paste the scrap of paper, write what she remembered of Florence.

The leather-bound notebook was so different from the home goods she bought at the Oglethorpe Mall. It was for her, not for some life she wished she could inhabit. "We're going to be late," said Giovanni.

The door's chimes rang as it opened.

4 / Lee

LEE WORKED ON THE contents of the thick manila envelope
all day. There were a hundred and fifty probing, awful, and
repetitive questions:

What is your favorite drink?

What sexual positions do you prefer?

What are you hoping to find on Sloppy Seconds?

Do you want to get married?

Have you participated in an orgy?

What is your favorite fruit?

Francine, reached via FaceTime—her visage grainy, orange lipstick arresting—confirmed that the show was indeed called *Sloppy Seconds*. Lee had sent an audition
package to *The Bachelor* years before (complete with a
video Jason had taken of her horseback riding in a string
bikini—oh, how it had chafed), and while she'd made it
only to the second round, new shows routinely dug through
old tapes. *Sloppy Seconds* was a forthcoming reality show
about ordinary people who had been dumped by famous
people. Now that Jason was famous, Lee (as the saying
goes) was a contender.

Hopped up on room service coffee, Lee scrawled answers. She made up tidbits she thought would appeal to the producers, creating a sexy vixen who was a bit unstable but had a heart of gold. She wrote until her hand was sore. She tried to ignore another set of questions:

Do I want to live in a "Malibu Beach Dream House" with seventeen other people, vying for love and prizes?

What about my baby?

Should I have flown to Malta?

Why am I here in my cabin when I could be in Florence, Italy?

In what way do I think this job would make me happy?

TO SILENCE THESE PESKY thoughts, Lee went for a walk, heading to the twenty-four-hour frozen yogurt station in the Aqua Zone. She sort of hoped she'd run into someone in her family, but knew they were probably in Florence without her. No one had even called to remind Lee about the tour, she realized, feeling left out.

Every lounge chair by the pool was filled, and Lee felt twinges of both revulsion and empathy as she gazed over the sea of bodies. It was like a nature movie: humans in captivity. She saw a man on the far deck smoking a cigarette. From a distance, he looked like Matt, and Lee walked toward him.

Lee remembered the night before Regan's wedding. Matt and Lee had shared a cigarette outside Elizabeth on 37th, where the rehearsal dinner was still going on. She'd been someone else then: a star shooting skyward, on the brink (she'd thought) of fame. Matt had dropped the cigarette to the ground.

It was raining lightly. "I'd stop all this," he said, "if you want me back. Please?"

"She's my sister," Lee said. She remembered being flushed with champagne and indignation, but flattered, too. "Don't you love her?"

"It's not the same. You're my Beautiful One, Lee," said Matt, using the nickname he'd given her.

Regan had taken Lee's first headshots, arranging Lee's hair to catch the light, brushing her eyelids with shadow from the Clinique counter at the Oglethorpe Mall. In the days before selfies, Regan had captured Lee's beauty. There was no question where Lee's loyalty lay. She had left Matt in the rain, marched into the restaurant. She'd pulled Regan into the ladies' room and demanded that her sister call off the wedding.

"Why?" Regan said. "Why would you say this to me? Why would you do this now?"

"He's not the right person for you," said Lee, stopping short of telling her sister about Matt's betrayal, the way he could be cruel.

"I see," said Regan, facing her sister. Her expression was dark, furious. "You can't even let me have one night," she said.

"This isn't about me," said Lee.

"It's always about you," spat Regan. She pushed open the ladies' room door and disappeared. Lee breathed in and out, trying to compose herself. When she felt calm, she walked outside and hailed a cab. She was back in Los Angeles by the next day.

Lee *was* the Beautiful One; she always had been. Winston had taught Lee that her looks were her strength. She was still relying on them, hoping to use them to secure a job she wasn't sure she wanted. She had nothing else: no family, no skills, no home.

5 / Charlotte

CHARLOTTE WAS WORN OUT. Instead of setting an alarm to make the day tour of Florence, she'd slept in, deciding after breakfast to simply wander around the port city. She felt proud of herself as she disembarked. Here she was: a modern gal on her own in Livorno, Italy! It was crowded and, okay, filthy, but a very nice Nigerian man sold her a faux-Gucci purse that sure did look like the real thing. Charlotte longed for Minnie, who would have loved Charlotte's chutzpah. What Charlotte wouldn't give to buy a fake Gucci bag for her friend.

Charlotte was walking down a crowded street full of cafés when she spotted Paros, her porter, handsome even out of uniform. He turned in to a coffee shop and Charlotte, feeling brazen, followed. ("You hussy, you!" she heard Minnie exclaim happily.) The shop was filled with young people smoking and eating gelato at the same time. It was strange to see Paros sitting at a small, circular table, his skin pale under fluorescent lights.

"Ciao!" said Charlotte, sashaying toward him and putting her hand on her hip.

"Charlotte!" said Paros. "Please, please join me."

"Don't mind if I do," said Charlotte. Paros wore street clothes, and old ones at that—faded corduroy pants, a jacket that looked like something a farmer would wear, odd shoes. He was, in fact, a farmer, he told Charlotte, after she had ordered an espresso. He had been a *retired* farmer, but then the Greek economy had collapsed, and with it, his savings.

"I had to go back to work," he said, stirring a sugar packet into his coffee. "My children depend on me."

"Mine, too," sighed Charlotte. "Well, I don't know if they depend on me, but they . . ." She shook her head, feeling deflated.

"They're going to be fine," said Paros.

"I know," said Charlotte, flustered. "Well, I can say *I know*, but to be honest, I don't know."

"I'm only glad I have held on to my home," said Paros, adroitly changing the subject. "I harvest olives and my home is a short walk to the beach."

"That sounds really nice," said Charlotte.

"What about you?" said Paros. "Tell me about your home."

"Oh," said Charlotte. "It's small but I do love it. My condo overlooks a golf course, rolling greens. I can drive a golf cart to church and to the grocery store."

Paros smiled. Charlotte smiled back. There was heat between them, a feeling Charlotte hadn't known in a long time. Did she dare to try to bring her lips to his?

"Kiss him!" said Minnie. "You're seventy-one years old! What are you waiting for?"

Like a heroine in a romance novel, Charlotte leaned across the café table, pursing her lips. But—and it almost happened in slow motion—as Charlotte's face grew close to Paros's, she saw that he was surprised and flustered, not bedroom-eyed and willing.

Charlotte reared back, humiliated, a small wail escaping her mouth. She stood quickly, rummaged in her purse for a few euros, and dropped them on the table.

"Stop," said Paros. "Wait, Charlotte!"

But she was halfway to the café exit. Oh, she hated herself.

"Charlotte! Come back," called Paros, standing up. His voice was so loud that people turned to look.

She rushed outside and began to run through the Livorno streets. Where was the ship? What had she done? *That's what you get*, said Louisa, *for thinking you're better than you are.*

ELEVEN

Marseilles,
France

1 / Charlotte

OH, HER BODY. CHARLOTTE had spent her life disregarding it—starving it, forcing it through calisthenics as her *Body by Jacques* cassette tape droned on, bearing children, suckling children, submitting to Winston's halfhearted ministrations, enduring hot flashes, mammograms, colonoscopies. Eating cheese and drinking wine. Biking once in a blue moon, playing golf. Her body (as long as it was skinny enough to fit into her size four clothes) was an afterthought. Everything worked, so why dwell?

She had never been to a spa. The thought of strangers touching her made Charlotte squirm. What was she supposed to *do* during a massage, just lie there? How dull and stressful. She was used to ignoring her body's sensations, not enhancing them!

And yet her Magnifico package had included an "Evening of Bliss," so here she was, sitting primly on an oddly warm chaise longue in a Splendido robe, nothing underneath but her Macy's underpants. To Charlotte, an "Evening of Bliss" would mean Chardonnay and Triscuits, complete with all three of her children and Father Thomas calling and leaving messages, assuring her she was loved and appreciated but not requiring her to *do* anything for anyone. And then a stranger with not too much chest hair would make love to her—mmmm, moving himself in and out of her, clutching at her, crying out her name. And then he'd tuck her in, kiss her sweetly, and depart.

The thalassotherapy pool, located deep in the under-belly of the ship, was like a sinister disco. Even the word "thalassotherapy" gave Charlotte the creeps. "Charlotte Perkins?" said a stout woman holding a clipboard.

Charlotte rose to her feet. "Hello," she said awkwardly.

"I am Norma," said the woman. "You are ready for your combo treatment SpaTopia, Hot Rock Sampler, Fantastic Feet Fantastic You."

It seemed a question, yet was spoken as a statement. "Yes?" said Charlotte.

"Good. We begin," said Norma. She turned and plodded down a neon-lit hallway. Charlotte's heart began to beat audibly in her ears. Why was it so easy for everyone else to forget they were underwater? This knowledge hit Charlotte at random intervals, making her woozy. *This is so wrong!* Her brain would scream. *I am UNDERWATER! HELP ME!*

Norma turned around to make sure Charlotte was following. Charlotte was not following. She was paralyzed, seized with terror. "I don't—" said Charlotte.

UNDERWATER! UNDERWATER! NOTHING ON BUT PANTIES! UNDERWATER!

"I don't think I am ready for this," Charlotte managed. "I don't like being naked," she said, or thought she said, sitting down, the revolting floor wet underneath her bottom. She was wearing panties, thank goodness, she was wearing panties. Where was she? Why was there a pool in the middle of a casino? Why were there naked people in a pool in the middle of a casino?

Someone was cradling her head, and Charlotte could have stayed with the present. She could stay but she just didn't want to. So much more joy lay in the past! The day she met him, the day he called for her, the way he touched her body, the one summer she was free! Paella, smelling of saffron, at a bullfight in Arles! Charlotte let herself fall into memory, so much richer than whatever on earth this wet casino was.

She was wearing a linen robe. The slice of Provençal sun from the window was warm across her lap. He put down his pencil. Within moments, he had parted her linen garment. She was naked, she was open, like the gift she would become.

THE SOUND OF FOOTSTEPS pierced her airy doze. Charlotte opened her eyes to find that she was lying down on a massage table, wearing her spa robe. "Ah," said a man in a white coat. "I'm glad you're awake. Do you have any remaining dizziness? Nausea?"

"No," said Charlotte.

"Well! It seems you had a bout of seasickness," said the man. "You might want to stay lying down for another hour or so, or we can bring you back to your cabin and settle you in with a movie and a cup of tea." He angled his head quizzically, an obsequious bird.

"Please call my children," said Charlotte. "I'm here with my children. I'm not alone on this cruise! If you just call them, I'm sure they'll come right away."

"Well . . ." said the doctor, shifting uncomfortably. "We did try to reach . . ."

"Did you try all of them? All three?" said Charlotte.

He looked around the empty room. "I'm sorry," he said. "We left messages, but . . ."

"Oh," said Charlotte. "I see."

"Would you like to be escorted back to your cabin?" he asked.

"No, thank you," said Charlotte, a familiar ache in the pit of her stomach. "I'm fine on my own."

"I could call your porter? I think it would be best."

"Paros?" said Charlotte, thinking of kind Paros. Handsome Paros. "Oh, yes, thank you," she said.

PAROS OPENED THE DOOR to the massage room quietly. Charlotte was dressed and ready, her purse in her lap. "Oh, Charlotte. Are you all right?" said Paros.

"I," said Charlotte. "My children . . ." She looked down, too tired, suddenly, to put a happy face on things. "I fell," she said, "and none of my children came to help me. I took them on this cruise, but I'm still all alone."

Paros looked grim, seemingly saddened by this news. He drew near, held out his arm. She hooked her own arm through his, leaned into him a bit. "Well, Charlotte," he said, "I'm here."

"You're here," said Charlotte.

"Forgive me for being afraid, earlier," he said.

"I do," said Charlotte.

Paros brought his face close, closed his eyes. She did not move away. And then he kissed her.

2 / Cord

BEFORE BREAKFAST AT SHELLS, before the Day Tour of Arles & Aix-en-Provence, Cord rose early, showered, and headed to the Friends of Bill W meeting in the Starlight Lounge. With Handy's encouragement, he'd taken an overnight, zillion-euro taxi to Livorno, blearily boarded the *Marveloso*, and forced himself to attend a Sundowners AA meeting. It was a nice group of alcoholics, and for lack of any better ideas, he'd set his alarm for the morning meeting before zonking out in his cabin.

The chair of the Sunrise meeting was a guy in a bathing suit and Cozumel T-shirt. He had long silver hair, which he ran his hand through as he spoke. "Hey. I might just go on and start," he said. "I'm Jacob and I'm an alcoholic."

"Hi, Jacob," intoned the four other drunks in the disco.

"I chose a reading today about control, because I'm still trying to control everything," said Jacob. "I mean *everything*. Like should my wife order pork chops? And should we stay on the Colosseum tour there in Rome . . . or just stop when we're tired? And should we have sex? Does she want to? Do I want to?" He shook his head. "I'm so tired, and it's supposed to be my vacation. This sucks," he said. "I want a drink, but I'm not going to have a drink. I just wish my brain would slow down. It's . . . it's just exhausting. Thanks. Thanks for being here, guys. Thanks for listening. I love you all."

"My name is Gerrie," said a beautiful young woman in a red dress. "Geraldine. I'm an alcoholic."

"Hi, Geraldine."

"I'm on my honeymoon," said Gerrie. "Yeah, and I'm terrified. I can't stop thinking about, like, what if my husband leaves me? What if we have kids and they . . . I don't know, they're sick or something? I'm trying to stop the 'stinking thinking,' I try to hug myself, you know? But for one thing, I don't want Ben to think I'm crazy. Anyway, I get it. I'm trying to give up control, too. But seriously, how beautiful are all those bottles of booze everywhere?"

They all laughed.

"I know what it would lead to if I had a cocktail," she said. "I get it. I've been there, puking in my mom's bathroom, blacking out . . . I know. But it's hard."

Cord nodded. It was hard. But sitting in this room, this nightclub still littered with empty drink cups, the sun streaming through the windows, he looked at the faces of strangers who understood. And the day seemed a tiny bit easier.

BEFORE HE WAS DUE to meet his family for their day tour, Cord called Giovanni again, but the phone just rang and rang. Cord left a message, maybe his thirtieth. He wrote another lengthy text. He was sorry, he was sorry, he was sorry.

CHARLOTTE SEEMED INFUSED WITH happiness. She stepped across the gangway into France wearing a fuchsia silk dress with matching kitten heels. Lipstick, gold jewelry: Cord and Lee had jokingly labeled looks like this the "full Charlotte Perkins."

"Oh, darling," said Charlotte, stopping to pose with Cord for the ship photographer.

"Now put your arm around your wife," said the young man, snapping away. His accent wasn't quite British— maybe South African? Cord had seen him running the limbo contest in the Aqua Zone the day before.

"Oh!" cried Charlotte. "You *devil*. He's my *son*."

"I would never have guessed," said the guy.

"Okay," said Cord, stepping away from the fake life preserver emblazoned with FUN IN MARSEILLES! "Let's move on. Where are my sisters? Where's Matt?"

"I don't know," said Charlotte.

Cord was irked. He'd figured everyone had been worried sick about him. He thought he would have been all they'd be talking about. But it seemed no one in his family had even noticed he was missing.

IN ARLES, THEIR GUIDE, an older woman in a white hat that seemed too small for her head, made them get off the bus to stand next to a low concrete wall and a muddy river. There was a bridge in the distance. There was trash at Cord's feet, an empty packet of French cigarettes and a squished French beer can. When the guide spoke, she paused constantly for dramatic effect.

"Gaze at the Rhône," commanded their guide. "Right very here—*this*—is the exact spot . . . where Vincent van Gogh painted . . . *Starry Night over the Rhône*. Marvel! Marvel!"

Cord could vaguely remember the painting, lush with a turquoise sky and silver-yellow stars. "I guess it's more *marvelous* at night," said Charlotte sotto voce, her tone jubilant. She seemed awfully cheery for a woman whose children were hurting. Or maybe she didn't know they were hurting. Maybe she didn't even see them.

Inwardly, Cord began to feel sorry for himself. But he halted his thoughts. He was thirty-six years old. Maybe it was time to stop blaming his mother for his troubles. Cord remembered the Serenity Prayer. It didn't say anything about pouting, wishing someone were different than they were. This sense that he was wronged was part of his problem, part of the way he justified drinking. Cord looked at Charlotte, who met his gaze and winked. It was what it was. He winked back.

"He was staying," said the guide, "at the place you know. It's called the Yellow House . . . on . . . la Place Lamartine. He was very sad. Despairing. And . . . he would come here, right here, and he would . . . paint the night sky."

Some loudmouth in a University of Texas cap asked the exact year.

"Eighteen eighty-eight," the guide responded. "Marvel. Marvel!"

It was hard to marvel, as Cord breathed bus exhaust and squinted, but he dutifully tried. Van Gogh! It was pretty amazing. Cord liked the French lilt of their guide's voice, too. She paused and then hit English words with high notes. Maybe he should find a Frenchman, thought Cord, since Gio was never coming back to him.

Martyrdom was a hard habit to break.

As they toured Arles, peering at ivy-covered buildings with pastel wooden shutters, Cord felt like he was wandering through a movie set. He half expected Audrey Tautou to peek out one of the windows wearing a kerchief and a flimsy blouse. Something about the cobblestone streets, the window boxes filled with flowers, the metal tables and chalkboard signs with specials written in script—*Plat du Jour Courgettes!*—well, it made him want to smoke.

Next to a carousel filled with actual French children, Cord slipped into a shop and bought some French cigarettes and French gum. He rejoined the group on the steps of a deserted, dusty arena. His mother was gazing up at the building, transfixed. Built in A.D. 90 of Mesozoic limestone, their guide said, the Arles Amphitheater could seat twenty thousand. The two-tiered structure had 120 arches. The guide talked about chariot races, bullfights, blood, and famous artists.

"He took me here the afternoon I met him," said Charlotte, leaning in and touching the sleeve of Cord's shirt.

"What?"

"He brought me here. They served us paella. Nobody could believe I was with him. Nobody else got lunch! Only we got paella."

Cord looked at his mother. She seemed upbeat and sane. She spoke with clarity. "I'm sorry, Mom," he said. "What are you talking about?"

He felt apprehensive, waiting for her answer. Was this how dementia worked? Your mother was seemingly fine and then, boom, she was telling you she'd gone to a bullfight in Arles?

Charlotte shook her head. "I just wanted to tell someone," she said. "I didn't figure you'd understand. And honestly, I don't care."

Cord barked—sort of a laugh, sort of a gasp—as Charlotte walked away from him into the amphitheater, stepping swiftly down the stairs to the first row of seats. She moved elegantly in her hot-pink dress. Cord felt a rush of affection for his crazy mom. Her life hadn't been easy: her snootiness was hard-won and (Cord knew) illusory. And now it seemed she was losing her mind.

"Picasso and his friends, all the painters, when they come here," said the guide. "They serve them . . . paella!"

His mother must have read it somewhere.

Cord entered the hot amphitheater and located Charlotte. "How would you feel about a little excursion?" she said. Her eyes were actually shining; she raised her eyebrows coquettishly. "Come on, let's go," she said.

Cord smiled. He wanted to be connected to her—he always had. But why? Why did he feel so responsible for her? ("Because you're codependent," he heard Handy say in his mind. "Accept the things you cannot change, brother.") But it wasn't fucking fair. He wanted to *mute* his exhausting need to protect Charlotte, not accept it!

He let himself be tugged outside the amphitheater and toward a taxicab. Was this acceptance or weakness? He'd have to ask Handy. Could they possibly be the same thing?

When they climbed in the taxi, the driver put down his copy of *Le Figaro* and started the engine. Cord felt disoriented. His mother spoke in French to the driver. He'd forgotten she spoke French.

The taxi drove out of Arles, into grassy hills. Cord saw hedges of rosemary, towering almond trees, scrub oak. The air was clean and dry, the light diffused and lemony. Tangles of lavender and thyme grew wild. "Where are we going?" he asked.

"There are some things I've been meaning to tell you," said Charlotte. Her tone was grave. The whole situation— the French taxi, the Provençal landscape so lovely it was almost surreal—struck Cord as suddenly terrifying, the folded mountains in the distance forbidding. Could Charlotte be ill? "What, Mom?" he said. "What's going on?"

Her face was not the same face he'd known, or maybe he hadn't looked at her in a while. There were deep lines, and her powdered skin—she didn't wear foundation—was so fragile-looking. Her blue eyes, unadorned; her face, untouched by Botox or plastic surgery; her stare absolutely direct, gazing at him—gazing *into* him. When was the last time he had locked eyes with Charlotte?

"I was sixteen," she said. Her voice was matter-of-fact. "I met him in a café, Le Zinc. He invited me to a bullfight. His brother picked me up in a convertible. And afterward, we came here. He wanted to draw me, he said."

"Are you talking about . . ." said Cord.

The taxi stopped, but remained idling. The driver spoke, and Charlotte answered. "He says we can't go any closer," she told Cord.

They climbed from the taxi. "There," Charlotte said, pointing in the distance. "See that castle?" Cord could see a magnificent fortress with faded yellow walls and reddish shutters, rising against the north slope of the mountain.

"I thought it was love," said Charlotte.

"Mom, are you saying . . . ?"

"He told me I was beautiful enough to stop his heart," said Charlotte.

Cord felt an eerie calm steal over him, the feeling he remembered from having exactly three gin and tonics. (The fourth led to a downhill slide.) Maybe Charlotte was mad and maybe she'd slept with a famous painter. What did it matter, really? Cord's father had been a difficult, tortured man, and if this excursion brought his mother joy, who was he to mess around with it? "I never loved your father," said Charlotte. "Or, I guess, he never loved me. It never occurred to me to wonder what I thought about it all."

Cord grimaced. He didn't want to get into it, his awful childhood. He didn't want to admit the thud of recognition her words created inside him.

It never occurred to me to wonder what I thought about it all.

He looked around at the slim green cypress trees, the lush hills, the dense sky. He looked at the gorgeous structure—the butter-colored walls protecting the castle from . . . what? Charlotte and Cord?

"Others had painted these hills, but now he owned them. That's what he said," said Charlotte. It was like she was in a lucid dream. "I was a virgin, before," she added, after a while. "It was painful. But I thought . . ."

Cord had seen pictures of his mother at sixteen. He remembered a shot of her in a schoolgirl kilt with knee socks, her look innocent but game. He'd never seen that expression in real life.

"What I remember the most is feeling as if it was all beginning. Everything was ahead of me when I came here. And you get to a point in your life, Cord, when you wonder if there's anything big left to happen to you."

"Mom," said Cord. "There's plenty ahead for you."

"What do you want?" asked Charlotte. "What do you really want, honey? Life doesn't go on forever, you know."

"I want to be happy," said Cord. And here—*here*—was the moment he could tell his mother who he was. After all, she was baring her own heart. "Mom?" said Cord.

"I want to be happy, too," said Charlotte.

Cord cleared his throat. "Mom?" he said again. But Charlotte hiked up the skirt of her dress, gathered breath, and started to run toward the château.

"Mom!" cried Cord.

The driver jumped out of the taxi, yelling at her to stop. Cord watched her, stunned. "Mom!" he cried. Charlotte did not turn around.

"She will be jailed!" said the taxi driver. "It is not for the public. *Arête! Arête*, madame!"

Cord took off, but Charlotte, kicking off her kitten heels, was fast. She ran until she reached the castle, then began banging on the door. "I'm here!" she yelled. *"C'est moi!"*

Finally, Cord caught up, breathing heavily. The driver was a few paces behind them. Cord pinned Charlotte's arms to her sides. The door was solid, enormous, shut tight. After a while, Charlotte wriggled free and began running back toward the taxi. She had lost her mind.

"What do I care?" screamed Charlotte. She spun in a slow circle on the vast lawn, arms open wide, cragged peaks rising above her. Sunlight bathed Cord's mother, making her glow. "He's dead!" she cried. "And I'm alive!"

Cord couldn't help but grin. Maybe she had been a famous painter's lover. Anything was possible. Even telling Charlotte his truth. "Mom," he said.

She turned to him.

"I'm gay," said Cord. "Giovanni is my love. I love him." Charlotte was still. She nodded—not shocked, but not pleased, either. "I love you, too," said Cord. He moved toward his mother and encircled her gently in his arms.

"Ah," said Charlotte, easing into his embrace, "lucky me."

3 / Regan

REGAN HAD STAYED UP until almost dawn, drinking tea and working on her scrapbook, laying out tiny watercolor paintings on the floor of the cabin, pasting tickets and menus and pages ripped from tour brochures. Sometime toward morning, she ordered a pot of coffee and a plate of croissants with butter and jam. As much as Regan yearned to visit France and sip an actual café au lait, she decided she would spend the day in her cabin with her art supplies. She had missed the way the hours slipped past as she transferred images from her brain to paper.

TAKING A BREAK TO stretch her legs, Regan opened the cabin closet to see that it was bare of Matt's clothes.

Her plan had worked. But as she touched the empty hangers, she felt a wave of fear. What had she done? She imagined the girls' faces when she told them and felt nauseous. Was she selfish for wanting a second chance? She was, surely she was.

———

HER *MORNING MARVELOSO* NEWSLETTER featured a Slimming Ionithermie Super Detox Treatment "created by a French biochemist" and available in the spa. After the detox, proclaimed the leaflet, "You will return home looking refreshed and rejuvenated and 8 to 10 Years Younger!"

Eight years ago, Regan mused, she had been the mother of a one-year-old, happily ensconced in her suburban lair, her days filled with endless lists of easily accomplished tasks. Essentially, her job each morning was to feed her small family and make sure that the house looked the same at 5:00 P.M. as it had at 6:30 A.M., when Matt had left for work. Also blow jobs, which she'd read in a magazine would keep Matt faithful and fulfilled. Every few days, Regan dutifully yanked down his boxers in bed, performed fellatio, and swallowed. When he'd fallen asleep, she went to town with the Listerine. In the morning, she made coffee and eggs and even *pancakes*, for the love of God. She'd thought she was happy.

But now, it was hard to look back at those days and see them as anything but pathetic. If Regan *hadn't* been creating the perfect house and happy marriage, what had been the point of all that effortful action? In retrospect, she seemed a cog in an assembly line, sucking and swallowing and scrubbing and sautéing, doing her part to make . . . what? Younger Regan seemed so energetic, so dumb.

Regan pulled on her pale pink robe, feeling sympathy for her younger, tender self. She remembered her rehearsal dinner at Elizabeth on 37th, when Lee had cornered her in the ladies' room, proclaiming that Matt was not the one for Regan, that she should call off the wedding. Now, Regan understood that her sister had been right.

Regan stared at herself in the bathroom mirror. Her hair was tangled, pulled into a topknot and secured with a number two pencil. Her fingertips were stained with color. Her skin was lined. She was going to be a single mother. She was going to need a job, a new place to live.

Regan opened her sliding doors. Standing on her balcony, the port of Marseilles before her, Regan felt as if she were inhabiting—just for a moment—the person she'd once dreamed she'd become.

4 / Lee

LEE'S BLEEDING HAD BEGUN in the evening. After she had emailed the files to Francine, Lee had gone into her bathroom to change and noticed scarlet stains. She got back into bed, curled up on her side, and prayed fiercely, understanding too late that this baby was all she wanted, all she'd ever wanted. *Please oh please don't leave me*, she told her baby. *Please oh please. I'll change.*

Waves of pain and so much blood. Lee grew scared and called Regan, then Cord. When neither answered, she called the ship's doctor, who came to her room and confirmed she had miscarried. He gave her pain pills and a sleeping pill, telling her it seemed the worst was over. She could check into the Medical Center, the doctor said, or simply rest in her cabin. Lee told him she would stay in her room, wanting to mourn in peace. When he had left, she changed her sheets and climbed into bed. She didn't take any of the medicine, feeling somehow that she deserved this pain, that it was punishment for being selfish and afraid. When the cramping eased, she fell asleep.

Upon waking, Lee saw that she'd missed a call. She could scarcely believe it as she listened to the recording. It was Jason, his message brief and kinder than she would have expected from someone she'd swindled. She could imagine him rubbing his eyes as he spoke: "Lee, it's me. I'm not going to call the cops, okay? I'm afraid and I'm worried. Who are these plane tickets for? Are you on the European cruise I guess I'm paying for? With three friends? I'm going to cancel the card, Lee. I'm not mad—you can find a way to pay me back. I'm worried, Lee, I really am. And I just . . . I just wanted you to know the card won't work anymore."

It seemed as if doors were closing along a hallway. First, Jason leaving, then her career narrowing to one sad possibility. Finally, the door that led to a life as a mother had slammed shut.

Lee had spent her life trying to shield her family from pain. Using Jason's credit card and purchasing a vacation package had been her last gasp, she saw now. Even Lee, the ultimate fixer, couldn't keep Charlotte from growing old. She couldn't save her sister's marriage. And, she realized, she wasn't going to be able to change—to become a mother, to become an actress. She'd tried her best, she truly had. But even thousands of dollars of plane tickets and excursion passes and fun days at sea hadn't been good enough.

She understood, as her father had, that there was only one answer. It suddenly seemed so clear. She had considered suicide before—swimming into fantasies of everything ending—but had always been able to pull her mind back from the idea. Now, it was obvious she needed a way out.

Lee's hands shook as she applied her makeup. For some reason, it seemed important that she look her best on her last day. She was, after all, the Beautiful One. Lee slipped into her gold sheath, put her hands on her empty body.

On her balcony, she considered the sea. As she had since she was a child, back when she believed she could be one, Lee admired the dazzling stars. But instead of a list of wishes, she had only one: for the unrelenting pain of wanting and never getting—of aching with no relief, of life—to end.

5 / Charlotte

CHARLOTTE'S *SPLENDIDO EVENING NEWSLETTER* announced the Passenger Talent Show. Charlotte thought it was odd that no one had contacted her about reading her essay, but when she checked the contest website again, there it was, clear as day: *The winner of the Become a Jetsetter contest will read his or her prizewinning story aloud at the Passenger Talent Show on the final night of the cruise of a lifetime!*

Charlotte dreaded returning to Savannah. She no longer wanted to do her own laundry, slice her own cheese, or pour her own Chardonnay. Sure, life aboard the *Marveloso* was like living in a bubble: four thousand people making a mutual decision to disregard the possibility of sinking. There were no choices or grocery shopping; there was no painful or difficult news. There was the thrill of waking each morning and finding a new view from her balcony. Oh, how she would miss the horn sounding, champagne glasses ringing together when the *Marveloso* pulled from shore.

Sadly, the trip had only reinforced the distance between Charlotte and her children. She didn't even know where they were—when she ate supper in her room, she'd expected a flurry of concerned calls but her phone had remained silent. There was a certain amount of relief knowing they probably wouldn't be in the audience during her performance, however, so Charlotte decided to get in touch with everyone in the morning, when it was all over and they could enjoy a last day of sightseeing after disembarking in Barcelona and before flying home to their separate lives.

The Teatro Fabuloso backstage area was smaller than she'd imagined. One wall was crammed with costumes on hangers—Charlotte could see tantalizing strips of leather and sheer black shirts. Such magic burst forth from these cramped quarters! She could almost smell the dancers' perspiration. Charlotte borrowed a can of hairspray and misted her coiffure, peering into a circular mirror surrounded by lights, cupping the ends of her hair, patting the curls into place.

Bryson approached with a clipboard. "Are you here for the talent show?" he asked.

"Of course I'm here for the talent show!" said Charlotte.

"Put your name right here," he said.

Charlotte was puzzled: Bryson didn't seem to know that she was the winner of the Become a Jetsetter contest. Before Charlotte could allay her fears, however, he took the clipboard and walked toward another woman, who was even older than Charlotte. "I'm singing show tunes," the woman said. "A medley from *Guys and Dolls* and *Carousel*."

"Fantastic," said Bryson.

After eight other passengers who apparently had talent,

or thought they did, which maybe (thought Charlotte) was the deciding factor, Bryson took to the stage with a few lame jokes about the ship's toilets (small) and his male member (large—ew, but also, hmm). Charlotte sighed and reapplied her lipstick. She cleared her throat, felt her heart pound as Bryson said, "And for the last act of the evening, please welcome Charlotte Perkins, reading an essay she calls"—he peered at the clipboard—"'The Painter and Me'!"

Bryson turned to Charlotte, beckoning her onstage. She blinked.

"Go on," said a stagehand, pushing Charlotte's back.

"But I won the contest," said Charlotte. "Why isn't he saying I won the contest?"

"Please, it's time," said the young woman.

"Charlotte Perkins?" said Bryson. A spotlight swung toward Charlotte, blinding her.

"But I'm the winner," said Charlotte.

"You are a winner," said the woman, speaking slowly, as if Charlotte were demented. "You are definitely a winner."

"I'm not demented," said Charlotte.

The woman took Charlotte's hand and yanked her toward Bryson.

"Here she is!" said Bryson.

"Who won the contest?" said Charlotte.

Bryson chuckled. "Welcome to the stage!" he said.

"The Become a Jetsetter contest," said Charlotte. "I won."

"What a comedian!" said Bryson. He leaned toward her, and whispered, "It was canceled. The contest was canceled. Okay? Nobody won. Now please read your essay."

He smiled at the audience again and put his arm around Charlotte. Her mind spun. If she hadn't won the contest, how was she on this ship? Was she dreaming? *Was* she demented?

"Are you ready?" said Bryson.

Charlotte unfolded her computer printout. The stage lights were hot on her skin. She flushed, confused and embarrassed. When she'd written these words, she'd felt as if she was typing up the story of her great love, a historic love, a love that celebrated her beauty and distinction. But something had changed in her since the night when she'd written in a fevered rush. Now the story seemed tawdry, a sad tale of a young girl seduced and abandoned. Her happiness had all derived from being chosen, being admired. The painter had used her, and she had let him.

Charlotte had once read a novel about the wife of a famous artist. The narrator wrote that she survived because she had never defined herself by the artist's portraits of her. The women who completely identified with the images her husband had created were destroyed, she wrote, because as soon as he lost interest, they no longer existed. Now, Charlotte gathered her strength to speak, to live long after her famous painter was gone.

The silence in the Teatro Fabuloso was crushing. "I . . ." said Charlotte. She closed her eyes and saw Louise's pinched face, heard her mother saying, *What a disappointment.*

"I . . ." she said, opening her eyes. "I thought I was loved, once," she began. She pursed her lips. "But love," she continued, ignoring her crumpled printout, "love is not something you have to wait for. It's not something someone can give you or not. It's . . ."

There were rumblings of discontent in the audience. Charlotte's shame curdled to anger, a clean flame. She suddenly tired of caring what everyone—what *anyone*—

thought of her. To hell with her mother and to hell with shame. She raised her chin. "I want to tell you about my first lover!" she cried.

That quieted things down. Even Bryson looked amazed.

"If you'll just sit still and listen," Charlotte continued, "I'll tell you all about it." The room grew silent. Charlotte began, "I was a beautiful girl when I first went to his castle. He was gnome-like, but in an attractive way. It's hard to explain, but I'll try." She had the audience in the palm of her hand as she read her entire story. Finally, she concluded with gravitas. "I am quite sure," she said, "the nude on a couch is . . . in fact . . . *moi.*"

A booming wave of applause washed over her. Charlotte was beside herself. She imagined Minnie was proud. Charlotte nodded, accepting the audience's adoration as it bathed her in happiness. She folded her essay.

Cheering from the audience was interrupted by a cry from the back of the theater. "Man overboard!" someone yelled.

"It's a woman!" screamed someone else. "Oh my God!"

Bryson rushed onto the stage. "Calm down," he said, pushing Charlotte aside. "We need to calm down." Audience members, shrieking and jostling for position, filled the aisles and rushed the exits.

"The end," said Charlotte into the microphone. Bryson led her off the stage, and she found it was easy to disappear into the crowd. But instead of heading to the lido deck to rubberneck at some tawdry disaster, Charlotte returned to her cabin, where she found a handwritten card: *I will be finished with work at 10:30 P.M., and would be honored if you would stroll around the deck with me. My cell number is enclosed. Yours, PAROS*

Charlotte sat quietly for a time. She had no idea where

her cellphone was—probably in her faux-Gucci purse or her evening clutch—so she lifted her cabin phone and dialed. She was done with waiting for pleasure to come her way. Tonight was her night, and she was ready to seduce a handsome man. She was more than ready.

TWELVE

Barcelona, Spain

1 / Charlotte

AS MINNIE HAD ENCOURAGED her to do, Charlotte greeted Paros in her nightgown. His eyes widened when she opened her cabin door. "Oh, Charlotte," said Paros.

"Hello," said Charlotte.

"You're beautiful," said Paros.

"Thank you," said Charlotte. "Would you like to come in?"

"I would, yes," said Paros.

Charlotte pulled the curtains shut, unplugged her phone, and found a soft-jazz station on her bedside radio. "I'd like you to make love to me," she said, feeling emboldened. Who was this forward creature? It was Charlotte! It was!

"It would be an honor," said Paros. He dimmed the lights. "Please lie down," he said.

"Oh, my," said Charlotte, happily following orders. "Do you think we're moving too fast?"

"Your wishes are my desires," said Paros.

"It's been a long time," said Charlotte, suddenly nervous.

"For me, too," said Paros.

"Well, we don't have forever to waste, now, do we?" said Charlotte.

"We do not," said Paros.

"Then let's get to the good part," said Charlotte.

He climbed into bed beside her and kissed her face, her lips, her neck. "I love your fragrance," said Paros. Charlotte felt as if she were dreaming. Her *fragrance?*

He trailed kisses down her rib cage to her worn-out stomach, her thighs. His lips were hot and each kiss felt like an electric shock.

"Oh," said Charlotte.

Paros raised his head. "No?" he asked.

"Yes," said Charlotte. And then he pressed his mouth into her most private place. Charlotte was horrified and also deeply thrilled. She felt a stirring that she'd known once or twice, but then the stirring gathered force.

"Oh, my goodness," sighed Charlotte. Her brain switched off.

She felt a swell, a wave, her heart exploding in her chest. She climaxed, and suddenly understood that all of the painter's poking had been nothing. Winston's fumblings had had little to do with Charlotte. Those men were only footnotes. But this, from her very own center, *this* that she had asked for, that she deserved—*yes! This!*—was just the beginning of Charlotte's love story.

2 / Cord

IN THE MEDICAL CENTER, lit by fluorescent lights, Cord sat on one side of his older sister, who was not dead. Cord and Regan had kept watch over Lee's slumbering body all night. "Mom's still not answering," said Regan. "Should I go get her?"

"I guess so," said Cord.

"Okay," said Regan, standing and stretching. She glanced at Cord's phone on the counter. "You have a million messages, by the way," she said.

"Any from Giovanni?" said Cord.

Regan looked through them. "No," she said.

"Then who cares?" said Cord.

"I'm sorry," said Regan. Cord shrugged. "Maybe it's not too late," said Regan.

"Maybe," said Cord.

"Maybe the kids and I will move in with you in New York," said Regan. Cord looked up. "It's a joke," said Regan. "But I don't know. It might be nice to leave Savannah. What do you think?"

"I can see it, Ray Ray," said Cord, allowing a tiny smile. He looked at Lee's face—her false eyelashes, faded lips.

"She's so much more than this," he said. "God, what happened to her out there in Hollywood? Who is this person? Remember when she used to write poetry in that spiral notebook?"

"She was my hero when we were little," said Regan.

"Yeah. She took good care of us."

"Until she left," said Regan.

Cord exhaled. "She was allowed," he said.

"You got away, too," said Regan. She blinked back tears. "But we couldn't *all* leave Mom, could we?"

Cord sighed. "Oh, Regan," he said. "I'm so sorry."

"It's not me you need to apologize to," said Regan. "That was a long time ago."

"You're right," said Cord, closing his eyes and thinking of Giovanni. "Give me a sec?"

"Of course."

Cord stepped into the hallway and scrolled through a dozen text messages. The New York Stock Exchange had opened, and today was 3rd Eyez's IPO. The most recent text was from Wyatt: *3rd Eyez up $10 to $35 already motherfucker!!! YOU ARE RICH.*

He was supposed to feel elated, but Cord felt only tired. He dialed Giovanni. Where was he at this minute? Cord could see him on their fire escape—or was it now only Cord's fire escape?—the way Gio played with his dark hair as he read library books. Cord ached with loss. He knew Giovanni wouldn't answer, but then he did.

"Yes?"

Cord's stomach seized. "Giovanni. Giovanni. I'm so sorry."

"I know," said Giovanni. "I know you're sorry, Cord. I do. But it's done. Please stop calling me."

"But I'm sorry," said Cord. "I'm so sorry."

"Goodbye," said Giovanni, hanging up.

Standing in an antiseptic hallway, Cord was somehow a child again, trapped inside one of the worst days of his life. His father had forced him to "play ball" in their backyard, one of Winston's naked attempts to make his son manlier.

Cord kept missing the ball, and Winston got more and more annoyed. In retrospect, he was probably eager to start his early evening routine of boozing till blotto, but at the time, all Cord understood was that his father wanted something from him that he could not—no matter how he tried—provide.

He couldn't catch the ball.

Instead of giving him softies, his father threw the ball harder and harder. Cord knew his father loved him, or wanted to. It wasn't that Winston was a bad man. And Cord didn't understand—not yet—that he wanted to kiss men, to love men and not women. He just knew he was a failure. He missed ball after ball, each miss making him run and rummage in the azaleas.

Cord could feel it now: the heat in his face. The scratches on his hands as he tried to find the ball, his worry that his shorts would ride too low as he bent over. The last time he rose, tossed the ball back to Winston. The grim look on Winston's face as he brought his arm back and threw the ball directly at his son.

The ball hit Cord in the face, and as it did, he split open. He could no longer remain inside the broken boy. He cracked off, and watched from above as the sad kid fell, his hands to his nose. Cord felt nothing as his father approached the boy without sympathy. Winston picked up the baseball, which lay a few inches from Cord. He whispered, "Pansy," and walked toward the house. Cord watched as the boy lay still on the lawn.

Get up, he told the boy now. *You can do this.*

He began to breathe heavily, feeling the searing pain of his childhood—the terror and shame. He could withstand it. He was strong and sober and he was not alone. Slowly, trembling, the boy stood. Cord called Giovanni again, his heart pounding.

"Hello?" said Giovanni.

"You're wrong about me," said Cord.

"Oh, honey," said Giovanni.

"I told her about us," said Cord, "and I'm winning you back. This is forever, Gio. This is forever. Will you let me try?"

There was a long pause. Everything, everything waited there. Finally, Giovanni spoke, his voice kind and filled with fearful love. "Damn you," he said. "Damn you."

It was as if Gio was speaking directly to the lonely voice, which grew silent.

Inside Cord, a small boy lifted his fists and cheered.

3 / Regan

AS SOON AS REGAN had seen a missed call from her sister, she knew something was wrong. And though Lee hadn't left a message, and did not answer when Regan tried to call back, one thing being a mother had taught Regan was to trust her gut. She ran to Lee's cabin and banged on the door. It was locked, so Regan called security, who arrived after an agonizing twenty minutes with a key.

By the time Regan entered Lee's room, Lee was already at the edge of her balcony, sobbing, saying crazy things, preparing to jump. The hapless security guard who had responded to Regan's call radioed for backup. A crowd had assembled on the floors below.

"Lee," said Regan, opening the sliding doors, trying to keep her voice calm.

"Don't touch me!" said Lee, crying out like a trapped animal. "Leave me alone! Don't touch me!"

"It's me," said Regan. "I love you. Please."

"You don't understand," said Lee. "Ray Ray, I'm just like him. I can't do it. I can't do it anymore."

"Just like who?" said Regan, trying to listen to her sister, trying to see the Lee she'd once known inside the desperate woman moments from plunging into the sea. (Or worse, onto one of the decks below.)

"Dad. I'm just like Dad. I can't do it. It's too hard."

"Dad?" said Regan. "You're nothing like him, Lee."

"He killed himself," said Lee. "I wasn't supposed to tell you."

Regan drew a stunned breath. But it made sense—all the darkness around Winston, the way Charlotte wouldn't allow them to talk about him. Lee's flight to California.

"It's okay," said Regan. "You're not Dad, Lee. Come back."

Lee turned around. Her beautiful face was pale and anguished.

"I've got you," said Regan. She held out her hand.

4 / Lee

WHEN SHE WAS A little girl, all Lee had known were summer hours to fill, Charlotte off playing tennis or cooking something in the kitchen. Lee listened to Casey Kasem's *American Top 40*, prank-called friends and strangers. When Winston was home, they got out—playing Cave Family in the backyard, wandering the streets of their hometown, buying pizza and ice cream and Jolly Rancher candies. Time was elastic, evening stretching forever before fading to sparkling night. The sounds of frogs and cicadas. The smell of pine needles and marshland. Ice slamming into Winston's cut-crystal glass. His voice a hot knife.

After Winston was gone: a smaller house, sure, but always thrumming with raucous laughter, cabinets of ramen noodles and microwave popcorn. Charlotte collapsing on the wicker couch after a day of showing houses to people who treated her like dirt. Regan brought her mother cold drinks. Cord splayed across the couch, listening to her stories. Lee flitted in and out, the telephone cord wrapped around her hand, always headed somewhere, applying lip gloss, smelling of Aqua Net.

She'd taken every one of them for granted, not known

how much she needed them, running away as soon as she was able. Lee was convinced her family was her burden.

She had wanted to die. Someone—some passenger with a high-res camera phone—had filmed her on her balcony. In the end, it was the movie of her suicide attempt that had brought her stardom at last. Uploaded to YouTube, watched millions of times, the video enabled Francine to ink a reality show deal before Lee had even left Barcelona.

It was all she had dreamed of during those hot, endless childhood summers: bright fame, the flash of photographers every time she left her Hollywood home, magazine covers, eventually receiving *real* roles in feature films just a few months after the debut of her reality show, *One of You to Love Me*.

In the video, she stands on a balcony of a megaliner, the Spanish sky wide above her, passengers freaking out below. Gorgeous Lee, unforgettable, barefoot in a gold dress. In the throes of what was later diagnosed as postpartum psychosis. Her hair whipping in the wind. Her mascara smeared. She opens her mouth and screams, "I just wanted one of you to love me!"

5 / Charlotte

THE MUSEUM WAS SURROUNDED by an ancient courtyard in Barcelona's Gothic Quarter. "Let's get in line," said Paros, who had met her, as promised, dressed in his farmer clothes. No matter—Charlotte could take him on a shopping spree at the Hilton Head outlet mall if things progressed. Paros would look fabulous in loafers and those Vineyard Vines pants, patterned with tiny, pink whales.

Charlotte and her children had stayed in Barcelona for three weeks, renting an Airbnb apartment until Lee's doctors felt she was ready to fly home. Charlotte and Paros had said goodbye when the *Marveloso* departed, and had reunited when it returned. "Are you going to be fired for fraternizing with a former passenger?" Charlotte had asked, flirtatiously.

"A large part of me would love to be fired," said Paros.

Charlotte put her hand to her chest. She wasn't sure if he was talking about the large part she was imagining.

Now, Paros kissed her forehead. They joined the queue snaking into the museum. Paros paid their entrance fees. So gallant! thought Charlotte. Also, she liked his silver money clip. Winston had always traded in rumpled bills from his wallet.

Once Charlotte was inside, the exposed-brick walls made her feel as if she were in a bunker of some sort. With the help of a paper map and two docents, Charlotte found *Nude on a Couch*. She stood in front of the work of art she had inspired. The painting itself was vibrant: purple and magenta, a young woman's face obscured, her breasts the focal point. Charlotte did have great breasts. But the woman in the painting was open, offering herself. She existed to please, to be savored, eaten up.

"Is it really you?" asked Paros.

Charlotte turned to him, surprised.

"I heard about your essay," said Paros. "My friend Jonas was working in the theater bar the night you told your story. He told me you were a star."

Charlotte turned back to the painting, flushed. "It was me, I suppose," she said. "It was me, once." She felt sorry for the girl who had inspired the painting, and with the sorrow came a gratitude that she had come so far—raised her children, brought them to Europe, found a new lover with whom she could savor the city of Barcelona. She had not been a woman after the painter had his way with her. But she was a woman now.

They looked at art for a while, and then Paros pulled Charlotte to him. She felt the length of his body against hers. What luck to have found him, to have let herself be found.

"I don't want to say goodbye," said Paros, into her hair.

Charlotte didn't speak. What could she say? *Let's get married?* She wasn't sixteen anymore, and understood that a wedding wasn't an answer to anything. *Let's move to*

Greece? Savannah? Paris? This seemed rash, even considering Paros's agile tongue. "Kiss me," said Charlotte.

And oh, how he did.

THEY MET CHARLOTTE'S CHILDREN and grandchildren at Dulcería de la Colmena, a charming cake shop along Plaza del Angel, its windows lined with rows of intricate, mouth-watering treats lit like diamonds. Charlotte took in the gold, filigreed letters spelling *Bombonería* (was there a better word in the world?) and *Pastelería*. Inside, she peered at a display of something called *turrón*.

"It's nougat," whispered Paros. He smelled deliciously of limes. "Some say it was eaten by athletes in ancient Rome."

She turned to him. "Which kind should I . . . ?" she asked.

"Ah, there is hard *turrón;* there is soft *turrón; turrón* with Marcona almonds, egg yolk, and caramel . . ."

As he spoke, Charlotte's eye caught a tray of powdered pastries. She read from the tiny card nestled among them, *"Buñuelo."*

"It's a donut," said Paros.

As Charlotte pointed, he ordered, and the next thing she knew, she was standing in the plaza, a paper box of treats in her hands. They ordered tiny, hot coffees at a nearby café.

"Happy family," said a guy with a Polaroid camera, hoping to sell them a photo. He stood back, framed the shot. "Happy family, smile!" said the man. Charlotte could see the image already: Lee, still shaken from her ordeal, about to leave them again; Cord, giddy and hopeful; Regan, already inhabiting her new persona as a single mother, flanked by her daughters, who had spent the day playing in the magical Park Güell.

When they were young, Charlotte had been so busy with her pain, with making money and driving the carpool. She'd resented her children as they climbed into bed with her, reading beside her, touching her feet with their own. She bought frozen pizzas and boxes of macaroni and cheese and fruit and milk and Entenmann's chocolate-covered donuts and her children ate it all, leaving Charlotte only crumbs.

They would leave her again—they would—and she would end up back in Savannah alone with her Chardonnay and her cat. But as the camera flashed, they crowded around Charlotte, her family: bedraggled, imperfect, ready to go home. They were enough, more than enough, as perhaps they had been all along.

Charlotte opened the paper box. The low Barcelona light cast shadows on the plaza. The smell of the *Pastelería*, rich caramelized sugar, mixed with the mineral tang of a fountain lined with hopeful pennies. Her children reached toward her.

When one hot, sweet donut remained, Charlotte took a bite.

Epilogue / 2018

HOLDING A CHAMPAGNE FLUTE of sparkling water, Lee took a moment to herself in her mother's living room, considering the oil portrait that hung above the fireplace. There Lee was, just six years old, her smile brilliant with fear. She could almost sense her father nearby, fiddling with his camera; she could hear Charlotte's high, nervous laughter. The salty Hilton Head Island air, thick with humidity. Regan's baby fingers, gripping tight. The feel of her brother's warm back through his polo shirt.

Perhaps Lee and her father were the same: both troubled, both sad, both needing chemicals in their brains that nature had not provided. But only one action separated father from daughter. One second in a lifetime of seconds.

Three years before, on her balcony high above the sea, Lee knew that she could no longer stand. She had no choice: she was going to fall. Before her, waves churned, promising an end to her pain. She inhaled, lifted her arms.

But then, behind her, Regan's voice. Lee turned and saw, as if inside a dream, her baby sister, silk dressing gown billowing, face sure and kind and open. Regan's arm outstretched.

Winston, on his last day, had succumbed to the fog. Lee understood, and gazed at the ocean with longing.

"I've got you," said Regan.

Against the allure of the fall. Despite the desire to be free. The memory of her father's blue face. The smell of ocean and strawberry shampoo. Regan's voice, whispering that she was beloved. Her sister's hand in her hair.

Acknowledgments

SPENDING MOST DAYS TYPING away in a closet wearing pajamas can feel lonely, even for a happy introvert. I am so thankful for my community of mothers, writers, and friends, including Beth Howells, Roz Gillespie, Terra Lynch, Susan Chopra, Jamie Perkins, Amelia Canally, Debby Wolfinsohn, Stacey Gardner, Biz Ramberg, Genny Mounce, Tina Donahoo, Caroline and Adam Wilson, Moyara and Stefan Pharis, Liz and Andy Gershoff, Doug Dorst, Owen Egerton, Mary Helen Specht, Dalia Azim, the LLL, the BFB, my Wednesday noon crew, Masha Hamilton, Andrew Sean Greer, Christina Baker Kline, Jane Green, Vendela Vida, Tomas Rivera, Leah Stewart, Jardine Libaire, Allison Lynn, Laurie and Drew Duncan, Paula Disbrowe, Emily Hovland, Erin and Tim Kinard, Jenny and Sean Hart, and Ben and Francie Tisdel.

Important note: Charlotte Perkins is wholly fictional and not based on my glamorous, beautiful, golf-cart-driving, Savannah-dwelling mother, Mary-Anne Westley. (Nor is Paros in any way based on her young, handsome husband, Peter Westley.) Thank you to my family, the Westleys, McKays, Bennigsons, Meckels, Shabers, Wards, and Toans, for the gift of embracing whatever springs from my imagination.

Heather and Russell Courts, the ultimate jetsetters (and the only couple I know who spent a first date riding Egyptian camels . . . I was there!), hosted my family in Athens and we cannot wait to return.

Michelle Tessler is a brilliant agent and treasured friend. Thank you for eighteen years—and counting!—of support, guidance, wild adventures, big dreams, steak frites, and invitations to Kauai. I can't wait to see what we'll get up to next.

I thought *The Jetsetters* was going to be an easy novel to write. I was wrong. I don't know what I would have done without Kara Cesare by my side for every page and every moment of the journey. Kara, you have taught me so much about character, plot, and bringing my whole heart to the work. I am very thankful for your editorial guidance, for our Plaza teas, and for your friendship. I am honored and thrilled to be surrounded by the best in the business: Gina Centrello, Kim Hovey, Kara Welsh, Benjamin Dreyer, Jennifer Hershey, and Jesse Shuman.

How lucky I am to be married to a man who, when I ask, "Should I drain our savings and take the boys on a Mediterranean cruise, for novel research?" says, "Do it." I love you, Tip Meckel, and though you say you'd rather be shot than go on a cruise, I'll continue to try to convince you otherwise. I am awestruck by our shining WAM, our brilliant THM, our wild SJM, and the sweet and fierce NRM.